# Silk

## The Bloodstone Series

## Chris Karlsen

# Chapter One

Dressing the dead required a certain dexterity and patience. William surveyed his work with pride. A pity no one would see his accomplishment. He doubted Isabeau's maid could've done much better.

Sweat beaded his forehead and he used his dead lover's embroidered hanky to wipe his face and the film of perspiration from his chest. The fire in the hearth had gone out while they made love, but even naked, the room was like an oven. He started to pour a glass of wine then thought better of it. Until the body was disposed of and the stage set for explaining her death, he needed to keep a clear head. Instead, he rummaged through the chiffonier hunting for petticoats. No respectable woman left the house without proper underpinnings. A bottom drawer was filled with lace and ribbon-trimmed petticoats. William took the top ones and managed to get them on and tied with far less trouble than he had with the dress.

"Thank God," William mumbled, snickering at the inappropriate application of the phrase. "Now riding boots."

The boot slipped on her tiny foot with ease. He laced it up and had the second one half on when he noticed the ball of stockings on the floor. "Bugger me."

The concept of heaven or hell held no interest for him. On certain holidays, Isabeau droned on about religion and turned a devout Catholic face to the world. If there was anything to her belief, then she was probably gazing on the scene from some perch in Purgatory and laughing. With that grating thought fueling every move, he removed the boot and started over, stockings first.

Finished with dressing her, William threw on the same clothes he'd worn earlier, crept downstairs and headed for the stable. On the way he looked east toward the ruin of the ancient hill fort that bordered his land. Pink streaks lined the distant sky. He'd have to hurry if he wanted to make it to the cliffs before the whole of Tintagel awoke.

He lit a single lantern and carefully placed it to the side where he wouldn't knock it over.

"Sir?" The stable boy stood at the base of the loft ladder rubbing sleep from his eyes, shirt askew and buttoned wrong.

William gave little start. He hadn't heard the boy stir.

"I can take care of the horses, sir. What did you need me to do?"

"Nothing, Charles. Go back to sleep. I'll saddle King Arthur and Guinevere. Isabeau and I thought it might be nice to go for an early ride." William laid a firm but gentle hand on the lad's shoulder. "Sleep. By the time I—" he corrected himself, "We return, the horses will be ready for feeding and brushing."

The boy nodded and climbed up to his hayloft bed.

Hurriedly working against the rising sun, William tacked up Guinevere, the mare Isabeau rode, and then saddled his big bay hunter. When he was done, he brought both horses round to the far side of the stable and tied them to a rail out of sight from the house.

William dashed back to the bedroom, taking the steps to the upper floor two at a time. Muffled voices came from the kitchen. Of the household staff, cook rose the earliest to begin the day's breakfast preparation. Soon the butler and his valet would be awake. He considered sneaking out of the house but dismissed the idea rather than do anything that might appear suspicious. A ride at dawn's light was out of the ordinary but not so strange as to provoke speculation and clucking by the servants, if he acted normal.

He wrapped Isabeau in a cloak and carried her down the main stairs. With every step, he whispered sweet words to his dead mistress and nuzzled her cool cheek. A smile played at his lips. To any staff member about, it looked like a romantic gesture.

After numerous tries, William secured the body to the mare in a semi-sitting position. Just getting her onto the horse's back turned into a monumental feat and by no means was he a weakling. He took a moment to catch his breath. The short time to sunrise didn't allow for more than a couple of moments. Next he tied her hands to the pommel and her feet to the girth. Isabeau still tipped forward but to anyone they might ride past, the position could pass for a deliberate effort on her part for speed. He'd pony Guinevere on a long line. All he had to do was keep both horses at the same smooth gait, a nice extended canter, or perhaps a measured gallop.

Castle Beach would be his final destination, the easiest spot to unload his baggage without discovery. The route there posed different issues. The foliage of St. Nectan's Glen offered excellent cover and slim odds of seeing other riders. It also added an additional thirty minutes to his journey. The fastest path took him out in the open where he ran the biggest risk of being seen. After a brief mental debate, he decided to use the fastest route and headed straight for the cliffs across the moor.

Guinevere galloped along with King Arthur while William maintained a steady pace, keeping St. Materina's Church in sight and on his right. The church was the midpoint between the cliffs overlooking Castle Beach and Tintagel village proper. The sun had just begun to peek over the horizon when he stopped. Seabirds had already flown from their nests and hovered over the fishing boats preparing to sail out. The absence of gulls, puffins, and other squalling local animal life magnified the roar and crash of the waves against the rocky cliff.

William dismounted and let Arthur graze on the scraggly grass. The fine stallion made an excellent shield as William untied and lifted Isabeau's body from Guinevere. With little effort, he rolled his late lover off the edge of the cliff and watched, grimacing, when her dainty body bounced off a rocky outcropping. True, he planned on packing her back to France, or to another of his associates. And true, he didn't see her death as a great loss, but he wouldn't have wished her bashed on the rocks, even in death. However, this was the most expedient way to rid himself of an inconveniently dead mistress.

*It shouldn't have come to this...*

#

The ebb and flow of the tide, the rush of water as it churned through the stones embedded in the sandy shore entranced him while the events of the prior evening played in his mind.

"Do you love me, William?" Isabeau pursed her full lips and glided across the carpet with a graceful sway. The sheer gown trailed behind her like a silken mist. She stopped between his knees and faced him.

"No darling. You don't inspire love. You amuse me, which is infinitely better." *You used to anyway.* William took a swallow of the rich claret and swirled the liquid around his mouth and waited for Isabeau's familiar routine. His denial of love always triggered a tantrum.

She'd tested his patience of late. First came the needy question, followed by his honest answer, then the dramatics, the feigned hurt, the pout, the demand for a physical show of desire. *Desire.* It's all there'd ever been between them. Recently, the edge to that passion had grown dull. Even the more unusual aspects of their lovemaking seemed stale, desperate and contrived.

She rubbed her calf against his.

"Don't. I'm not in the mood," he said and moved his

leg. "It's a big house Isabeau. Surely you can find something to entertain yourself with other than me."

"I don't want to." Spoiled and demanding, she could be a petulant child when denied. She rubbed the other leg now.

William groaned. He didn't feel like fucking her tonight. He'd risen with the sun and spent the entire day with Harold, the estate manager. They rode the perimeter of the thousand acres that belonged to Foxleigh Hall. Poachers, a constant irritant had become bold over the past few weeks, venturing deep onto the property, shooting badger and deer, even the does, leaving the fawns to die. *Bastards.*

The traps were set—not to attract animal life but human. He'd gone inland to Launceston to hire extra guards, the precaution of distance a necessary evil. In all likelihood, the violators lived in one of the nearby villages, which eliminated using men from the area as possible sentries.

"Just let me sit and enjoy some peace and quiet."

"You're cross. Maybe you should eat." Her winged brows dipped into a furrow of false concern.

"No." Too tired to eat when he returned, he'd waved away the tray of food the maid brought to his private chamber. But Isabeau had no way of knowing he refused dinner since he always ate alone and she never disturbed him. Everyone in the household knew he hated sharing a meal or a table with others present unless a social situation forced him. The sounds people made when they ate disgusted him. Nor did he find idle conversation over food particularly engaging. No witty discussion could compensate for the smacking, slurping, swallowing noises. These offenses were compounded by the glimpses of half-devoured food of folks who felt the urge to speak while eating.

"I'm not hungry. I'm weary. Were you the least bit observant you'd have noticed?" William ignored the sour face she made and laid his head back against the cushions of the chair and closed his eyes. He sat still as stone, holding the wineglass by the globe, not sleeping but resting his eyes.

Close to dozing off, he spread his legs farther apart, so his feet were flat on the floor. The only sound came from the occasional pop of wood in the fire as it burned. The heat from Isabeau's body and the silk of her gown as it brushed his knuckles gave her away as she knelt in front of him. She removed his riding boots and began unbuttoning his shirt. He opened his eyes to watch.

She peered up through thick lashes, her unlined complexion glowed and her moist lips glistened. *The face of a penitent and the morals of a peahen.* A pleasurable combination most nights. She'd deliberately worn the ribbons loose and her gown had slipped from her shoulders. The soft garment split apart below her navel, exposing creamy pink and white flesh. Those thighs, shorter and plumper than an Englishwoman's, produced surprising strength when it mattered, aiding him in burying himself deeper within her.

"I love you," Isabeau said and stretched forward so the tips of her breasts skimmed his wool trousers and the nipples pearled.

"Don't be silly. You love my pounds, shillings, and pence, well, not the pence so much," he clarified with a light chuckle. "You love the jewelry I give you." William picked her hand up and fingered the cameo ring he'd bought her for Christmas. "And, you love the fine clothes, and the sex, but you don't love me."

She pushed off his legs and stood with remarkable speed. With a long sigh, he straightened, ready for the torrent of indignation she'd no doubt hurl at him.

The moue returned, only more pronounced. "How dare you tell me who or what I love. Why must you be so cruel?" Isabeau stomped a barefoot while one fat tear escaped down her cheek. "You break my heart," she added with a dramatic lip quiver. "Why don't we marry? I could be a good wife, a good mother. You could learn to love me. I already know many ways to please you."

"I can learn to play a bagpipe too. That's not going happen either." A lifetime with the temperamental, possessive Isabeau— the thought almost gagged him. William raised a hand palm up in hopes to stay her emotional declarations. "Don't."

"Make love to me. Let me show you how devoted I am."

"Isabeau. I want a hot bath and sleep, in that order."

"Make love to me. I will make you forget your weariness." The gown puddled at her feet as she slid it off. Naked except for stockings and satin slippers, she touched herself, teasing her skin with fluttery strokes. William's cock involuntarily twitched and jumped a little at the tempting sight. *Carnal creature.*

"No, you won't. You'll want to play games, like you always do," he said low, confident she wouldn't deny the accusation.

She propped a foot up on the arm of his chair, tilted her head and fingered the nest of dark curls between her legs. William sipped the claret and followed the path of her fingers with his eyes. He finished the wine and set the goblet onto the leather top of a side table.

"You like games." Isabeau pointedly shot a glance at the tented front of his trousers. "You especially like me on all fours, tied, restrained and at your mercy, *oui cher?*"

His body warred against him. Part of him wanted nothing more than to lie quiet, but part, wasn't quite as spent as the rest. It had sprung back to life with the minx's teasing and now throbbed for relief.

"True, I like a variety of things. However, were I to forget my tired bones, I'd like to do something completely different this evening." He paused. Isabeau tipped her head, a quizzical expression on her face. William anticipated her curiosity. "Tonight, I'd like to fuck like every other bloody Englishman, with you on your back and me on top groaning and pumping away for a minute or so, then a nice sleep."

A sneer touched the edge of her mouth, then Isabeau laughed. "You English, you are so uninspired, a pity for your women. My soul cries for them."

"Yes, unimaginative lot that we are, we have somehow managed to colonize much of the world."

She took his hand and led him to her chamber. He didn't object. Upstairs Isabeau unbuttoned his trousers and pushed them down. William stripped out of the legs and held still while she undressed him the rest of the way.

She dropped to her knees and eased the sides of his underwear down to his ankles. He stared at her bent head and wondered how hair that looked so inky in the daylight could reflect so much gold and red in the light of the gas lamps. He leaned forward as she wrapped her warm hand around his cock and toyed with the tip. She wet the end with her tongue then blew on it with her warm breath.

Threading his fingers into her hair, he pushed himself between her parted lips and moaned when she sucked him in further.

When he could take no more, he pulled her up and kissed her. The hard edge of her teeth pressed along the seam of his mouth, painful, almost cutting. She fell backward onto the bed, holding onto his arms and dragged him down on top of her.

She'd done what she said: made him forget his exhaustion. About to explode, William entered her, thrusting, stroking. Isabeau with her incredible sense of drama, jerked her head to the side and scooted away like a crab toward the pillows, dislodging him. "You know what I want."

He panted above her, his arms bracketed her hips. "Yes, I know what you'd like. I told you before we started I had no interest in playing games tonight. I'm tired. Let's be done with this." How dare she do this now, he swore to himself. If he were a different kind of man, a less refined man, he'd force her, roughly if necessary. He'd teach her how unsound it was to ignite a man's baser desires then deny him satisfaction. After tonight, he'd find another lover and send her back to London or Paris, the sooner, the better. "Finish!"

She grabbed a favorite red silk scarf from the stand by the bed and held it out to him. "Do this for me and we shall both finish gloriously." She gave the scarf an impatient shake.

William debated whether to give in to her demand or simply finish himself off. A refusal allowed him to retain the power between them, but he lost much sexual gratification, to give in he relinquished his authority to the rapacious witch.

He suppressed his resentment and snatched the scarf from her hand and sat back on his heels. She lifted her head so he could wind the silk ligature around her small neck. William had to loop it twice to get it snug enough. He gave each end a tug to check the tightness, the amount of play. Isabeau raised her arms above her head, like a slave girl tethered to a pole. She closed her eyes and sighed. Her sooty eyelashes fluttered against her cheek.

He studied the nimble beauty. Would his next mistress be a willing partner of the rarer sexual arts? Isabeau showed him things he'd only heard discussed by some of the men at his club. Strange things, erotic and different, they spoke of rough and tumble love play usually performed by expensive whores. He had several mistresses over the years and numerous liaisons in between. None of his paramours came close to Isabeau in imagination. It's the one thing he'd miss.

She whimpered, and the sound brought him back to the moment. One of her kneecaps prodded his buttocks as she spread her legs. The scent of her readiness inflamed his desire. He trailed his fingers across her belly and she shivered at the touch, tiny goose bumps rose along her pale skin. She grabbed his wrist and laid his hand on one end of the scarf. "Do it."

He wrapped an end in each hand and pulled. His fingers crept up the silk and he tugged a bit harder still. The material pressed deeper into the flesh of her neck. Bright pink dotted her cheeks and radiated down to her jaw. The veins in her temples popped out and pulsed in time to her heartbeat. She moaned, pushed her hips upward and writhed against him. Her soft pubic hair tickled his testicles. Isabeau's unsubtle way of letting him know she wanted him inside her. He obliged.

Her hands encircled his wrists. She tugged hard outward, harder than usual. A choked sigh escaped her. He paid no attention. This was standard. Isabeau always insisted he maintain pressure until she signaled for him to release his hold. In the past, when she reached the edge of consciousness, she'd beat along his upper arms. This time she thrashed her head back and forth, something he hadn't seen before. Her eyes bulged in an unattractive way and she clawed at him. Her nails gouged the skin on his hands, drawing blood.

She hurt him and he wanted to slap her. He almost let go of one end of the scarf to do that. Instead, he pulled tighter. Isabeau tried to insert her fingers into the spot where the material crossed over. Her mouth opened and shut, soundless and fishlike. She swatted at the mattress wildly. Red-faced to the point of being near purple, she bucked beneath him.

She fired his blood with her lack of inhibition. Never had she responded with such intensity. Raw power surged through him, primitive, animalistic. He pumped hard. Ready to climax, William clenched his fists, twisting the scarf one last turn. Odd, feathery touches tapped his biceps, feminine and subtle grazes, and then she went limp. Spent, he released his hold and collapsed on top of her, his heart pounding while he caught his breath.

Isabeau didn't move and her head stayed turned to the

side. She hadn't cried out the way she normally did when sated. Perhaps she was disappointed with his effort. He gave the thought a mental shrug. At the end of the day, it really didn't matter. He'd arrange for her departure first thing in the morning.

William rolled over and slung a sweaty arm over his eyes. He tried to decide which was worse, telling her tonight the affair was over or waiting until morning. The idea of doing it after such a rambunctious sexual endeavor seemed bad form, but he wanted to get it over with. He turned onto his side, prepared for histrionics, caterwauling, great tears and verbal abuse.

"Isabeau, look at me. I've come to a decision and it will likely distress you." Nothing. She didn't stir. "Isabeau?"

He shook her by the arm. Still no response. William let go and her arm dropped listless to the mattress. He raised her arm again and let go. Again, it fell listless. He straddled her and patted her cheeks. Nothing. Her head twisted without resistance first right then left depending on the direction of his pat. He slapped her harder. Nothing. Vacant eyes stared fixed on the ceiling. He bent an ear to her chest. Nothing. William leapt from the bed, snatched a silver mirror from the dressing table, and held it under her nose. Nothing.

"Bitch." William hurled the mirror against the wall. "Bitch, whore," he raged and paced along the side of the bed. "I will not allow you to make my life a nightmare."

#

"This was your doing. I told you to leave me alone." William stood with his hands on his hips and took one last look at the broken female form. He braced his legs wide apart, tipped his head back and drew in several deep breaths of salt air. He loved living near the sea. The dawn held the beginnings of a fine spring day. Too bad he'd spend it and the next several cooped up at his estate, mourning the death of a woman he didn't love. The expectations of polite society grated on the nerves at times like this.

In the east, a sliver of sun appeared. The hour to raise a hue and cry for help had come. He'd stretched his visit to the beach out as long as he dared. Now, he'd ride hell bent into the village demanding help in rescuing his beloved Isabeau.

The clatter of the two horses galloping echoed off the cobblestones village street so it sounded like four. Candles were lit in the hamlet's windows, men and women not already at work came outside to see the cause of the commotion.

"Quick, you must come. There's been a terrible accident." William dropped Guinevere's lead rope and reined in King Arthur hard. The stallion's rear hooves slid on the mist covered stones. William turned him in a circle until the horse found purchase on the edge of a cobble and stopped slipping.

"Please, my lady's mare spooked and thrown her. She's fallen off Trebarwith Strand. I fear she's seriously injured." He directed his plea to several men standing at their gates.

Curious children peered around their mother's skirts at him while men grabbed lanterns and rope. Some of the men ran behind King Arthur on foot, a few had work horses handy and rode. One or two others ran to small boats and would row, paralleling the crowd to the spot where the lady fell. Often victims of cliff side falls had to be relocated by water, when carrying the injured person up the rocks was too dangerous. The women who didn't have infants to feed followed in groups, chattering, eager to witness the excitement.

\#

William pressed firm fists into his lower back and arched. The stretch eased the weariness that settled down his spine from the arduous retrieval of Isabeau's body. He briefly considered taking a few minutes to write in his journal but couldn't find the energy. Exhaustion consumed him. The previous day's work on the estate, and the events of the night had taken its toll on his system. While her body lay in the parlor where in the morning it would be dressed one last time, and before collapsing onto bed, he visited Isabeau's chamber one more time. There, on the pillow he'd so often fell asleep on, lay the silk scarf, where he'd tossed it. He picked it up with the intent of burning it in the privacy of his chamber. The silk slid over his palms, through his fingers as he wove it between them. Whisper soft yet deadly, an unusual combination. The thought amused him and he stuck the scarf into his pocket. Rather than destroy the delicate weapon, he'd store it in his bureau as a token of the night, a reminder of the lovely but foolish Isabeau.

He'd ordered the maid to clean the chamber and pack everything. The maid and his valet, Burton, who met him as he left the room, did their best to console him in this dark hour. William thanked them for their efforts. Fully clothed, he lay down and closed his eyes, grateful for such a caring staff.

*May 15, 1888*

*She let it go too long. A ladylike fist banging on my upper arm, our usual signal would have sufficed. Instead, she heated my blood with her wildcat gyrations. The writhing, the intimate press of her swollen folds against me. Inspirational. There'd been no cry, no complaint, only a breathy gasp, that sensual moan. The struggle. The force of her fight. The glassy sheen to her eyes, the way they widened, more and more. Ecstasy. I've never been so hard. I'd have stopped had I known, then again, perhaps not. A moot point. She's dead. An accident, but still...*

Journal entry of William Everhard

## Chapter Two

London-Gardens of the British Museum
May, 1888
"Inspector Bloodstone."

Rudyard turned. A policeman several inches shorter than him and square built stood at attention. The young ones always did when first meeting Rudyard. A phenomena he attributed to his being awarded the Victoria Cross. The prestigious medal struck awe in the raw recruits. When given to him, the queen's letter read: *For extreme valour in the face of the enemy.* For his part, when asked, he explained he'd only done what was necessary in battle. The medal remained in its original leather presentation case alongside the envelope with the royal seal and the queen's decree inside. Both sat in the top drawer of his bureau next to his socks.

"At ease constable, this isn't the army. What's your name?"

The young man's shoulders dropped down and forward a fraction as he unlocked his knees and moved his feet apart. "Clive Northam, sir." His face brightened. "You requested a photographer." Pink bloomed across his cheeks. "For important pictures of a homicide they told me."

"I did and they are."

Photography didn't interest Rudyard, too much rigmarole involved with setting up each shot. But those fellows he met who studied the art were fairly fanatical about it. He had to admit the photographs came in handy. Back at the station, he liked having them to refer to during the investigation. One day they might be useful evidence in court.

Northam lifted the wood-based camera by his feet and held it snug in the crook of one arm while he grasped the tripod stand with his other hand. "Where would you like me to start?"

Rudyard pointed. "I want several of the victim: her position, the state of her clothing, and the immediate area around her body as well."

Too heavy an application of starch by the laundress, irritated an old war wound on his throat. In spite of his lack of interest, observing the photography was enough of a distraction to help Rudyard resist the urge to dig a finger under his collar and satisfy the nagging itch.

When Northam finished Rudyard said, "Thank you. Stay nearby. I may have you take some others shortly."

"Sir." Northam bobbed his head once and stepped away to talk to one of the constables manning the perimeter keeping civilians from the scene.

Rudyard knelt next to the body. Sprawled out face down in front of a wrought iron bench, her legs spread, one arm bent with the palm flat on the grass, the victim's other arm was extended, the gloved fingers curled. Scattered by the tips were loose grapes. Death's pallor had crept into her chubby face except on the purplish cheek touching the ground discolored by lividity.

The victim's reticule contained two shillings six-pence, enough to steal if robbery was the motive, an embroidered handkerchief frayed at the edges, a comb made of bone missing three teeth, and a vial of lavender water. She carried no paperwork to indicate who she was or where she lived. One of the museum's day shift guards said he'd often seen her strolling through the gardens in the early morning hours. They exchanged greetings but she never told him her name. He never saw her walking with anyone.

The guard told him she was well spoken with no noticeable regional accent. She sounded neither upper crust nor lower class. He pegged her for a London girl.

Rudyard tugged the glove from her left hand. She wore no wedding ring and her fingernails were short but nicely filed. He removed her other glove and turned her hands over. Both palms were free from workhouse callouses, nor were they red and rough like a laundress's. She didn't look downtrodden or haggard. From the look of her dress, which was simple, well-worn but clean daytime attire, Rudyard eliminated the possibility she was a prostitute. Closer examination revealed a tear on one cuff that had been repaired skillfully. He ran his thumb across her fingertips and found tiny pricks in the skin, some fresh and some healed over. They were concentrated around her cuticles, a result of seamstress work in all likelihood. He'd seen similar punctures from sewing machine needles. The borough was rife with clothing manufacturers. She might've been employed by any one of a dozen. Once the photograph of her was developed, he'd have the junior constables take on the tedious job of showing it to the numerous factory bosses.

Rudyard ran his hands across her back but felt no exit wound from a bullet. He rolled the body over to look for another cause of death. Stabbing might, or might not, produce a large quantity of blood, depending on the number of times she was stabbed and how much her clothes absorbed. He saw no visible wounds by a gunshot, a knife, or other sharp instrument. She hadn't been beaten, at least he saw no evidence. Strangled perhaps? After a brief fight with the tiny buttons on her high collar, he spread the sides apart. Just below the top line of where the collar started were the thumb-sized bruises over the woman's windpipe.

"We have antemortem bruises on her throat. Have a look," he told Archie Holbrook, his new partner.

Archie already had ten years of service with the Metropolitan Police when Rudyard joined the force. But Rudyard had seniority in the Criminal Investigative Division, having been a homicide investigator for the past five years. Seniority notwithstanding, he expected a puffed up attitude on Archie's part. Instead, Archie had proven an excellent partner with a genial personality and a strong willingness to learn.

Archie knelt on the other side of the body and pointed to a circular bruise, darker and smaller than the thumb-sized. "Nasty business, choking. Our killer pressed her collar button mean-hard into the skin to make such a bruise."

Both detectives stood. "One can only hope that with such a vicious throttling, she passed out after several seconds," Rudyard said.

The woman's skirt, along with her petticoats, had been tossed up, exposing her legs and lace-frilled drawers. Archie bent and pulled down on the skirt and petticoats.

Rudyard stayed his hand. "Wait." He picked up a metal disc from the ground and examined it.

"What's that?"

"A button. It looks like it's from a uniform jacket."

"Recognize the detail?"

Rudyard shook his head. "No, the facing is worn but it could be a lion's head. Hard to say for sure, I'll need to see it under a magnifying glass. Once she's transported to the morgue, I'll also want to take her knickers and petticoats for evidence. Her clothing, although in disarray, reveals an interesting clue about her killer."

Archie looked the victim up and down, his brows knitted together. He turned back to Rudyard with a puzzled expression. "I don't see how her clothes tell us anything."

"What's your sense of smell tell you?"

Archie bent closer to the body and inhaled. "It tells me the killer spent himself either before or after attacking her. As her drawers are still tied at the waist and don't appear fumbled with, I'd guess the attacker didn't have time to complete a rape."

"That, or the rotter can't control his base needs or himself, spilling himself as soon as he was free of his trousers or close to it," Ruddy said in his matter of fact way. "Unusual information but possibly useful."

Some of his more religious colleagues thought him cold. Comments Rudyard shrugged off, no need to wear the seriousness of a crime like a permanent hair shirt.

He and Archie rarely socialized together off-duty. Most often Archie went straight home to his two small children and devoted wife, Margaret. But he enjoyed the occasional wager, be it on a game of darts or the occasional game of Whist.

"A pint says if we find him, we'll discover our killer can't perform manly duties the usual way," Rudyard challenged.

"You're on. I'm always happy to take a pint off you." As was his habit when deep in thought, Archie scratched at one of the thick mutton chop whiskers trimmed to blend with his equally bushy mustache. "Well Ruddy, wager aside, let me play Devil's Advocate here. Should we get someone who looks a good suspect, how do we get him to...you know...show us this weakness?"

"Haven't a clue."

Archie grunted. "Didn't think so. I'm going to enjoy that pint." He waved a hand toward the museum's second floor windows overlooking the garden. "In spite of the sexual component, I doubt our man knew her personally. If that were the case, she'd have been attacked in a more private spot."

A more immediate question came to Ruddy's mind. Was this a crime of opportunity or planned? When the weather permitted, the popular museum gardens were crowded with visitors all day.

"I'm thinking the murderer lives or works in the area and knew she often came to walk here in the morning. He planned it. I bet he waited for her every day until she finally showed today."

A stream of the foulest of curse words came from

further down the footpath. The responsible party out of sight at first, then a wiry fellow, held high so only the tips of his shoes touched the ground, burst into view. Two constables, their truncheons swinging back and forth from beneath their uniform caped coats, each with a hand under the man's arms walked him toward Rudyard and Archie. All the while, the man continued to heap verbal abuse and threats against the Peelers. The man sported a swollen nose, a dark blue and purple black eye, with a matching colorful lump on the forehead. The bruises were too vivid to be fresh. They couldn't have come from the constables who had him in tow.

As they approached, the taller of the policemen carried a lady's straw bonnet in his other hand.

"What's this then?" Archie asked.

The Peelers lowered the man so his feet were flat on the ground. The shorter constable without the bonnet gave the dirty-faced suspect a rough shake. "We found him trying to sell the lady's hat, which got our attention right away. Where would the scruffy devil come by a hat unless he stole it?"

"Heard a woman was murdered this morning and thought this..." The tall constable raised the bonnet up, "might belong to her as it's in too good of shape to be discarded without reason."

The man tried to wriggle from their grasp to no avail. "I told them I found it by the fountain, all by itself. No lady was around asking about a lost bonnet. I found it, I claimed it. Nothing wrong with that."

The odor of sour beer and sweat soaked clothes thickened the air. Ruddy moved to the right where he wasn't directly downwind of the filthy rascal. "The fountain, you say."

There was only one fountain in the gardens. It was bordered by a flower bed with tulips the same shade as the pink one stuck in the headband. If the devil wasn't the murderer, then it was possible the hat wound up away from the victim by one of a number of means. A slight breeze off the river could've carried it the small distance. Or, it might've been dropped by the killer. Although, why the murderer would care about the hat was beyond Rudyard. "What's your name?"

"Davey Wilkey."

"If it turns out the bonnet belongs to our murdered lady—" Archie shot a glance at Ruddy. Both knew a hat that maybe belonged to the victim wasn't much evidence.

Ruddy gave the tiniest of nods, giving Archie permission to proceed. "And seeing how the victim's property was found in your possession." Archie stepped closer to Davey. "You'll be dancing the hangman's jig for it."

Davey's unbruised eye widened. "I was in custody until an hour ago. I told them that." He tipped his head toward the short constable, who'd shaken him a moment earlier. "I was cutting through the garden on me way home, when I sees the hat."

"He did say he was in lockup. We've got a runner going over to Paddington Station to inquire," the taller constable said. "Thought it a good idea to bring him over to you for a bit of a chinwag while we wait for the runner."

Still saucer-eyed, Davey insisted, "Done a lot of things in my life, not all righteous in the eyes of the law, but I never killed nobody. No sir."

"What were you arrested for?" Rudyard asked.

"Got into a fight at the Bishop's Hat pub. Might've bashed the Peeler who broke it up on the nose." A twitchy, suppressed smile played at the corner of Davey's mouth.

That explained his black eye and the lump on his head. Good for the Peeler for getting in his own drubbing, Ruddy thought, remembering his rough and tumble days walking a beat.

"Which way did you come from when you entered the garden?" he asked.

"Russell Square."

From the look of where the victim lay, it appeared she'd come from the opposite direction and was headed for Russell Square. The fountain was between the square and where the murder occurred. If Wilkey was telling the truth, and Rudyard believed him, then he wouldn't have seen the body, but he might've seen someone leaving the scene.

"Was anyone around when you found the hat? Did you see anyone at all?" Rudyard pressed, hoping for the smallest clue.

Wilkey shook his head.

"You're sure?"

"No one. I swear I'd say if I had."

"There's the Paddington runner," the tall constable said and waved the man over. "Well?"

"He was in custody since before midnight and only released an hour ago."

Rudyard took the bonnet from the one constable. "Let him go. Thank you though. It was a good observation."

Wilkey dashed off without a look backward.

"Quick question." Rudyard looked from one constable to the other. "I take it you patrol together." They nodded. "And this is your patch?" They nodded again. "How long does it take for you to walk your beat?"

"Twenty minutes, sir," the short one answered with a worried frown—"provided we don't go on a call or aren't waylaid by a citizen inquiry. Our sergeant says twenty minutes is average."

"Relax," Rudyard held up his hand. "That's about how long it took for me to cover my post when I was in patrol. I'm trying to establish if the attack was planned. I'm thinking our murderer knew the timing of your routine."

"The timeframe is pretty consistent, sir. Day watch in this part of the borough is generally quiet," the tall one added.

"Thank you, you can both go."

The two constables went back on patrol, the runner from Paddington walking with them as they left.

"You don't happen to know where this millinery shop is by any chance?" Rudyard showed Archie the stamp on the inside of the bonnet's band.

"Mrs. Porter's. I do know where it is."

The surprise must've shown on Rudyard's face. Archie reminded him of a more youthful Father Christmas. One who had little familiarity with lady's business. Rudyard asked him about the shop as a courtesy not expecting an answer. "You do?"

"Her late husband was the silversmith, Samuel Porter, over on Tottenham Court. She took over his space when he passed and set up her millinery shop. My Margaret has an Easter bonnet from her."

"Perhaps we'll get lucky and Mrs. Porter will recall the bonnet's buyer and know who our victim is?" Rudyard said, without much hope.

## Chapter Three

Rudyard and Archie went straight from the crime scene to Mrs. Porter's Millinery. Rudyard had never met a hat maker. He'd met two dressmakers on a previous investigation. Both ladies were older than his mother, prune-faced, and impatient to have him on his way when he'd come to question them. His presence, whatever the reason, was an intrusion in their respectable, God fearing lives.

Horse-drawn carts of all types crowded the road. Here and there, hansom cabs wended their way through the traffic, depositing and picking up passengers as they did. Pedestrians crossing the street stepped with care to avoid horse manure and other unpleasantries, while those on the sidewalks worked their way around costermonger's stalls.

The shop was located in a narrow, old building its red bricks now soot black from the coal smoke that poured from thousands of chimneys and fouled the air. Mrs. Porter's Fine Millinery was painted in fancy scroll style across the top of the small shop's display window. Four fancy lady's hats mounted on feminine silhouettes filled the window space. All were different styles and individually embellished with ribbons, silk flowers, velvet bands, and feathers. A curtain hung behind the displays blocking the view of the activity inside from passersby.

Rudyard ran his finger along the inside of his starched shirt collar making certain it was straight. He used his reflection in the glass window to check the knot of his tie. A man's level of professionalism was judged first by the impression his appearance made. Assignment to the Criminal Investigations Division gave inspectors freedom from itchy wool uniforms. Quality attire was a small luxury he allowed himself.

"You're a regular Beau-Ruddy-Brummell." Archie didn't give two whits for how he looked as long as his clothes were clean and comfortable.

Brummell, the late English dandy, was still thought the most fashionable man of the century. The one all who aspired to dress well compared themselves to.

"Had I his money, I'd outshine him any day of the week," Rudyard smiled, confident in his assessment.

An overhead bell on the door jingled as they entered. Archie removed his bowler as soon as he crossed the threshold. Rudyard hated hats. He wore them only when social convention demanded it or when the weather turned frigid. After his years in the army, he'd had enough of helmets and hats to last a lifetime.

Two women huddled over a wide-brimmed bonnet with a white ostrich feather poking from the band. The plume was long enough, and fluffy enough to guarantee annoying interference with anyone standing close.

A petite woman with dark brown curls, clusters of which had escaped her many combs adjusted the hat on the other woman's head. The petite one stood on a wooden green grocer's crate to do so as she talked in a gentle but firm voice, assuring the woman the style was the latest from Paris. Attractive, with large brown eyes, a turned up nose, and too full mouth, Rudyard guessed she had several years on him. He figured her for a well-preserved forty. Far younger than the ancient dressmakers he'd dealt with in the past, she had to be an employee of Mrs. Porter's.

The employee eyed Rudyard, then Archie, then gave Ruddy another fast once over, flushing bright pink when her eyes met his. She quickly shifted her attention back to her customer. If she meant to be subtle, she failed. Even Archie saw her quick perusal, judging from the smile and brow wiggle he shot Rudyard. For a day that started off with an ugly murder, it was looking brighter. She didn't wear a wedding ring but she didn't look the spinster type. He guessed she was a widow like the shop's owner. London was filled with widows. The field narrowed when one counted the attractive ones, it narrowed further still if the lady possessed a healthy, lusty interest in one. At least he hoped there was some heat behind her perusal of him.

She glanced over at Rudyard again, then glanced down at the victim's straw bonnet in his hand. She excused herself from the customer, stepped down from the crate, and came over.

"I see the hat you're carrying is crushed across the crown. Were you looking for a replacement?"

"No. I'm Detective Inspector Bloodstone and this is Detective Sergeant Holbrook. We'd like to speak to both you and Mrs. Porter regarding the lady who bought this hat."

"I'm Allegra Porter. How can I help you?"

"Our questions are better suited for private conversation. We'll wait while you finish with your sale," Archie told her.

"Thank you, I'll try to hurry the purchase along." A short time later, the customer left the shop wearing a satisfied smile and her new hat.

Mrs. Porter hung the *Closed* sign up and led he and Archie to a cubbyhole of an office in the rear of the store. "What did you need to know about the lady I sold this to?"

"Do you remember her?" Archie held the hat out to her but she didn't take it.

"Yes." She took a short breath, held it for a few seconds, let it out, and then took another. Rudyard suspected she was afraid to ask what she wanted to ask. "Did something happen to the lady who owned the hat?"

"Yes," Rudyard said.

"What?"

"She was murdered this morning."

The color drained from Mrs. Porter's face. "Murdered." She sank into the desk chair and brought her hands to her face. "Merciful heavens."

Violence rarely touched the lives of the *good* citizens of London, or so they believed. Archie didn't care for the abrupt tone and harsh honesty Rudyard employed with witnesses. For his part, Ruddy had little patience for pussy-footing around while investigating serious crimes.

A sad look replaced her initial shock as Porter looked from the hat to him. "Poor girl. How awful."

Archie touched a hand to her shoulder and said in a gentle voice, "We'd appreciate anything you can tell us about her."

"She's...was a seamstress for Garfield's. She'd come into the store a number of times and tried on most of the hats but never bought any. I knew, of course, money was an issue. I think she only owned two dresses and both showed they'd been mended often."

"If she couldn't afford your hats, how'd she wind up with this one?" Archie asked.

"It's not uncommon for my better customers to wish to sell a hat back to me once it is out of season. I prefer not to buy them back, but I'd rather that than lose a customer. This one," she gestured toward the bonnet, "is a return. I felt sorry for the girl and sold it to her at a deeply discounted price."

"Did you happen to learn her name?" Ruddy asked.

She turned to Rudyard. "I don't recall off hand, but I will go through my receipts and see if I can locate it."

"I'll check with you tomorrow around the same time, if that is good with you," Rudyard said. Once the investigation part of the meeting was done with, he'd ask Porter to dinner. That was his plan anyway.

"Where can I contact you if I find it?" She pushed a curly lock of hair from her face. "To be brutally honest, I'd rather you didn't come to the shop again. Many of my clients have delicate dispositions, Inspector. They live quality, orderly lives. Unfortunately, a necessary evil in your line of work requires you to function with the seamier, more sordid types in the city. Much as you may not wish it, I fear some is bound to...to..."

"Rub off?" he finished for her.

She nodded, doing so with an expression of authority. The face of a person certain in her opinion.

The belief wasn't uncommon. When he first started on the job, the attitude troubled him and he attempted to defend the work. He gave up early on and over the years the attitude lost most of its bite. Although, hearing Mrs. Porter repeat it stung.

"You may find me at Holborn Police Station. I'm there most days until early evening."

"Thank you for understanding." She stood and opened the door. A not so subtle signal for them to leave.

Outside Archie put his bowler back on and said, "Sorry, Ruddy. I'd have sworn she had her eye on you for a romantic reason."

"Not important."

"I wish you'd let my missus introduce you to one of her available lady friends."

"Absolutely not. I appreciate the thought, but no. I'm not lonely or starved for feminine companionship."

"What if I guarantee Margaret won't pester you with matchmaker questions?"

"You cannot guarantee such a thing. She will pester me. It is a woman's nature. Every time she sees me, it'll be a barrage of questions...*Do you think you'll be asking her to take tea with you? Or, do you think you'll be asking her to dinner? Do you think she's pretty? Everyone at church loves her. I can see the two of you on lovely Sunday walks together.*"

"Ruddy—"

"No."

# Chapter Four

Mrs. Goodge—Ruddy's motherly, round-as-she-was tall, landlady met him at the front door of the boarding house. She always did on evenings he came home at a decent hour. He'd lived at Mrs. Goodge's for five years. She liked having a policeman on the premises. Because she did, he rented the top floor's two-room flat with a private bath, for little more than what her other tenants paid for their single rooms with a shared bathroom.

"Mr. Bloodstone, you're here in time for dinner. I hope you'll join us for a change. We've lamb stew tonight, very tasty if I say so myself."

"It smells wonderful and I'm certain it tastes even better, but I must decline. I've a prior commitment."

Over the years, he often used the excuse. Rarely was it true. In all that time, he ate twice with the rest in the dining room. Twice was enough. He had nothing against Mrs. Goodge or her tenants. They always exchanged friendly greetings when they passed in the hall. But sharing the table with them reminded him too much of his home growing up. He loved his brothers and sisters but ten children vying for food every meal was chaotic and never enjoyable. Once she said grace, his mother served his father. After his father's plate was filled, what remained on the platter came to the children. The older ones served themselves first and then passed the dishes down to the younger children. As second from the youngest, many nights he fell asleep with his stomach growling, having had to make do with a few vegetables, and a hunk of black bread soaked in the gravy and drippings that remained. If his father's customers paid on time, Sunday dinner had meat, most of which didn't make it to his end of the table either.

Like the childhood meals, eating with them was all arms reaching, elbows bumping, and loud chatter. He simply preferred to dine out, usually at The Boot and Bayonet, a favorite pub. Although on occasion, he'd bribe Mrs. Goodge with a nosegay of posies to bring a tray up to his rooms. Tonight, he'd head over to the pub as soon as he changed.

Standing in front of the mirror, he removed his tie and the starched collar from his shirt. The scar had itched all day, to the point of being raw and sore. The spear mark had puffed up and the skin around it had turned pinkish-red. Ruddy rubbed a cream that helped with the itch and calmed the chafed tissue down. Relief came quickly as he changed into a looser-fitting casual shirt.

#

Ruddy closed the pub door. He stood still for a moment to let his eyes adjust to the gaslight dimmed by the haze of pipe and cigar smoke. From behind the bar, Morris Thornley waved to him with his one good arm. His left arm, shattered by a Russian gun at Balaclava, had been amputated at the elbow. An accounting of how many Russian rounds struck him, varied with the number of pints he downed.

Unable to remain in the army, the veteran of the 11th Hussars or Prince Albert's Own, as they were known, Thornley scraped together the money to buy a rundown pub. Before he opened, he hired Tom Graves, a young private who'd been drummed out of his regiment following a scandal.

With Tom's help, walls were painted, tables added, chairs refurbished, and the kitchen fixed up so Morris's wife and granddaughter could prepare meals. He changed the name from The Two Roses to The Boot and Bayonet. The sign outside showed two Martini-Henry rifles with bayonets attached crossed over a pair of worn hobnail boots. Morris held firm to the philosophy that all commissioned officers had goose shit for brains. He wanted a place where rank and file soldiers felt welcome, both those in active service and veterans. Through word of mouth, he let it be known, *no officers*. It worked. His clientele was almost all enlisted and none ranked higher than color sergeant. He removed the old owner's wall paintings of hounds on hunts and replaced them with posters of dogs in the various military uniforms of high-ranking officers.

Ruddy waved back and made his way through the gallery of different breeds dressed as famous generals, colonels, majors and the like. Morris chose one of a cocker spaniel for General Thesiger, or as Freddy Thesiger was more commonly known, Baron Chelmsford. Rudyard served under Chelmsford. He'd have picked a nervous little dog, perhaps a one of those hairless Chinese Crested dogs instead...a dog that would hesitate to act, as Chelmsford did that January day years ago. The day his indecision resulted in the massacre at Isandlwana. Not one of Ruddy's friends survived the slaughter.

He sat at the small table farthest away from the dart board and card games. Laughter and joking from the customers traveled across the room to where he was, but it blended into a constant hum easily ignored.

Morris came over with a bar towel and wiped the table top off. "What's the special today?" Ruddy asked.

"Fish pie and roast potatoes."

He liked fish pie, but the smell of Mrs. Goodge's meat stew had him hungry for a heartier dish. "Is there any pork or beef pie?"

Morris shook his head. "Not tonight, maybe Sunday. Got some bangers and mash, or fish and chips."

"The fish in the pie fresh?"

"Caught today."

"I'll have it then."

"We've apples just in from the West Country. I'll

bring you wedges and a slice of cheddar for dessert."

"Thank you."

Morris left. Ruddy dug out his Waterman Fountain Pen from his breast pocket and rolled his shirt sleeves up a couple of turns. The American made pens were expensive and guaranteed to be leak proof. He ordered two in hopes the company was right. He hadn't found a leak proof pen yet and had the ruined shirts as evidence. Next he took out his field notebook and drew two lines down one page. At the top of each column he put a symbol. Good suspects went under the plus sign, bad a minus sign, and possibles under the question mark.

First shift at the garment factories started at eight in the morning. The museum guard said the times he saw the victim it was close to seven-thirty. Assuming they could confirm she worked as a seamstress, it was safe to say she cut through the gardens on her way to the factory. He stared at the blank page. Who begins his work say around the same time?

Market men started their deliveries hours earlier, at first light. He put the flower, vegetable, and meat drivers in the minus. Chimney sweeps worked only daylight hours. He put them in the plus column then drew a line through the entry. Early mornings still had the bite of chill. People kept small fires going while they dressed and readied for the day. Flues held their heat until midday, which eliminated chimney sweeps. In the questionable column went shop keepers who dealt in dry goods, clothing and shoes. Most shops didn't open until midmorning but the owners likely arrived early to handle other business. The strongest possibilities were with tradesmen like roofers, maintenance men, and carpenters. They generally didn't begin their work until the family who hired them or the business owners and employees were up. He filled up the plus column with as many repairmen as came to mind. He'd have to find time the next day to walk around the surrounding streets and make note of where any building workers or tradesmen were on site.

His dinner came and he ate leisurely and slow. Who else could he add or eliminate? He put cab drivers in the minus column. They didn't have set routes. For one to know the victim cut through the gardens, they'd have to have been in the right place at the specific time more than once to know her habit.

He relaxed against the slats of the chair back, stumped to think of more for the plus list. June, Morris's granddaughter, came with his dessert and to clear his dinner plate. No sooner had she picked the one plate up and set the other down than an argument broke out across the room. The flipped table with the card game hit the floor with a loud bang and accusations of cheating were shouted. The friends of the accused player stood and challenged the friends of the accuser. They answered by charging the first group.

Morris and Tom dashed from the bar.

"Need help?" Ruddy asked as Morris went by.

"Feel like mixing it up?"

Ruddy rolled his sleeves up another turn. "You know me." He handed June his pen. "Take care of this."

The three waded into the donnybrook, pulling combatants apart as they tried to get to the two who started it. Everyone continued to throw punches. Ruddy knocked one young private on his butt. When the soldier scrambled to his feet, Ruddy drew back and knocked the lad down again. When someone shoved him hard from behind, he pivoted, and took a roundhouse he hadn't seen coming to the side of his mouth. He reeled slightly from the force then delivered a stronger blow back, breaking the nose of the fellow who'd punched him.

The soldier, a fresh-faced corporal, was the one accused of cheating. The corporal immediately stopped fighting to hold his bleeding nose. While he whimpered, Ruddy delivered a one-two hit, the first to the man's jaw, and the second to his stomach, knocking the wind out of him.

Tom, whose own nose dripped blood, had a buddy of the accuser by the scruff of the neck and half-dragged, half-shoved him toward the door. Morris may have only one arm but it was a powerful one. He had delivered a blow to the accuser's chin and another to the eye that had Ruddy wince. Both accused and accuser were thrown out with a boot in the ass from Ruddy and Morris.

"Where's their wager money?" Morris asked the friends of the two who remained in their seats and out of the fight, still drinking. The two pointed. Shillings and crowns were scattered over the floor from when the table was overturned. Tom picked the coins up and handed them to Morris who put all of them in his trouser pocket. "This will pay for the drinks they've downed and any damage."

"Some of that's ours, you know," one dared to tell Morris.

"You're welcome to take it—well, you can try."

None moved.

"I thought as much," Morris said and went back to the bar.

Ruddy stepped over to the spittoon and spat out blood. He ran his tongue along his gums feeling for the cut where a tooth sliced the inside of his lip. "Bloody hell, that skinny bugger got me good," he said, tasting more blood. He gave the tooth that suffered the brunt of the punch several test wiggles with his thumb and forefinger. A cut would heal, but a loose tooth might abscess and need pulling. He really did not want to run around with a big gap in his mouth. It'd show every time he smiled, which would be a pity since most women told him they liked his smile. The tooth didn't move a bit, nor did the ones surrounding it. He sighed, relieved. "Thank heavens."

Morris poured three shots of rum. He handed one to Tom, and put another in front of Ruddy. "Your dinner is on the house, of course. Glad to see you can still go toe-to-toe with the lads."

"I occasionally spar with a few of the fellows in training at a local ring." He downed the rum in one swallow and found the glass immediately refilled. He wrapped red knuckled, swollen fingers around the drink this time.   It occurred to him that the attractive and opinionated Mrs. Porter would say, policeman or not, he was part of the growing class of ruffians.

"What are you grinning at?" Morris asked him.

"The possibility I might be a ruffian at heart, policeman or no."

"Might?" Morris scoffed. "Doesn't matter which side of the pugilistic pillow you lay your head with the law or without, if going to bed with bloody knuckles doesn't bother you, you're a ruffian."

## Chapter Five

Cornwall, England

"Burton, I'd like to leave for London at first light tomorrow." William didn't look up from the brochure as he gave additional instructions to the valet. "Send cook and one of your gentlemen ahead to assist the staff there to ready the house."

His decision to go into the city was twofold. One, the city offered a nice change. He liked discussing politics with other members of the House of Lords who belonged to his club, Boodles. Two, he had no desire to hang around the estate and continue to act morose over Isabeau's death.

"I assume I will be traveling with you sir?" Burton asked, his demeanor a bit less stoic than usual.

"Of course," he said, laying a hand on the valet's jacket sleeve. "Where would I travel without you? Only Americans and bourgeoisie leave home sans proper staff. I meant to say *we* will be leaving at first light."

"I never doubted it." Burton beamed, as much as an English valet would allow himself. "Shall I order the brougham prepared?"

"Yes, but we're only taking it as far as Penzance." William hovered over a bowl of fresh cashews. Popping a couple in his mouth he chewed slowly, savoring the creamy flavor of the rich nuts. He wolfed down several more, brushed the salt from his fingers and stuck his hands in his trouser pockets. He tried to limit his intake to one handful.

The expensive nuts had to be imported from India. Fresh ones were difficult to come by in London, even more so in a remote shire like Cornwall. He consistently violated his restrictive self-imposed rule since he took a handful every time he passed a dish.

"We'll take the railway from there to Paddington. It's easier on my kidneys than an extended coach ride. Besides, the Great Western has added two new passenger cars. I'd like to examine them. Since the financing came from Parliament, it never hurts to check on how one's money is being spent."

Humming a cockney pub song he'd heard in Launceston, William grabbed another handful of cashews and headed for the stable. He'd ride out and meet with Harold to see how the new guards were doing patrolling the grounds for poachers. In his absence, Harold had permission to prosecute any violators to the fullest extent.

#

"Sir—" Burton stood just inside the library door. "A gentleman to see you."

"Who is it? I'm trying to finish my correspondence before the journey," William snapped. "You know I don't relish these interruptions." The role of polite host didn't hold a lot of appeal for him on most nights. Tonight was no exception. Gone were the riding jacket and the waistcoat along with his cravat that got tossed several brandies ago. He enjoyed his solitude. All day he looked forward to a quiet evening before going to London. A nice late night snack had already been brought to him, which he'd have to have removed now.

"It's Mr. Goddard."

"You should've said so. Show him in."

William put a check mark by the old French manuscript and closed the bookseller's pamphlet. He laid his dinner tray of bread, cheese, and fruit on top of a table in an unlit corner of the room and waited for his friend.

"Dennis, how the devil are you? It's been ages since I've seen you last." He waved his hand toward one of the club chairs. "Please sit down. Brandy?"

"Love one. I apologize for not visiting sooner. Meant to come over the other day when I heard about Isabeau. Terrible tragedy."

William tipped his chin in a single nod and handed the drink to Dennis who took the snifter and sat back.

"You wouldn't happen to have a cigar," he asked, tapping at different coat pockets. "Seem to have left mine home."

"I do, a fine Montecristo, brought in special from the Caribbean." William flipped open a wooden humidor on his desk and trimmed the end of two cigars with a monogrammed cutter.

"Nothing worse than a beggarly neighbor," Dennis said with a self-conscious laugh. After a couple of puffs the Montecristo stayed lit. On the fourth puff, he blew out a long, blue trail of smoke that made rings before dissipating in the air. A wispy cloud quickly filled the room between the men and their cigars.

"Don't be silly. So tell me, how is everything with you? How's the family?" Unlike Dennis, William inhaled, held it, then blew the smoke over the end of his cigar. The tip flared bright orange momentarily before fading.

"We're all quite well, thank you for asking. Family is why I'm here. Faith is coming back from America soon and her mother and I wanted to invite you over for a welcome home party."

"I'd love to attend, if I'm here. I leave tomorrow for London." The mention of Dennis and Amelia's daughter brought an easy smile from him. "Adorable, sweet, little Faith is returning."

"She's not little anymore. She's a lovely young woman now, if I do say so myself. But then, it's been three years since you've seen her, only one for her mother and me.

I dare say, you're in for a surprise."

"I'm intrigued. I'll make double the effort to be here. When is the party?"

"The end of June."

#

The Green Dragon Inn sign swung and creaked in the wind that blew from Mount's Bay. William stepped down from the brougham and held his silk hat tight to him, not bothering to don it as he was instantly assailed by the chilled breeze. "See to the luggage Burton, I'll register us, provided I don't get blown to Lands End first."

"Shall I pick the tickets up at the station after?"

"Yes, good idea," William said and dashed to the protection of the inn's doorway. "Make sure they're for the 9:00 a.m. and not the 7:00 a.m. I can't bear the riff-raff one must wade through on the platform of the early train."

Burton straightened to his full five-feet-eight, and sniffed, turning the corners of his mouth down. "It goes without saying sir."

The door to the coaching inn opened. William was forced to step out of the way as the landlord escorted a weeping young woman from the premises. A threadbare bonnet cast the woman's face in shadow. A few strands of light blonde hair, almost white, escaped and hung in long curls to her shoulders. For a brief moment William contemplated inquiring as to what the trouble was about, but immediately rethought the wisdom of getting involved in a matter that wasn't his concern. For all he knew, the woman might be a thief who stole from the proprietor or the patrons of the inn. Better to mind one's business he told himself. He'd have all the excitement he desired in London. He turned his back on the little drama, sliding past the man and woman and into the reception area.

After registering, he ordered a meal sent up and a hot bath prepared. Weary with a sore back from the carriage ride, William spent the rest of the evening in his room, retiring to bed early.

The following morning he left the First Class passenger's waiting room to join several men for a game of cards, perhaps ecarte or vingt-un. They seemed the sporting type, amenable to a wager or two. On previous occasions, he'd been especially lucky at vingt-un.

From behind a barred window nearby, William overheard the ticket master say in a firm tone, "Third Class passage is four shillings, tuppence."

"Please, could you not make an exception, just this once? It's imperative I reach London."

"If I make an exception for you, then I will have to do so for every peddler and wastrel in the shire. Now, move along miss, before the queue behind you grows longer."

William turned to see who the ticket master had taken such a harsh tone with. A drab bonnet caught his eye. It looked remarkably similar to the one worn by the young lady ousted at the Green Dragon. He started to walk on, after all, what were the odds it was the same female? There was no shortage of ugly hats in England, this was just another. Then he saw the pale white-blonde hair, which had leaked out the sides. He stepped closer. Could it be? He owed it to himself to at least get a good look at her face.

William watched her leave the station, the opposite direction of the platform. Her shoulders sagged and she carried a single tapestry bag in a hand that trembled. Where could a woman in such dire straits go? She bowed her head and drew the back of her hand over her eyes probably wiping away tears.

He vacillated about helping. After all, the woman's troubles weren't his problem. She wiped her eyes again and he decided to offer her some financial help, if nothing else.

"Miss, can I be of assistance?" he called to her fleeing back, just loud enough to be certain she heard. The Viscount Carton rarely raised his voice, even in anger.

She shook her head and said a low, "No," and kept

walking without a backward glance. As a rule, people didn't make a habit of ignoring him, William found her behavior disconcerting. "Miss." He easily caught up and snagged an elbow.

She stopped. "Sir, I appreciate your offer. However, I doubt you can help. You..." Deep pink colored her cheeks when she finally lifted her eyes to his. Clearly, she recognized him from the inn.

The problem was money, he knew but he wanted to hear if she'd tell the truth. He flashed his most engaging smile, one that never failed to charm. It lent a boyish innocence to his face. William knew it and often used the effect to suit his purposes. He untied the ribbon and pushed the bonnet from her face. "Why don't you let me decide if I can help or not? What's your name?"

"Catherine. Catherine Owensmouth."

"A fine Welsh girl." William brought her bare hand to his lips. Most women wore gloves. A safe wager she sold hers. "I'm William Everhard. Now that we know each other-" he teased, earning the ghost of a smile for his effort. "Tell me what you need."

"I must get to London and I'm seven pence short for the fare."

William studied her. She had bright blue-grey eyes and lashes that were fair but long and spidery. The lovely eyes held a hollow emptiness of defeat. The lost gaze of hunger and despair. He'd seen it often enough in the city. Her smooth skin had a translucent quality and was stretched tight over gaunt cheeks. Her cracked and chapped mouth might have been pretty once.

"I'm going to London also. Would you give me the pleasure of your company on my journey?"

"I have no way to repay you, Mr. Everhard."

"Please, call me William. Allowing me to pass the tedious hours of the ride with you, pays your debt." He pulled her hand through the crook of his arm. "Shall we?"

Catherine hesitated and blinked up at him with doe-like eyes lit with hope. "Thank you. Your kindness overwhelms me."

"As your beauty does me," he said, lying. He'd known a fair number of exceptional beauties. Hers didn't equal the same standard. But, she had potential. He sent Burton to the ticket window to pay for her fare.

"Come, we'll miss the train." The smell of unwashed bodies and food in various stages of either ripeness or decay almost knocked him over. Tickets in hand, Catherine glanced up at him when he cringed and made no attempt to hide his grimace as they neared the platform. He brought a handkerchief to his nose and took several rapid, deep breaths. The scent of the starch used by the laundry maid relieved the immediate anxiety he felt by the foul odors of the lower class crowd. Since childhood, his highly developed sense of smell had been more a plague to him than a boon. Weather permitting, his household staff always opened the windows of Foxleigh wide and kept them open during the day. His love of the fresh sea air was well known.

Catherine needed a wash too. She hadn't been offensive, not like the folks on the platform. Her hair and nails were clean, but a faint musty odor wafted from her clothes. She wore the same dress she'd worn the day before. William noticed the odor when she passed him in the doorway at the Green Dragon and again today on the station stairs. He'd see to obtaining a hot bath for her when they stopped for the night in Exeter.

The uniformed porter held the door to the First Class Carriage and assisted them up the few steps. Burton already verified the baggage had been loaded. William led her through the Second Class passenger car to the dining car. She took one step inside and he almost bumped into her when she unexpectedly paused to breathe in the rich scent of baking bread.

With a firm hand on the small of her back, he escorted

her to a table set with fine linen and heavy, useful crockery unlike the fragile and elaborate porcelain found at Foxleigh. He didn't bother to ask if she wanted to eat. He waved aside her protests and ordered cheese biscuits, double rashers of bacon, eggs, and mushrooms sautéed in butter. "Please, eat. If you'll excuse me, I have some business to attend and will join you in a short time."

"But Mr. Everhard, William—"

He continued on his way knowing she'd be frightened to be left alone so soon. It couldn't be helped. Later, if he kept her, she'd adjust to his repulsion toward people eating. William headed for the smoking carriage to enjoy a cigar. There should be enough time to read the papers. Even if the London Chronicle was a week old, or the Times two days past, there was bound to be some useful tidbit.

A half-hour later, he reentered the dining car where Catherine sat waiting, her breakfast dishes cleared away. The waiter brought a fresh pot of Darjeeling for her along with a pot of Jamaican coffee for him with fresh cups of fine china. William had ordered the tea and coffee on the way to the table.

William made idle conversation about some of the boring human interest stories he'd read while subtly observing how she comported herself. He wanted to evaluate her social skills and background. She poured her tea and drank with the manners and poise of a young woman brought up in a house of at least middle income. In spite of her current poverty, she spoke like someone with a modicum of education, no arbitrary dropping of consonants and vowels.

Her dress was a modest shirtwaister, simple. The coarse weave and quality of its wool he would've refused for any member of his household, and certainly himself. The dull grey color did nothing for her, but then he doubted it would do much for anyone not in line to see the undertaker. He couldn't imagine what a modiste called the color, but if asked, he'd call it, dead dove grey. The white lace collar and cuffs gave her a prim appearance, staid and old-maidish. He thought she'd look brilliant in sapphire blue or emerald green.

"Why are you so determined to go to London? Do you have a husband or fiancé awaiting you there?" he asked, seeking confirmation of what he'd already guessed since she wore no ring and had no money. Had she belonged to someone, they'd have sent her funds.

"No, I have no one. My family lives in northern Powys." She sipped her tea and cast her gaze downward then off to the side, any place but where it might collide with his scrutiny. "I hope to find employment in London, perhaps in one of the educational institutions for girls. I'd prefer one of the upper-class schools. Unfortunately, I hear they require a certificate. I imagine I'll have to settle for nursery level."

The nuances in her statement didn't escape him. One doesn't travel to London from the north via Cornwall. She had to have a reason for the circuitous route. He'd wager she'd been employed somewhere in the vicinity of Penzance, probably as a governess. And, if she'd been a governess, why wasn't she seeking another position with a wealthy family? Interesting, he thought, and suspect. Something had to be amiss. The story was a lie or at best, a partial truth. "Were you employed nearby?"

Catherine stared into her teacup and whispered, "Yes," so softly, William had to lean forward to hear her.

"As a governess?"

She nodded.

"Look at me." William took the cup and saucer from her hand. Very tentatively, she raised her face to his. "What happened?"

"I was turned out without a character reference."

William took a swallow of his coffee to hide his smugness over having been right. "Shall I tell you what I think happened or do you want to tell me your version?"

She bristled with false indignity before she agreed to give her side. "I was employed by the Richardson family of Mousehole. Have you heard of them?"

William shook his head.

"Mrs. Richardson believed her husband was bedding me. So, she dismissed me last week without the salary due me or a reference, only my modest possessions. She didn't even allow me to say goodbye to the children."

"Did you?"

"Did I what?"

"Bed Mr. Richardson."

Silence.

"I see the answer is yes. In that case, perhaps we can work out an arrangement. How old are you?"

"Twenty."

William guessed her to be about that age. He'd also been sizing her up physically since they'd been talking. By his calculations, some of Isabeau's clothes might fit Catherine. His late mistress was several inches shorter but rounder all over. A good seamstress should be able to make the changes needed. He presented his offer: "You'll never get the job you seek without a character reference or a certificate from the Secretary of Education. We can be of use to each other. I am in the market for a mistress. You have already been one man's. Why not mine? In exchange, I'll see to your living expenses, a modest house in town—"

"London?"

"Yes, also clothes, and a small household staff. As to the paperwork you need, I'm acquainted with the Secretary. I will find out about the examination you'll be required to take."

She listened to his offer, neither shock nor repugnance showed in her face. He liked that she hadn't played coy or pretended interest in the floor or her lap. "How do I know you will do what you say?"

"You don't." Impertinent creature for one in such a

drastic situation. Had he been in her place he'd have asked the same thing, but that acknowledgement didn't make him less annoyed. He wasn't in her place, he had means. "If the arrangement is not to your liking, I will bid you adieu." He reached into his inside pocket and removed a substantial stack of pound notes. William peeled off several. "London can be a difficult and dangerous city for a young woman. If you allow me, I'll leave a modest sum of money with you, enough to keep you in food and shelter for a few weeks."

She stayed his hand with hers. "I haven't said no." William paused.

"I accept your offer." For the first time since they met she smiled, fully, giving him a glimpse of straight, white teeth. The haunted expression in her eyes disappeared. She looked sweet-faced and younger than twenty. "The train stops overnight in Exeter. Does our agreement begin there?"

"No. I prefer you to be better prepared." She stared at him quizzically. Who could blame her? Any number of wild scenarios must be running through her mind. "You need a bath and your hair needs a fresh wash. I want it fashioned like a lady your age, not that severe headmistress style. And, you'll need a dress or two until a seamstress can redesign or alter more."

"I have another dress," she said in an apologetic tone and smoothed the skirt of her shirtwaister. "If you wish me to wear that instead."

"Don't tell me, it's made of the same wool but an equally boring color?"

"It's brown."

William reached over and rubbed the material between his fingers. "You dress like an upstairs maid." His fingers lingered inside her sleeve and he caressed the soft skin of her inner wrist. He tipped his head so his lips almost touched her ear. "I don't fuck the servants," he whispered and chuckled at her sudden intake of breath. From the corner of his eye, he saw the beginnings of the smirk she stifled. The rough language had been a little test. She'd passed. He'd chosen well. Pleased, William sat back in the seat. "Talk to me. Tell me about yourself."

She stared blankly and hunched her shoulders. "I'm not sure what to say."

"We'll start with something simple. What sort of literature do you read?"

The light in her eyes dulled and apprehension replaced it. "Why are you interested?"

"I read a great deal. Collecting antiquarian books is a passion of mine and I enjoy literary discussions." His explanation didn't eliminate the concern in her face. "As a governess, you must read, you must have some experience with the subjects you teach."

"Yes, of course. I...I...what if..." Her voice trailed off and her eyes dropped to a place in the middle of his shirt.

"What if—what? You don't like the same things?" William asked in an offhand way and signaled the waiter for another pot of coffee, his had grown cold. She had no way of knowing the question was another test of her truthfulness. He knew the answer. She feared offending him.

"Yes. Some men—"

William cut her off. "I'd be disappointed if you turn into one of those simpering, addle-pated females who never has an opinion unless it's mine. We shall be over before we start. You will tell me what you like and don't like in all things. In time, you will know what I like and dislike both in public and behind closed doors." Catherine's expression hadn't changed and he wondered if the full impact of his words had escaped her. He'd soon find out. "Now, you first. Favorite authors?"

"Victor Hugo, Jane Austen, and let me think there's a couple I favor almost equally, hmmm...Charles Dickens."

"Tell me, you aren't one of those social reformers, nattering away about raising up of the whole of the East End?"

"Well, since we're being honest, yes, I do believe the government needs to devote more effort to serious reform."

"You aren't a Marxist, are you? *That* would be perverse. Viscounts aren't supposed to dally with Marxists," William said, jokingly and waved a dismissive hand. He liked Hugo and had been very moved by *Les Miserables*. He even found Austen's *Pride and Prejudice*, a worthwhile read. Dickens on the other hand, he considered a dreary drone and couldn't fathom how the man managed to get published, let alone find an audience. "Name another author."

"You'll probably have something horrible to say but I like Mary Shelley, *Frankenstein*. I haven't read her other works." Catherine's eyes narrowed, as she peered over the rim of her teacup and waited for him to respond...in the negative, he surmised.

Contrary to her fearful expectations, William found himself cheered by her choice. Not many women read horror or enjoyed the genre. "Now, that is interesting. You liked *Frankenstein*. So did I, a lot."

"Poor fellow, he roused a sympathy in me I hadn't anticipated when I began the book." She smiled up at him, obviously pleased by his reaction. "Your turn, William."

"Byron, Swift, and Milton, Milton being my favorite."

"By your favorite, do you mean his entire works or *"Paradise Lost*?"

"*Paradise Lost*. I enjoy all his work, but that one the most. '*The mind is its own place, and in itself can make a Heaven of Hell, a Hell of Heaven.*'" He could almost see the wheels and gears of her feminine mind turn, reducing Milton's presumption or in the case of "*Paradise Lost*," Satan's, to a philosophy she could understand. "What do you think?"

"I think it sounds like a man's excuse to do wicked things."

"Well said, my dear."

*Journal entry*
*May 25, 1888*
*London*

I purchased a seventeenth century book yesterday. Written in French, the book itself is an unusual blend of herbal medicines and a necromancer's potions. As interesting as that is, my curiosity is even more piqued by the scrap of loose parchment I found tucked between pages at the back. I believe it's a formula of some kind. I will talk to Mr. Ingram, the chemist, later this week. Perhaps he'll recognize the contents.

Catherine surprises me daily. Already we dabble in the more exotic sexual practices of our Eastern Colonial Cultures. What she lacks in finesse, she makes up for in enthusiasm. I look forward to introducing her to my favorites and rekindle the flame I felt only once. Strange, how an act which had such tragic results would also have such profound positive effects as well.

## Chapter Six

"If everything meets with your approval, we'll go on to Albion's cafe. You'll like the place. It's quite fashionable and not far from here, on Great Russell Street. Everyone who's anyone is seen there." William picked up his gloves and hat and headed for the vestibule of the townhouse he purchased that week for Catherine. He hadn't waited for an answer nor bothered to spare her a second glance. The possibility she might not like the furnished house he provided never occurred to him. It never occurred to him she might feel anything but gratitude. Only at the door did he realize she wasn't right behind him.

"Catherine?"

"Yes, I'm ready."

Her *yes* resonated more as a hiss than an acknowledgement. Then, she hit each clipped syllable of a snappish *I'm ready* with the force of a footpad's club.

While he waited for her to join him, he took his time putting on his gloves, tugging first at the seam along the back of his hand. The leather stretched taut and tight as he flexed his hand. Next, he pressed the leather between this fingers down and ended with a final pull on the seam at the inside wrist. He used the time questioning whether or not to ask what she was in a twist over and decided he might as well. "What are you unhappy about?"

"I don't understand why you've set me up in a house so far from yours. I'm practically dressing on the steps of the museum."

Did the mutinous Catherine think close proximity to each other made the odds of deeper sentiment on his part better?

"You're being silly. Belgravia isn't far. I can get here in less than half an hour if my driver avoids the crush of carriages on Oxford Street or Tottenham Court Road."

"What about your former mistress? Did she stay with you or did she have a separate residence?"

William picked at non-existent lint from his coat, and then lifted his eyes to meet her haughty stare. He studied her for a long moment and wondered if merchants were polluting women's face powder with some corrupt ingredient that made them disagreeable. He cursed the recent spate of truculence he'd endured with Isabeau and now, it appears, Catherine too. The former he could do nothing about, the latter he'd fix immediately.

"Have a care how you speak to me, and never question me."

She blinked and bobbed her head in understanding.

He shifted most of his weight onto the heel of a stylish, square-toed boot and spun around to open the door. "I'm leaving. You may stay or go, your choice."

"I want to come," she said, in a breathless, girlish voice and laid a light hand on his arm. She had the intelligence to implore him for forgiveness with big, contrite eyes. The ploy worked. His irritation ebbed and a twinge of remorse for his harsh words passed over him.

In the same breathy way, she asked, "Are we meeting someone?"

"Yes, a friend from the House of Lords. I have a stop in Stepney to make first. The borough is derelict and unpleasant. Life is cheap. Wait in the carriage. You'll be safe in the brougham or should be, and the driver will be with you. I won't be long."

On her tiptoes, Catherine kissed his cheek. "I'll be good." She adjusted her new bonnet and tied the ribbon while she brightly chatted away. "I'm terribly excited to meet your politician friend but not as excited as I am to go to a fine cafe. I've never been in one, only the occasional pub and tea shop. Do I look all right?"

"Yes, the emerald green of your dress compliments your complexion. I like you in bright colors."

\#

As the carriage rumbled east, William pulled the brougham's window curtain back and checked his orders were followed by his driver. Although, he demanded obedience from the staff, it never hurt to verify. He'd been explicit.

"Avoid Smithfield Cattle Market at all costs." The broad roads on the border of the market were a shorter and straighter route. If empty, they'd save a noticeable amount of time. *If they were empty.* Drovers and animals going to market clogged the immediate vicinity much of the day. The bleating and lowing combined with the filth and mire they left behind assaulted his senses. He hoped travelling at the dinner hour eased the congestion.

The sight of Stepney that greeted him from the window proved only slightly better than Smithfield. Street sellers hawking everything from tin utensils, to small packets of "fresh" roasted meat treats. He found the noticeable lack of stray cats by the fish sellers rather unsettling. Sharp ribbed dogs skulked along the curb. Every once in a while one stopped and snuffled at a remnant thrown into the gutter, or yelped as a costermonger's cart rolled over a paw or tail.

Catherine leaned forward to peer around his shoulder. He laid his arm diagonally across her chest and pressed her back into the cushioned seat. "You needn't be exposed to the sight of this rabble."

William let the curtain fall into place, having no desire to have his senses further assaulted by the extraordinary depth of poverty.

In a hushed, respectful voice, she asked, "May I ask why we are in Stepney?" She'd taken pains to let the question sound inquisitive and nothing more.

"I am visiting a charity hospital."

Her head snapped to the left and Catherine stared wide-eyed at him. Her lips twitched, but she resisted asking the questions he knew she desperately wanted to pose. He suffocated a laugh as she struggled, torn between satisfying her raging curiosity and not wanting to risk his ire. She'd hear what his motivation was when he met with Lord Montague, so he might as well end her suffering.

"I am giving a reform bill to a friendly member of Commons to present on the floor of Parliament. Don't know who yet. My opposition will have his bill put forth by another MP, a bill that diverts available funds from my cause to his. I want to use one or two charity hospitals as arguments against him and his cause. I need to know what points to make, what the greatest need is for the hospitals."

"You spoke against reform on the train."

"No. You didn't listen. I spoke against reformers."

Her brows dipped together briefly. "I didn't realize one excluded the other." Her face brightened with sudden enthusiasm. "Since we're discussing reform, it seems to me the government needs to acknowledge more than one cause."

"This is exactly why I dislike reformers. The problem with most—" He pointed at her. "You all want a world of change instantaneously. You're never satisfied with small but consistent improvements. Nor do you ever offer a viable suggestion for achieving change. Trust me darling, the government is well aware of the abundance of worthy causes and institutions to put precious sterling into. The problem is choosing the right ones first and finding the pounds to allocate."

The carriage came to a halt. William moved the curtain back and saw a brick building not unlike a dozen other tenements on the street. The only difference, a blackboard hung above several windows proclaiming the place to be the East London Hospital for Sick Children. A small crowd of young women who looked old beyond their years and rail thin older women stood with children of all ages on the sidewalk.

William opened the door and had one foot on the steps when he felt a tug on his sleeve.

"May I come? I am quite fond of children," Catherine asked not letting go of his sleeve. "I believe I'll be as safe with you inside the hospital as out here."

He hesitated, his analytical gaze flickered over her, taking her measure. He didn't worry over exposure to illnesses. He came from the healthiest of families and was rarely ever sick. The children inside were the poorest of the poor and suffered all manner of diseases, nothing like the children she was governess to. She might be part of the trade class and savvy enough to be a fine lover, but she'd still been sheltered. The cumulative effects of visiting such a place might trouble her for weeks. He had neither the patience nor the inclination to coddle a faint-hearted or grievously ill mistress.

"Please William, let me go with you."

"Fine," he agreed against his better judgment. "Be aware, I've no mind to listen to blubbing or to endure morose moods because you've seen a side of life not meant for your eyes."

She kissed his cheek and said, "Thank you."

#

The atmosphere at Albion's was subdued. Few tables were occupied this early in the evening. London's upper crust preferred to eat later, a habit they denied acquiring from the French. A chamber quartet played a calm Bach selection. William requested a table by the windows that overlooked the lush indoor garden belonging to the British Museum's Library and Reading Room. The museum brought in flora from all continents. According to a press release, it had been the current curator's idea to show off the varied species to an appreciative café clientele.

Catherine touched her fingers to the glass tittering like a young girl. She oohed and aahed over the exotic displays of flowers and trees. A strange sense of triumph filled William. He'd opened the door of a new world to her.

She reached over and wrapped her fingers over his. "What a lovely place. Can we come often?"

"If you wish. There are many other fashionable cafes for you to visit also."

The waiter hovered like a haughty sentinel as William ignored him and kissed the back of Catherine's fingers. After a moment, the waiter cleared his throat. William let go of Catherine's hand and turned his attention to the server. "Good evening."

The waiter stared straight ahead. The ties of his white apron circled the thin man's body twice and ended in a large knot to the front. A clean linen towel lay draped over one arm bent at ninety degrees across his abdomen.

"Sir?"

"A bottle of your finest Medoc."

"We're not having dinner here?" Catherine asked.

"No. I've provided you with a fine cook. She'll prepare whatever you like later."

"Why did we come here if we're not going to eat?"

"They have an excellent wine selection and I thought you'd be pleased with the ambiance. Did you not understand when I said not to question me?"

"I understood." She eyed an elegantly carved cart under a painting of the queen. "There's a berry scone on the pastry tray over there with a pot of clotted cream. I love clotted cream. May I at least have a scone and cream?"

"I'll order one boxed and you may take it home when we leave. Now, you need to be quiet for a while darling. Lord Montague is coming over."

The pasty-faced Lord always reminded William of Humpty Dumpty. His girth deceived those who didn't know him into thinking he was a jolly simpleton of an aristocrat and easily fooled. No one enjoyed this assumption more than Montague, who never bragged, but belonged to the Royal

Microscopical Society, an elite group of science oriented intellectuals.

"I say Everhard, how the devil are you doing?" His bold perusal swept over Catherine. "Quite well, I see. Don't sit there like a bump old boy, introduce us."

"Catherine Owensmouth, may I present Godwin Montague." William gestured in the direction of his associate. Catherine proffered her hand.

The stout Lord bowed and brushed her fingers with his lips. "Call me Montague, everyone does," he said with a wink. The waiter positioned an extra chair at the table so the men could face each other. "Do you still intend on pursuing your plan to increase the food allotment at the charity hospitals?"

"Absolutely, starting with the children's hospital in Stepney."

"Seems a waste of effort to me. They get two meals a day. How much can a sick child eat? I doubt most have the strength to finish what they're given now."

Doctors blamed their illnesses on many causes: squalid conditions, close contact with vermin of all sorts, tainted food and water. William believed lack of nutrition contributed as much as the other causes. "I've been there. I've yet to see a child who hasn't a hollowed out stomach. Feed them better and the strength will come." Montague huffed. "I also intend to ask for an increase in the heating allowance. By the time I left today, my fingers were icicles. It didn't matter how warm it was outside."

"Still don't see the point, Everhard."

"Think about it. Get them healthy and they are contributing part of the workforce rather than a drain on resources."

"Perhaps, you're right. Along those lines, I heard an interesting rumor, has the ring of truth though." Montague glanced over at Catherine.

"She's all right. Go on."

"Fawcett will help push your plan through Commons, but he'll want a quid pro quo."

"No surprise there. I want nothing to do with his quid, pro, quo. He'll want me to support his prison reform law, help convince the Lords of its merit." Fawcett's politics rubbed him the wrong way as did the man. "The purpose of prison is to discourage crime. His reform will have the whole of the East End breaking windows and stealing ladies reticules to get into Newgate because the food and accommodations are better than the workhouse."

William sipped the Medoc the waiter had brought and mulled over his options. Fawcett had been in Commons a long time, his influence would be a big boon. But at what price? "I'll have to find support elsewhere. I can't in good faith agree to upgrade the facilities for those lawless among us. Not as long as we have so many unfortunates who haven't resorted to crime."

"You have an uphill battle if you go against him, Gladstone's related by marriage."

"I know. I know. All these monies he wants for cutpurses and footpads take away from worthy causes like the East London and Evelina Hospitals to mention two. I'll give him a battle royal."

"I've no doubt you will. I look forward to a most entertaining debate. Until then, Everhard." Montague grabbed the hat and walking stick he came with, nodded to William and added a little bow to his nod at Catherine and left.

"When we're finished here, I want to stop at a chemist friend's on the way home."

In the carriage, William removed her glove and pulled a small velvet box from his pocket, dropping it into her palm. 'I meant to give these to you before Montague arrived and forgot. They're cameo earrings, I thought you might like them."

## Chapter Seven

Ruddy hummed the exciting last minutes of the 1812 Overture as he worked to shape the hot metal. This section of the music mimicked cannons being fired, which he fancied when working iron. He matched his hammer strikes to the pounding of the big guns he heard in his head. He never cared for, or learned the first half, so he couldn't hum to it. In his opinion, the opening took too long to get going. Most of the time, he preferred the jauntier music hall tunes.

Four hard blows followed by three lighter taps after each and he needed to put the iron piece back into the forge fire. When the curved arm piece turned white hot, he pulled it from the coals.

"Inspector Bloodstone," a female voice he didn't recognize called out.

Ruddy laid the hot iron and tongs on the side of the anvil and turned. What the devil? The last woman he expected to see stood under the trellis. Never had a victim or witness from one of his cases ever come to where he lived. "Mrs. Porter. What are you doing here?"

She eyed his leather apron. "That looks like a farrier's apron. Are you some type of blacksmith in your free time?"

"No, my father's a blacksmith. This is one of his old aprons." Sweat trickled into the corner of his eye and stung briefly before he wiped his sleeve across his damp face.

"Was that Tchaikovsky you were humming?"

He nodded.

Out of the unflattering light of her shop's gas lamps and in the afternoon sun, she appeared prettier, softer and fresh-faced. Soft and pretty didn't mean it was all right for her or anyone to know where his home was.

"How did you know where I lived?"

Her face flushed pink. She blinked owl-like several times and clutched her reticule close. "I went to Holborn Station first. I explained to the sergeant at the desk that I had important information for you. He said as it was part of a murder investigation, he didn't see the harm in telling me where to find you. I imagine he felt a small widow lady wasn't much of a threat to you. I-I didn't think you'd mind."

"Lucky us. I didn't know we had a seer among us."

"What do you mean?"

"He divined you were a widow," he said with a smile, enjoying her discomfort.

She drew herself up like a pigeon on a stroll. "Do you want my information or not? I can just as easily leave you to your metal works and a note with my news at the station."

"You're here now. What did you want to tell me?"

"The murdered lady is Georgina Ellis. I found her address." She brought out a slip of paper from her skirt pocket and approached Ruddy. "Here."

He took the paper from her. "Thank you."

"I'll be going now."

"Good day, Mrs. Porter."

She stopped by the old garden chair and picked up his sketch pad. She looked from the pad to the bench he was working on and back to the pad. "Did you draw this pattern? I'm always interested in fashion of any kind."

"Yes. It's my interpretation of a flower that grows in India."

"Is that curly-cue piece still hot?" She put the pad down and stepped toward the forge.

"Yes. Very." He caught a whiff of lavender as she moved past him.

"What's this piece?"

"The arm rest for a garden bench."

"Do you do a lot of this type of thing?" She pointed to the ornate iron back attached to the wooden seat.

"Yes."

"Why? Don't your investigations keep you busy?"

"I spend many hours a week trying to solve crime, but even I have off time, Mrs. Porter, as I'm sure you yourself have. I like working with the steel and iron. I do some repair jobs but mainly I make decorative garden pieces. I like the creative process involved and it relaxes me. I like not thinking about crime and criminals."

"Do you work on commission? I know someone who might like to hire you."

"Generally I do, but this bench isn't a commission. It's a surprise for Mrs. Goodge, my landlady. She often crochets out here and only has that rickety chair to sit on."

"Did your father teach you how to work with iron?"

"Yes."

"Why not become a blacksmith too?"

The forge fire had begun to ebb, the coals losing some of their bright orange. He tugged on her arm and she moved back. "Embers." He poked the fire, spreading the hottest coals out and away from each other.

"Why not be a blacksmith too?" she asked again.

Why she wanted so much information, he couldn't begin to comprehend. The questions were harmless though and didn't bother him to answer.

"Two of my older brothers work with my father now. There's only so many blacksmiths needed in the part of Wales I'm from. That and I didn't want to go to bed every night in misery with an aching back. My brothers handle the heavy draft and plough horses and my dad does mares and ponies."

Mrs. Goodge came from the rear of the house into the garden. "Working hard, I see, Mr. Bloodstone." She smiled at Mrs. Porter. "Where are your manners? You should cease toil when you have company. Have you offered your guest tea?"

"No. I didn't think this a social visit."

"You should offer none the less."

"Would you care for a cup of tea?" He expected Porter to say no.

"I'd love one." She extended a gloved hand to Mrs. Goodge. "I'm Mrs. Porter by the way." Unlike men, the women barely touched fingers in greeting.

A tiny frown formed between his landlady's brows at hearing the 'Mrs.' then disappeared. "Mrs. Goodge, it's lovely to meet you. Now, about that tea—"

"Mustn't keep a lady waiting, Mr. Bloodstone," Goodge said.

He let out a heavy sigh and hoped Porter saw and took the hint. Tea with the hat maker would be a total waste of time, of that he had no doubt. At best there'd be a long period of idle chitchat, and at worst, silly feminine jibber-jabber. What could she possibly want to talk to him about, certainly not the investigation?

"Mrs. Goodge will show you to the parlor," Ruddy said. "Excuse me for a minute. I need to put my apron away and I'll be down directly."

In his room, he washed his face and hands, ran a comb through his hair, and changed shirts. He went downstairs with fingers crossed Porter wouldn't stay long.

When he joined them, the conversation revolved around the latest fashion in hats from Paris, the unseasonably warm spring, and Queen Victoria's broken heart. Newspapers dubbed her, *The Widow of Windsor*. Although, twenty-seven years had passed, she'd never gotten over the death of her husband Prince Albert.

To his relief, Porter left after one cup of tea. Ruddy saw her to the door, thanked her again for the information on Georgina Ellis, and said goodbye. He was midway up the stairs to change back to his metalworking clothes when Mrs. Goodge stopped him.

"Mr. Bloodstone, you were very quiet during tea. I'd have thought you'd speak up and invite Mrs. Porter to the Kensington Gardens pond. Clearly, she wanted you to. She mentioned she liked it there, twice, and that she went on Sundays."

"She also doesn't like the police. She told me that herself so I see no reason for the two of us to get together." He started up again.

"Mr. Bloodstone—"

"What?"

"She's seems a lovely person and I worry you won't find a nice lady to share your life with. I fear you'll end up a lonely old man. If you don't wait forever to marry, you're young enough to have a house full of children. Cherub-faced tykes to bounce on your lap, and hug, and kiss, sons to pass on your name, wouldn't you like that?"

Mrs. Goodge meant well. "Don't fuss over my being a lonely, old man. I appreciate being alone many days and nights. And, if I feel the need to hold a wiggle worm of a child on my lap, I have more nieces and nephews than you can count on all your fingers twice over. I have only to return to Brecon to fill a fatherly longing."

"Please, for me. Invite the lady for a simple lunch."

Meeting the lady couldn't go anywhere. To people like Allegra Porter, he was a necessary evil. Goodge didn't understand that and she'd no doubt ride this horse into the ground, if he didn't make an effort. "Oh, all right. On Sunday, I'll go the pond. But fair warning, I shan't stay past noon and I have one condition. You must promise not to ask me to do this kind of thing again."

"I promise. She'll show. You'll see." Goodge bustled off toward the kitchen with a big smile.

"Lord, what have I done?"

#

Kensington Gardens pond was immensely popular with young boys from the borough. They came on weekends with toy sailboats and pretended to be Admiral Horatio Nelson or a pirate of no special origin.

The two boys next to Ruddy chose pirates of "the worst sort. Men would shake and ladies would swoon at the sight of our skull and crossbones."

"Good choices, mateys," Ruddy told them. Were he that age again, he'd choose to be a pirate too. From what he read, they had more fun than most.

"My boat," a boy about five-years-old cried. The sail of his toy had snagged on the hand of a marble nymph, part of a circle of nymphs at the center fountain.

"George no." A young woman grabbed the little boy as he climbed onto the stone surround of the water. He fought in his mother's arms, his high-top shoes catching in the folds of her dress. "Let me go."

"I'll get it." Ruddy took his morning coat off, folding it neatly and setting it onto the stone bench. He sat and removed his boots and socks and rolled his pant legs up, showing an indecent amount of male calf. A few ladies turned away at the sight. More did not, but they were subtle in their scrutiny.

The pond wasn't deep. The water hit just above his knees. The slimy bottom almost had his feet flying out from under him more than once.

Ruddy waded out to the fountain and untangled the canvas sail. The boy's mother held onto his waist as he jumped up and down encouraging Ruddy to hurry back with the boat. When he reached the edge, the boy took his toy and immediately set it to sail again, this time away from the treacherous nymph's hands.

The mother gave Ruddy a throaty *thank you*, peering up at him under the brim of her straw bonnet. She was tall, blonde and pale as milk with large blue eyes.

"You're welcome." Neither her expression of gratitude nor his response bore the tone of simple courtesy.

Ruddy straightened his trousers and put his socks and

boots back on. He glanced around and didn't see Porter in sight, which was fine with him. At the same time, he didn't see a husband or father rushing to the boy's mother's side.

"Mr. Bloodstone," a voice he now knew to be Allegra Porter's rang out. Eyes straight ahead, he silently cursed his bad luck. For a few pleasant moments, he'd thought she wasn't going to show.

He turned and waved. She smiled and waved back. Ruddy slipped his coat on and turning back to the young mother asked, "Do you and your son come here every Sunday?"

She smiled. "Most. But he's my nephew, not my son. I'm not married."

"Oh..."

"Your lady is waiting."

He winked. "Another day perhaps."

"Perhaps."

He walked towards Mrs. Porter who stood in the shade of a large oak and thought about the wasted weather. A sunny, cloudless day, a light breeze blew off the Thames. It was a perfect day for stripping down to his undershirt and working on the garden bench. Over his shoulder, he gave the spot he'd left a quick, wistful glance...or, perfect for chatting with a rosy-cheeked blonde. Good morning, Mrs. Porter." Ruddy buttoned his coat and smoothed the front so it lay flat. Then, rather than offer Porter his arm, he clasped his hands behind him. Not rude, but not the most gentlemanly thing to do.

"Please call me Allegra. May I call you Rudyard?"

He shrugged. "If it pleases you. Shall we walk?" He gestured toward the popular park's promenade.

"What a splendid day, don't you think?" She leaned in to him enough to touch her shoulder to his bicep. When he didn't respond, she bumped his shoulder again, engaging his attention. If his lack of offering her his arm bothered her, she didn't show it. Just the opposite, she looked up at him with large brown eyes displaying unexpected warmth.

Suspicious, he said, "Yes, it's quite nice," and searched her face for a clue to her odd behavior.

They walked along in silence for a short time when Ruddy could stand it no more. "What is this about Allegra? Why am I here?"

"It's an awkward topic, but I admit I planted the seed over tea."

"Don't play coy. You did more than plant a seed." He stopped and laid a light hand on her arm so she stopped too. "You obviously wanted me to come to the pond. I am mystified as to why."

"I did. I was very unkind to you when you came to my shop. My judgment of your profession was harsh and unwarranted when aimed at you. I am sorry I insulted you."

What the deuce? Part of him was desperately curious as to what instigated the change in her attitude. An equally large part of him whispered, *let it go. Do not pursue this.* The warning burned its way to the front of his brain and got beat back. The policeman in him couldn't ignore the change. He glanced around, mentally flip-flopping.

Regretting every word, he asked, "What's brought about this sudden enlightenment? Your position on the police was pretty clear but a few days ago."

"I know my apology sounds insincere."

"It sounds like a trap."

"Trap you how?"

"I haven't the foggiest notion." He shoved his hands in his trouser pockets rather than throwing them in the air and walking away. With no potential gain for her, he couldn't see how it was a trap, but what else could she be up to? "Tell me something sensible about this meet or I'm leaving."

"The news rarely, if ever, prints a story commending the police. Over the years, I formed a negative opinion of them."

"You're not alone, comes with the territory. You were

quite clear on how you feel about us. No need to put too fine a point on it." He fingered his watch chain tempted to check the time. "Apology accepted. If you're finished Mrs. Porter—"

"Allegra."

"Fine. If you're finished, Allegra, I'd like to go."

"I'm not."

Good Lord, but the woman was a blister that refused to pop.

"Yesterday a madman with a meat cleaver snatched a woman walking down the street and threatened to kill her. A constable arrived, and with no weapon other than his truncheon, pulled the woman from the man's clutches and confronted him. The man wielded the cleaver wildly, challenging the constable who stood his ground. The bobby blew his whistle several times and another constable responded. The two of them wrestled with the armed man and brought him under control."

"They did their job and did it well. How does this relate to me?"

"I realized I'd painted all of you with a nasty brush. The first constable's handling of the madman was impressive but it was seeing not what he did so much, as what he was willing to do."

Sentiment of this sort, although appreciated, was also uncomfortable. Ruddy never knew what to say or if an answer was even required. Worse, the comments came from a woman. What women said and what they meant often contradicted each other.

After a moment of fumbling for a response, he said, "It's nice to see your view of us isn't as skewed as before. It's been a pleasure speaking with you. I'll be on my way now."

Her hand shot out and she clasped his wrist in her palm with surprising strength. "Don't go yet. I hoped you'd join me for lunch." Her thumb caressed the back of his hand.

"My treat."

What did she mean by that? He looked right and left as though the truth behind the invite would fall from the sky. If one of the music hall ladies he socialized with said that, he'd know what was meant and how to answer. But hearing it from a very proper widow stumped him. Deciphering the rabbit warren that made up the minds of most women was never his strong suit. All he could do was ask for clarification. "Allegra, are you flirting with me?"

Her thumb stopped its stroking. "Um, yes. Am I not doing it right? I've never flirted. Never had to. Mr. Porter and I married young. Our courtship was short."

Ruddy's brows lifted a notch. Maybe she wasn't as proper as he thought. "I'm no expert but I understood your meaning, so I'd say you did fine. Lunch sounds lovely. However, I will pay. I prefer a lady's *treat* to be more than cucumber sandwiches."

"We are of one mind in that regard." She looped her arm through his and pressed close.

"I'm still curious. I find it hard to believe one young bobby's actions triggered a...I'm looking for the right word here, this rush to be with me."

"I've been widowed for some time now. I miss a man's touch. In spite of my unkind words to you the day we met, I didn't find you unattractive. I assumed you weren't one to go to bed in your cups every night. You were well groomed. All qualities I like. It's not easy to find men who fit."

"I see. Because I'm not hideous, not a drunkard, and appear to bathe regularly, you picked me. How you flatter me."

"It sounds awful when you put it that way." She squeezed his arm tight. "Are you changing your mind about my *treat?*"

"I'm not an ugly derelict, nor am I a fool. Nothing's changed."

*Journal Entry*
*May, 1888*
*London*

*The French alchemist's book has proven most interesting. The sorcerer claims he has the secret to eternal youth. A compound he created that makes men feel much younger than the mirror reflects nor suffer the effects of their gradual loss of strength.*

*I am not a braggart when I say in spite of my forty years, I remain strong and cut a dashing figure. But—how nice it would be to enjoy the stamina and raw power of my twenties. The formula looks simple enough. The chemical composition based on one's own without the change aging brings about.*

*Before I leave, I shall stop in and see the chemist, Mr. Ingram. I am anxious to hear what he deduces the formula to be.*

## Chapter Eight

William's coach rumbled along on the old smuggler's road toward Foxleigh Hall. The route was a major thoroughfare to the shire's southeastern cities and pitted with cavernous holes. He stared out the window in disgust after a rear wheel hit the edge of one, nearly jarring him off the seat.

His brougham passed a work crew. The same crew he'd passed a couple weeks earlier on his way to Penzance. He also noticed they were mucking about the same area. For reasons he couldn't understand, the horrible craters never seemed to get done over. If he hadn't been in such a hurry to get home, he was tempted to stop and ask them what exactly did they do with their spades. Instead, he plotted to invite the Earl of Denby out for a weekend. Let him get bounced around for hours on end. That ought to get all the holes from here to the county's eastern border filled.

A woman's scream interrupted his satisfaction with the plan. He pulled a pistol from the secret compartment in the floor, cautiously stuck his head out the window and tried to see down the road. If a highwayman had a carriage stopped ahead, he was prepared. The brougham came to an abrupt halt as the trouble came into his line of sight. It didn't appear to be a robbery. A woman, presumably the one who screamed, struggled with a cart driver. They tussled for a few seconds before the man jerked a whip from the female's grasp and began striking the carthorse over her yells and objections.

William tucked the pistol in his boot and jumped from his carriage. The cart man got another two blows in against the animal's flanks when William grabbed the whip from him. The man whirled around in time to see the strike aimed for his face, but not in time to raise a defensive arm. The braided thong caught the man's cheek, splitting the skin under his eye. The strength and downward force of the blow staggered the man.

"How dare you take a whip to this horse." He studied the animal for injury. His lips tightened at the bloody welts and the half-starved condition of the gelding. Ribs protruded at its girth, the flank had sunken in and two bones over the point of the croup stuck out. The driver had loaded the wooden cart to capacity with heavy limestone. It would have been an incredible burden for any horse smaller than a Shire, let alone a starved Cob.

"Unhitch the horse and tie him to the rear of my coach," William instructed his driver who'd already joined his employer on the ground.

"That's my horse and if you touch him I'll have you arrested for theft. I ought to have you arrested anyway for interfering with a man and his property," the cart man said, dabbing at the lash mark with a dirty handkerchief. He stuck the blood spotted rag into his pocket and squared himself up.

William pulled the man up by his shirt front until he stood on his toes. "I ought to have you flogged."

"This is an outrage. The viscount will hear of this, those stones are meant for his estate."

"I *am* the viscount."

William let go so fast the man stumbled backward, arms flaying the air and into the side of the cart. He gaped at William for a half a heartbeat, then turned his attention to the female. "What about her? She ain't no viscount and she kept me from disciplining my own beast."

For the first time, William took a good look at the woman standing off to the side. A plumed hat lay a few feet away on the ground, giving him a full view of her face. When he first observed her struggles, he envisioned the lady to be older, well into her thirties. The wrongness of that assumption just settled into his brain when she rushed forward and silk jacketed arms wrapped around his neck before he could speak.

"William."

"Faith?" He felt a nod against his neck. She leaned back just enough to allow her to tip her head and grace him with a bright smile. He held his hands at her waist at arms-length to get a longer look at her.

The thin waif he'd last seen was gone. In front of him stood a lovely young lady, perhaps the loveliest in Cornwall. Under his hands, the curved waist and shapely hips of a grown woman warmed his palms through the material of her clothing.

Faith slid her hands down his biceps, over his wrists and buried her fingers inside the hollows under his thumbs, squeezing his large hands in her smaller ones. "Oh William, how splendid of you to come along when you did. I couldn't bear to watch the brute beating that innocent horse. If you hadn't driven by, I don't know what would've become of the poor creature." Still clutching his hands, she gazed up at him with wide green eyes. "You saved its life."

Struck dumb, he'd never been at a loss for words before. "You flatter me," he said, finally finding his tongue. "Send your carriage away. I'll take you home. But, come and have tea with me at Foxleigh, first."

"I don't know," Faith teased and tapped a forefinger against her cheek. "It sounds terribly improper, taking tea alone with the handsome William Everhard, the Viscount of Broken Hearts." She interrupted as he started to protest, "I'll do it."

"We won't be all that alone, there's—"

Faith pulled away. "Oh mercy William, it never occurred to me, there might be a viscountess. I thought since my parents never mentioned you married, you hadn't."

"I haven't. However, my full staff will be about, much to my regret, we won't be completely alone." He drew Faith close, tugging her arm through the crook of his elbow. William assisted her into his carriage himself.

The cart driver walked around the rear of the brougham, giving the tied horse a wide berth. He lingered out of William's reach. "How am I supposed to get to the quarry," he asked, his tone defiant and surly. "And that horse cost me two...three pounds."

William tossed five guineas on the ground. "For the horse. Now, walk, while you can, because if I ever see you on or near my estate, you'll find yourself crawling."

The man touched the slashed cheek already discoloring, spat on the ground and started down the road. William climbed inside and pulled the curtain closed, then focused all his attention on his guest.

#

"You're staring." Faith removed the velvet jacket and made herself comfortable in one of the wingback chairs.

William hovered in the doorway of the drawing room awaiting the butler. "Sorry, I can't believe how you've changed." He took his time and let his eyes travel the length of her. Your hair for instance."

Faith self-consciously patted the curls that had fallen forward over her shoulder. "I know. Mother warned me it would turn. I had hoped she'd be wrong and it would stay lighter."

"I like this better."

"Do you?"

"Yes. It used to be the color of new straw, now it reminds me of orange blossom honey. It's richer, warmer— sets off your eyes." He wanted to take the ribbon out and loosen the golden locks. He wanted to stroke them and see if they were as heavy and soft as they seemed. He stepped in her direction.

"You rang sir," the butler said from inside the door.

William stopped mid-stride. "What tea did you prefer?" he asked Faith. "I have a new shipment of Oolong, they say it's the champagne of teas. I have several others, if you rather."

"I'd rather a coffee," Faith said.

"Coffee?" he asked, surprised by the request. He didn't know any ladies who enjoyed coffee above tea.

"Yes, whatever coffee you're drinking. As I recall, you always preferred coffee."

She blinked up at him, slowly, and a tiny smile tipped the corners of her mouth. If he didn't know better, William might have guessed she was flirting. A delightful prospect if true. "Coffee it is." He pulled the other wingback chair around so they sat across from each other at the small table while they talked. "I thought you weren't returning until the end of June. Your father mentioned a party for you then."

"That's when a small welcome home dance is planned, yes. But, I've been back for several days." Faith toyed with the feminine bow at the throat of her blouse. "Now that I'm home for a while I'd like to beg a favor of you."

Whatever she asked he'd agree to, the reference to her stay not being permanent pricked his curiosity. "What do you mean a while?"

"Ummm...there's a good likelihood I will be leaving for America again next spring."

He relaxed. Next spring might as well be the next century, many things could happen to change her mind. "Name your favor and if it's within my ability, I shall grant it."

The pot of coffee arrived. Faith clapped her hands together and confessed her mother didn't allow her to drink the beverage. Proceeding to add cream, she drowned the dark liquid until it was lighter than the skin on the back of William's hands.

She took a sip and peered over the rim of the cup conspiratorially, "I want you to teach me to ride."

The strange request confused him. She rode. She'd ridden since childhood. He added a spoonful of cream and drank several swallows of his coffee, trying to figure out the reason for her odd request. He couldn't. "You know how to ride, which tells me you're up to mischief. What are you plotting?"

"I am not plotting. I am planning a surprise, so obviously this arrangement must be a secret." Faith set her cup down and scooted up in her chair. Beneath the table, her knees almost collided with his. "Please, promise you'll at least consider what I want you to do."

Every cell of his body screamed at him to say no. His lips parted with that precise intention-intention being the operative word. "I promise."

"I want to learn to ride astride."

"No." Even as he denied her request, he briefly fantasized her in those form-fitting chamois breeches women wore under their riding habits. Maybe if they only rode on his estate...he gave himself a mental shake.

He never understood why her parents sent her to America to begin with and to Chicago of all cities. The wild west as far as he was concerned. "In England, ladies ride sidesaddle. Do women in Chicago ride astride?"

"Most don't, but some do and those women get around so much easier. The city is still in the midst of reconstruction from the great fire in 1871. It's a very exciting time there."

William checked his temper at her reference to Chicago and talking as though she would return. "You ask a lot. Your father, I can always bribe with fine cigars and brandy. Your mother, on the other hand, will have my hide if she finds out."

Faith leaned closer, inches from his face, her lips a hands breadth from his. She shook her head side to side a bit faster than the average metronome and waggled a finger back and forth. "They're not going to find out though, are they?

He stared into merry eyes almost as dark as his coffee. The devil was a woman and Faith one of her most beautiful minions.

#

"No!" Either Faith ignored or didn't hear the shouted order. William ran to where she came off the horse, hitting the ground with a thud he heard from a hundred feet away. His heart in his throat, he charged past the high row of shrubs. All around the estate various forms of fencing were used. Tall hedgerows, like this, marked undesignated areas and aided in discouraging trespassers. The short hedgerows bordered the sheep enclosures, and wooden rails lined the horse pastures. None were intended to be part of a steeplechase event, which he would inform Miss Goddard of in no uncertain terms, if she wasn't badly injured or worse. The possibilities tore at his insides.

William never lost a foot race in his youth and he still had a good deal of speed. His long strides ate up large chunks of field and left deep divots in the soft ground as he rushed toward her. She lay in the grass, flat on her back. A few steps more and he'd be close enough to drop down begging all the saints he didn't believe in to let her be unhurt.

Faith groaned and propped herself up on her elbows. She looked up at him as his knee hit the ground.

"Are you all right?" he asked and clamped her jaw between his thumb and fingers in a perfect horizontal "c," and inspected her face.

She managed a tight nod.

He lessened his grip on her chin. With the other hand he squeezed and prodded along her arm, ribs and leg. Then, he switched hands and repeated the process on the other side, quelling her protests with a sharp glare.

"What the deuce did you think you were doing jumping that high hedge? I ought to wring your neck." He released his hold and waited for the explanation he'd never find adequate.

"I knew I could do it. I wanted to experience the

sensation of gliding like a bird in flight."

"Yes, I see how well you did. You almost killed yourself. And, I don't even want to estimate how many years you took off my life with the bit of daring-do."

The willful minx stuck her chin out and folded her arms. "I will make it next time. I would've this time except I wasn't balanced or far enough forward in the saddle."

"You imagine two weeks worth of practice has enabled you to handle a risky jump like that?" William grabbed Faith by the forearm and jerked her up with him as he stood. "For your information, there'll be no next time. There may not be another lesson, period."

She didn't understand, couldn't understand. If she'd been killed or badly hurt, he'd never forgive himself. Not to mention, the extraordinary coincidence of his former mistress dying a mere six weeks earlier in a "riding accident."

"William, please don't be angry with me. I'm not afraid of heights or speed. I never have been. Besides, I've taken jumps sidesaddle, you know I have. I'll master them riding astride too. You'll see."

"I don't believe it's a good idea..."

Faith fisted her hands around the sleeves of his shirt and pressed herself against him. "Please William, please don't send me home. I do so love riding with you. I'm free to be me, here."

His fingers rested lightly on her waist wanting to encircle it. Too soon. Too forward. "All right, but you must promise to listen to me. If I say you can't do something, then you can't."

She rose up on tiptoes to hug him close then stepped back and away, beaming with delight. He wavered. His weight shifted to compensate for the unpleasant emptiness left when Faith let go. A brief rush of cool air teased his shirt where she'd clung. Brushing herself off, she jogged over to her lesson horse. A bolt of emotion seized William and he recognized how precious she'd become to him. More than once since her return he'd found himself smiling as he went about estate business but thinking of marriage and life with her.

*Journal Entry*
*June 1888*
*London*

*Another night without sleep. In my restlessness, I started reading, Le Guerisseur et Le Sorcerer, the book containing the formula for youth. My French isn't expert enough to translate verbatim but I gather it's an insanity debate between, Andre Patric, the healer and Gaston Malleville, the sorcerer. Malleville authored the compound. He claims it tricks the mind and therefore the body into a youthful state again. He goes so far to claim it can be a recipe to treat madness, if used properly over time. Patric argues such trickery eventually destroys the mind, which can absorb only so much manipulating.*

*I hated leaving Faith but at least Catherine seemed genuinely pleased to see me. I was too tired both nights to reach a state of arousal. Too tired. Both nights. What the devil has sapped my energy?*

## Chapter Nine

"Mr. Everhard." Ingram ran a hand through his thin layer of remaining hair and came from behind the counter. "The formula you asked me to decipher, I'm afraid I can only identify two of the ingredients. The one—" he hesitated, glanced around and lowered his voice, "—is a mystery to me."

Strange behavior. The furtive gesture had William glancing around himself to see if something was amiss.

The chemist reached into the pocket of his work apron and withdrew a folded piece of paper. "I know of a doctor who might be able to tell you what it is. I must warn you, sir, the man is a renegade. His theories are not accepted by London's medical community."

"Ingram, what are you saying? What do you think this compound is? Start by telling me the two elements you know."

"Yes, yes, of course, sorry," he said, still in a hushed voice. "A small amount is almond oil which has been mixed with a substantial portion of papain." He must've realized from William's blank expression the substance papain was unknown to him. "Papain is derived from papaya," the chemist explained.

"Why would someone combine the two?"

"If I had to guess, I'd say the almond oil is a facilitator of some kind. I suspect it helps the other elements work their way through the body."

"This papain, what does it do?"

"It's a protein-cleaving enzyme."

William shook his head, still confused as to what Ingram was implying.

"I'll explain as best I can. In certain organisms these enzymes help speed chemical reactions in cells. This discovery is all very new. We only learned about papaya being a source for the enzymes a few years ago."

William shrugged off the information. "That's it? Why all this secrecy?"

The chemist stared at him like he was an imbecile. "I have another customer, a Mr. R.L. Stevenson, he's written a few travel stories. He too, has many questions about different chemical compounds. The things he asks are peculiar and uncommon, combinations not unlike this one. Perhaps you might wish to speak to him."

Appalled at the suggestion, William told him, "Certainly not. If I wanted all of London to know my business, I'd take out a column in the Gazette. What about the third element, the one you say I need to speak to this unsavory doctor to learn more?"

"I didn't say unsavory. Renegade is the proper word. Some, me included, believe his theories accurate just too advanced for the current academics and doctors."

"You didn't answer. What do you suspect the third ingredient is?" William asked, unsure if the man was being deliberately obtuse.

Ingram took so long to answer, William thought a response would never come. At last he said, "I know what I think it is, and I'm afraid I might be right. Please, do us both a favor Mr. Everhard and speak with this doctor."

"Tell me this: do you think this formula can successfully restore youthful vigor?"

"I don't know. If it truly restores that sort of vigor, then no. But I do fear Mr. Patric's warning about tricking the brain. Since I don't know what the third element is, I worry about the side effects of long term use. Is it possible to cause irreparable damage to the mind? Maybe."

The overhead bell on the door jingled and a prim

woman barely glanced at the two men before walking to the rear of the shop. Ingram scurried back to his mixing area and involved himself in the blending of powders.

William waited until he got into his carriage to unfold the paper with the doctor's name. His curiosity about the potion required satisfaction.

As the coach ambled over the cobblestones, William decided he'd meet with the doctor. He'd send a message to this renegade to come to the Rose and Crown pub, on Blackfriars Road, across from the Thames, nowhere near his home or club. He wouldn't take a chance he might be recognized talking to someone whose character and reputation were so questionable.

He relaxed against the seat's leather back and watched the fashionable crowd on Regent Street. Lambeth's Jewelry Shop came into view. He rapped on the roof signaling his driver to stop. The shop was a favorite of his and offered a wide array of pieces.

A cameo pendant of the Three Graces caught his eye as soon as he entered. A perfect gift for Faith. He'd give it to her at the welcome home party her parents planned.

Lambeth ran a black velvet ribbon through the stem of the pendent and attached a gold clasp to the choker. The jeweler carefully arranged the necklace in a bed of satin lining set into a box of velvet dotted with seed pearls. Lambeth made it a point to add the extra flourishes for the best customers.

#

Bodmin Edge Manor

"What is all this bickering in my normally peaceful home?" Dennis Goddard confronted the two most important women in his life who stood blocking the buffet with breakfast offerings.

"Father."

"Dennis."

His daughter and wife spoke over each other.

"Faith." He raised a silencing finger. "You'll let your mother speak." Dennis turned to his furious wife. "Amelia, what is this about?"

"Your daughter wants to announce her engagement at the welcome home party. I told her I've planned it for the start of October to co-ordinate with Devlin's arrival from Chicago." Amelia withdrew a lacy handkerchief from inside her cuffed sleeve and dabbed at the corners of her eyes. "It will ruin all my plans if she gets her way. I tried to explain that the excitement of a Christmas wedding will have faded if we announce too soon."

He made no pretense to appear as if he had to think about the solution. "Your mother has a point. Why is it so important for you to make your engagement public before Devlin can sail here?"

"All the other girls will be announcing betrothals at the end of summer. I didn't want to stand and listen to them drone on and on and not be able to discuss my fiancé." Faith pleaded her case adding drama to her cause with the open hands of a religious supplicant.

The ploy hadn't worked as a child and it didn't work with her father now. "You'll survive, and I venture, be grateful you waited."

"Father—"

"Discussion over. I want to eat my breakfast."

Faith stomped out of the dining room bemoaning the unfairness of parental judgments forced upon her.

Dennis and Amelia loaded their plates and sat at the table. "I'm anxious to meet this Devlin fellow. My sister reassures me he's a fine young man," Amelia said.

"I don't much care for the fact he's in trade."

"It's not like he's laying the stone work himself. He has his own company with quite a few master masons working for him."

"The fact he's deeply involved in the city's

reconstruction and his company is financially solid as the day is long makes him sound a solid prospect for our Faith," Dennis said, more to take the edge off his concern than anything else.

"She seems happy. I know you worry about her living so far away, but it was your idea to send her to Chicago," Amelia reminded him.

"I wanted her to see someplace besides this shire, a place different in all ways. I didn't think she'd fall in love. I always assumed she come back and marry William." Dennis dipped a sliver of toast into the soft egg yolk. "She loved him from the time she could walk. When she started to flower into a young woman and still carried a tendre for William, well..."

Smiling, Amelia patted his hands. "I thought they'd marry too. William is the finest man I can think of, *now*. At the time, however, he was quite the young libertine. We did what we believed best."

"He's never said it out right, but I have often felt he assumed they'd marry too. I've wondered sometimes if that wasn't why he never seriously pursued the eligible girls who flocked around him."

Amelia refilled her husband's cup of tea. "Perhaps. There's no point in dwelling on it. What's done is done. I'm sure William will be happy for her."

#

The Rose and Crown didn't differ much from the Cornish pubs William frequented on occasion. Like those in Boscastle, or Port Isaac, most of the patrons were dock workers, boatmen, or cargo clerks. He found a table that gave him an unobstructed view of the door and allowed him to keep an eye on the crowd of common men. He'd dressed down and taken a hired carriage, precautions a wise stranger to the area would employ. He'd ordered ale and when it arrived wiped the edge of the tankard with his clean handkerchief before taking a sip.

A small man in a rumpled frock coat stopped a few feet inside the pub and surveyed the room. He wore decent black leather gloves, his face wasn't blotched and ruddy from outdoor work and he nervously worried a metal watch chain on his waistcoat.

Now that he'd seen the nondescript fellow, William chuckled. After Ingram's warning, he'd pictured the *renegade* to be a broad-bodied man, lantern jawed, with sunken, skeletal eyes, not this mousy chap. William stood and waved until the man noticed him and came over.

"Dr. Frobisher?"

The man studied William as if he half expected to have his throat cut. His eyes darted to the left then right before he finally sat on the stool William pushed his way.

"Would you like something to drink? The ale is tolerable. I don't know if I'd trust the spirits."

"A Guinness will do. I'm not fond of socializing so I'd like to know why you wish to meet with me. The faster this is over and I can be on my way, the better. No offense, sir."

"None taken. I got your name from the chemist, Mr. Ingram." Frobisher appeared all right with the information. William continued, "I found a formula in the back of an antiquarian book. Ingram can decipher some of it. He thinks you can break down the last element." William showed the doctor the compound details.

Frobisher took the paper and removed a pair of wire-framed spectacles from inside his coat pocket. "I believe I recognize the last ingredient. If this is what I think, it's difficult to come by, and we're not sure of the effects."

"By effects you mean on the mind or mind and body?"

"Both. Can the mind convince the body to do what it normally wouldn't or is unable to do? Maybe. I also believe behavior can be controlled through the enhancement or introduction of certain chemicals to the brain. I'm working on proving the theory."

The possibilities of the mysterious formula fascinated William. The nature of the book, a tome written from a healer's and sorcerer's view, then couple it with the unusual attitude of Ingram, and it made for an enticing puzzle. "You say it's hard to come by, rare, How rare? Could someone of means obtain it with relative ease?"

"I said it was hard to come by, not rare." Frobisher folded the slip of paper but didn't hand it back. "May I keep this copy?"

William nodded yes, and added a caveat, "But answer my question and tell me more about the chemical."

"This I suspect is a hormone that comes from the pituitary gland in the human body. That's the most simplistic explanation. We don't have enough cadavers to obtain the fluid and test for all the possible effects. It has remarkable ability to repair injured tissue and shorten healing time. I speculate it might have untold uses in helping with brain disorders."

"I take it you don't refer to the harmless imbeciles or those sad simpletons who walk among us on the street talking to imaginary friends?" Frobisher didn't seem the type to concern himself with such commonplace folks.

"No, nothing so mundane. I'm thinking of a couple of my patients. One is a young mother who killed her child. This woman speaks to no one but the dead child. When she's not, she rocks incessantly to the point where she will soil herself in order to continue her vigil. Another, a man, is obsessed with fire. He has an uncanny ability to find matches and must be kept under close watch. There are others, worse ones."

Nothing the doctor said warranted him being ostracized by the medical community. William guessed the man left some key issue out. A number of theories as to what that might be crossed his mind. He wanted to hear the reason from Frobisher. "Why are you persona non grata among your colleagues?"

The doctor finished his beer and for the first time since entering the pub, smiled. "I do not belong to any men's clubs, which, I'm sure you are aware is a must if one hopes to rise in London society."

"That's not the only reason, Frobisher. I'm not a fool, don't treat me like one."

"The few proper physicians who might not care about my social standing don't approve of my extracurricular studies at the asylums. The dominant philosophy is lunatics are best put away where they don't offend the sensibilities of the good people of London."

The doctor didn't have to mention names. Several members of the Medical Society belonged to Boodles and they'd expressed those sentiments often. "Go on."

"I also have the bad taste to make the East End charity hospitals the home of my practice."

*Practice*—probably the doctor's euphemism for experiments. "Ah, interesting choice. I imagine few people miss the paupers who die in those places. You probably get quite a backlog of dead bodies awaiting burial."

Frobisher handed a passing barmaid his tankard and shook his head no, when she indicated a refill. "We have better supply than the medical schools, especially on Mondays, but fewer than you suppose." He got up. "You never gave me your name sir."

"It's not necessary. I will get in touch with you doctor. I'm very curious to hear what your final analysis of the formula is."

Frobisher touched the brim of his hat and left.

#

William had the hired carriage take him to Catherine's rather than home. All the way there he thought about the conversation with Frobisher. Were the doctor's theories about salvaging lunatics valid or did the doctor just have lunatic theories? Hours later he rolled out of bed, his mind on more personal matters.

Catherine slipped her arms around his waist, her breasts warm against his naked back. "Come back to bed, William."

"I will in a while." He stood and pulled a chair up to the window, watching the few night owls staggering down the street. The night breeze ruffled the lace draperies exposing his nakedness to anyone walking below. At this late hour, and in the dim light cast by the gas lamps, he didn't worry about being seen. He didn't care if he was.

Catherine sighed. The bed creaked and he listened to the rustle of linens as she shifted under the covers.

"William, have I stopped pleasing you?"

What could he say? He had no desire to hurt her feelings. She pleased him. Until the recent incidents, he never failed to spill himself in her. It just wasn't the same. Lovemaking hadn't been the same since the last night with Isabeau, since that long moment of ecstasy. Lord knew he tried to recapture the excitement. Catherine even let him take her to the edge with the same silk scarf. Of course, she had no idea of the scarf's history. Why wasn't it enough for him?

Maybe a change of scenery would help. "Maybe we'll go to Henley-on-Thames for a couple of days. You'll like Henley, the countryside is lovely. We'll rent a punt and sail down the river in the afternoon."

Optimistic about the day, he came to bed. Catherine teased and worked to arouse him and failed. "Don't." He'd made love to her twice. That should've been enough. "For God's sake, leave me be now."

## Chapter Ten

"I'm going to have to shoehorn the tale out of you I see," Archie said.

"I haven't a clue what you're talking about." Ruddy knew exactly what Archie referred to. The station house was a hotbed of gossip. Mrs. Porter's appearance there stirred the pot.

"The Saturday sergeant told me the widow Porter came round asking for you. Said she was all done up with a pretty bonnet and a spot of color on her cheeks."

"Nothing of note there. She's a milliner, one would expect her to have nothing but pretty bonnets."

Archie went blithely on, "He said he told her where you live as she didn't look dangerous. Did she come by?"

Archie was as much a gossip as any old woman. "Yes. That's how I found out where the victim lived. I've since spoken to the desk sergeant about telling people where I live."

"It didn't end there though," Archie said, with a solid poke in the ribs. "I heard you rendezvoused with her at Kensington Gardens the next day." He'd pronounced it ran-day-VU. Archie's Yorkshire upbringing came out whenever he pronounced anything in French.

It seemed he was surrounded by windbags. "Who told you that?" Ruddy demanded.

"Mrs. Goodge, while I was waiting for you to come down this morning. Go on then, give your partner the story."

"We went to lunch and spent a pleasant afternoon together."

After another shot to the ribs, Archie rattled on, "Show her the ins and outs of police work did you?"

"If you poke me one more time, you'll be seeing the *ins and outs* of my fist. This conversation is over. There it is," Ruddy said as he and Archie approached *Lady Poole's Home for Women.*

"Dreary looking place."

The red brick, three-story building had more bricked up windows than useable ones. They waited for a carriage to pass, then jogged across the busy road. "On her small wages, it's probably all she could afford."

"With no more window tax, you'd think they'd uncover some of the sealed ones. Newgate Prison gets more light," Archie added.

"Look at the upside. At least she had a warm place to lay her head at night. I imagine not every woman she worked with had that advantage."

They rang the bell attached to the wall next to the door. The brass bell reminded him of the one at his childhood school with its loud unpleasant clang. After a short wait, a prim looking, grey-haired woman in a dull brown dress with a white lace collar opened the door.

"How may I help you," she asked.

"You would be..."

"Mrs. Poole, the proprietress."

They identified themselves, and Ruddy handed her his calling card. "We're investigating Georgina Ellis's murder. We'd like to see her room."

Poole opened the door wide. Archie removed his hat and they stepped into the vestibule where a line of wool coats hung on wooden pegs. A strong waft of bacon and the clinking of cutlery came from a room down the hall. The residents having breakfast no doubt. But bacon? For boarders? Quite an extravagance. A ripple of envy passed through Ruddy. Unable to resist he asked, "Do you serve bacon to your residents?"

"Certainly not. I'm having a rasher of bacon with my porridge. The ladies are given porridge for breakfast. Toast and jam as well, if they pay extra."

Of course, he thought with a measure of cynicism. The luxury of bacon would hardly be offered out of generosity to the lady tenants.

"Terrible business, what happened to that poor girl," Mrs. Poole said.

"Yes, it was. Before we go to her room, perhaps you'd answer some of our questions."

"Anything. Although I must tell you, I didn't know her well and can't offer you much insight."

"Still, we have to ask," Ruddy said in a firm tone, knowing Poole, like Mrs. Goodge and every nosy landlady in the city, made it a point to know everything about the comings and goings of their boarders. "Did Miss Ellis have a suitor or gentlemen callers?"

"Not that I know of. If she did, she never brought them here, even to say goodnight." She straightened, clasping her hands together in front of her waist. With an *I'll brook no slander* posture and ramrod stiff, she told him, "I run a respectable home, Investigator. Men are not allowed inside."

"No one questions your standards, Mrs. Poole. We're certain a man committed the crime. We simply need to eliminate a beau or suitor as the possible murderer."

"The fact a man did it was never in question, now was it?"

"We don't assume anything without evidence."

Her shoulders lowered a fraction and she leaned forward. "What was done that you know it was a man? Was she defiled?"

For a woman who had little information to give, she brimmed over with morbid curiosity.

"We aren't allowed to discuss evidence in an ongoing case."

Archie brought out his small notepad. "Did Miss Ellis

have a quarrel with any other man she might've known or worked with?"

Poole shook her head. "Again, not to my knowledge. She was a quiet girl. Never caused no trouble with anyone here."

"How long had she lived here?" Archie asked.

"Two years. While here, she went to work six days a week, came home at a decent hour and was quiet as a mouse. As I said a few minutes ago, I don't have much to tell you. Would you want to see her room now?"

"Please." Ruddy stepped close behind Poole as she led them upstairs, his stomach rumbling the entire time for bacon.

The victim lived on the second floor in a room she shared with three other women. All the white iron beds had a moderately thin mattress and small pillow. The beds were set two to a wall and faced each other. Quilts of different patterns covered the beds, which brought some cheer to the room, giving it a functional rather than Spartan look. The far wall had a small wood burning fireplace. At the foot of each bed sat trunks of wicker or leather. The setup was similar to many barracks he'd stayed in, only it smelled better.

"Which was her bed?" he asked. Poole pointed to a tidy one with a patchwork quilt made from floral print cotton flour sacks. "And her dresser?"

"Here." She tapped a narrow-three drawer dresser with a basin and pitcher on top.

Archie searched the dresser while Ruddy went through Ellis's wicker trunk.

Nothing in the trunk or the dresser revealed any more than they already knew about the victim.

"What are you doing?" A young woman stood in the doorway, looking from Ruddy to Mrs. Poole.

"These two gentlemen are police inspectors assigned to finding Georgina's murderer," Poole informed the girl.

"Did you share the room with her?" Ruddy asked.

"Yes."

"What's your name?"

"Betsy...Betsy Kerrigan."

"Betsy, did she ever mention a special man? Give it a strong think. Even if she didn't call him special, you'd know if he was or not. Nor does it have to be a man she favored. It can be a man she wanted to avoid."

The girl sat on a bed across the room. "She did like someone special."

"We need to know everything she said about him," Archie said. "Do you know his name?"

"I don't want to say and be the one who pointed wrongly at someone."

Ruddy stepped closer. "If another girl dies at the hands of this man, do you want to be responsible for her death because you refused to give us information?"

She shook her head. "She never called him by name, not that I heard at least. They'd occasionally meet at the fountain in the museum gardens. He'd walk with her to Russell Street. Our factory is on Russell so they parted there. Sometimes he'd bring her flowers or sweets."

Sweets. That was in line with the small bunch of grapes they'd found by her hand. "Did she describe him?" Ruddy asked.

"No. She just said he was handsome with nice teeth."

"There's a first," Ruddy whispered to Archie. "A suspect with nice teeth."

"She said he had fine features like a proper gentleman," Betsy added.

What would a working girl like Ellis consider *fine features*, Ruddy wondered?

"Did she say anything else about him?"

"Only that he had deep blue eyes."

Archie continued to jot notes. "Was there a special day or days they met at the gardens?"

"No. She never knew when she'd see him."

"Had she a diary?" Ruddy lifted Ellis's mattress, hoping for the convenience of finding one. As children, two of his sisters stored their diaries under their mattresses, which he and his brothers stole and read aloud on a regular basis.

Kerrigan shook her head.

He gave Betsy his card. "If you think of something you forgot, please don't hesitate to contact me. I'd like to speak with the other ladies who share this room. Please ask them to contact me as soon as possible."

"Inspector—"

Ruddy stopped in the doorway and turned. "Yes."

"I don't know if it's important or not, but she mentioned once that he dressed like a swell. Of course that doesn't make him a swell." She looked Ruddy up and down. "You're dressed smartly and you're just a Peeler."

He ignored the comment. "Thank you, Miss Kerrigan. The information might prove more important than you realize."

He and Archie bid Poole and Betsy goodbye and left. Outside Ruddy told Archie, "Let's talk to the guard again. If he saw her several times, it seems he would've seen a well-dressed man loitering by the fountain early in the morning."

## Chapter Eleven

Ruddy took a large swallow of, in his opinion, the Boot and Bayonet's best ale. Morris told him more than once that most of his customers agreed it tasted like dirty sock water and he only kept it on hand for him.

"Interesting comparison. Point out which chaps tried the sock water," he'd told Morris at the time.

His mind drifted back to the only real evidence—the button Ellis had in her hand. Ruddy had shown it to his tailor, who confirmed his belief it came from an inexpensive uniform coat. A check of regimental insignias proved the button didn't come from a British military unit. Bloody hell, but he hated the thought of trying to chase down a foreign soldier, or worse, a sailor. They came in and out of port daily. When in port, the men scattered, most to pubs and bawdy houses. He'd never met a sailor with plans that included a museum visit.

His list of men who wore uniforms to work varied widely and was longer than he expected. He started with train conductors, postmen, doormen at fine hotels, and ended with constables. He had to include them in spite of his reluctance to believe one of his own capable of the murder. He eliminated officers from his agency, London Metropolitan. Their constable's buttons were equally as cheap but a different design. That left City of London's department. Contact with one of theirs always left him with his teeth on edge. Too lofty and full of themselves was a sentiment shared by most officers in his department. Men from the two agencies avoided each other. Their Wood Street headquarters had been the last stop of the day.

Ruddy hadn't reached the front desk when Nathaniel Napier, one of their inspectors called out, "Well, well, if it isn't Bloody Ruddy Bloodstone, hero of Roarke's Drift. These two are new," he said, gesturing toward a pair of constables standing by the desk. "They're ripe for a regaling of the story." He'd turned to the two young policemen at the desk and jerked a thumb in Ruddy's direction. "Got a V.C., he did."

Ruddy despised Napier with his unearned arrogance and constant snide comments.

"Nothing to tell, but since you're so damned interested, why don't you join up and get one of your own? I'm sure her majesty can find a place for you." Ruddy tapped his forehead. "Oh, that's right, you can't. It might actually require you to go into battle."

Napier bolted up, knocking his chair down in the process. "Are you calling me a coward?" He came round to stand arm's length from Ruddy.

"You know what you are. You don't need me to point a finger. If that label fits, then yes. If not, then no."

Napier rolled one cuff of his shirt and started on the other. In the background, Ruddy noticed one of the constables had gone.

Ruddy removed his suit jacket and handed it to Archie while Napier still stayed out of reach. "You want to have a go, Napier?" Ruddy asked and rolled his cuffs as well. "Let's do it."

Chief Superintendent Effingham, Napier's boss, came rushing from his office. "What is going on?"

Ruddy stayed silent and waited to hear what Napier would say.

"Nothing sir, just of bit of nonsense between rivals. Isn't that so, Bloodstone?" Napier turned to Ruddy with a half grin, crooked as it was insincere.

"Like Napier said, Chief Superintendent, we were having a bit of fun with each other," Ruddy confirmed.

"I don't believe either of you, but I'll let the subject drop. I suggest you get on with your business here and be on your way," Effingham told Ruddy and returned to his office.

Napier and Ruddy rolled their shirtsleeves down again. Afterward, Ruddy removed the button from his pocket and peeled away the cotton cloth. "This isn't one of yours by any chance?"

Napier shook his head. "Not ours."

Relieved, Ruddy eliminated a London constable as a suspect. He mentally crossed officers from outside London off the list. Enforcement in the smaller villages was sporadic. A Peeler from one of the villages would have no reason to be in the city while in uniform.

The young constable who'd told Effingham what was going on, hovered with his partner in the background. Napier turned and pressed his finger into the officer's chest. "Nobody likes a tattler. Be careful who you cross lad."

"Watch yourself, Napier. Apparently, there's a bigger bootlicker than you in your midst." Ruddy said and pocketed the button.

"One day, Bloodstone—you and I."

"Looking forward to it."

"Why's he so determined to get into fisticuffs with you?" Archie asked once they were outside.

"We've never got on. He's their station's boxing champion. I think the prospect of knocking me on my bum will give him even more bragging rights. The Victoria Cross thing grates on his pride."

Events of the day and the potential satisfaction of giving Napier a bloody nose dwindled. Questions about the murder crept back into his thoughts. Morris joined him at his table in the rear of the pub with a Guinness, the popular beer of choice in hand. "You've got the look of a man whose thoughts are a long distance from London."

"No, sadly my thoughts are fixed here in the city. I'm trying to figure out a clue. Ellis's roommate said she'd sometimes meet with a well-dressed man, a man of means the victim indicated. They'd meet up at the fountain by the British Museum."

"Don't know the spot but then the museum isn't my cup of tea."

"Not the point. I'm saying it's odd. What member of the upper class chooses to stroll through a public garden other than Hyde or Regents, where they can see and be seen by one of their own?"

"I agree the wealthy prefer the parks filled with others of their kind but it doesn't mean a man can't enjoy someplace different."

"We interviewed the guard again. The one that discovered the body walks that half of the building. He told us the majority of their male patrons are natty dressers, but he never saw a man like that loitering by the fountain."

"My guess is: the man is married and can't afford to run the risk of being seen by a friend of his wife's. Or, he might live or work in the area and the spot is convenient."

"Or, he's a murderer who's noticed the victim walking through the park on a regular basis, saw it as an opportunity and cozied up to her."

Ruddy took another swallow of his ale, mentally debating the merit of each theory. "I don't think he lives in the area. If so, he'd have cut through the park more and been seen by the guards. Not sure about the married man having a tryst idea."

To Ruddy's way of thinking, if the man was married and looking for a tumble, he'd have met her someplace other than the gardens and at a better hour.

Instinct drew him back to his original sense of the culprit and crime. "I feel like this was a crime of opportunity. I've thought it all along and can't shake the sense."

"If he was just seeking a victim, then why haven't you had more murders like this?" Morris asked.

Ruddy downed the rest of his beer and put his tankard on the edge of the table where June would refill it. "Everyone has to start somewhere. She might be number one."

## Chapter Twelve

When the hired carriage pulled up in front of the asylum's colonnaded portico, William remained seated. He hadn't expected such elegance. The building stood nearly a block in length. Fashionable white limestone trimmed the roofline, and white marble columns topped by Ionic capitals graced the entrance. It might have been a museum except for the fifteen foot wall that surrounded the structure and burly guards at the gates.

He stepped from the coach wondering whether the architecture wasn't wasted on lunatics, assuming the interior was as stately as the exterior.

The guards would have allowed him in had he identified himself. Instead, he chose to wait outside the gates for Frobisher. When he made no attempt to enter, they watched him from their posts with suspicious, beady eyes. He paced and his vexation grew with each step. He was reminded of the Bengal Tiger in Regent's Park Zoo who paced incessantly. Perhaps the big cat hated being watched too.

Five minutes after the hour, Frobisher showed. "Where the devil have you been," William demanded.

"I am only a few minutes late."

"I was on time. I put great store in promptness. Do not keep me waiting again."

There'd be no again. Today's visit to the asylum was the last stop before he made a decision about the formula. Whatever he chose to do, he'd ultimately sever the relationship. In the beginning, he expected the doctor's compound to be a cosmetic or a typical tonic found on a charlatan's shelf. Then, between Ingram's odd behavior and

Frobisher's optimism, he thought there might be more to it. Frobisher insisted it was a powerful restorative to calm the most unsettled of minds.

"Lead on," William said.

The guards knew the doctor on sight and opened the gates, touching the brim of their hats as they walked through. William noted, compared to the Bow Street Runners, or even the average constable, the guards were a motley duo. Their ill-fitting uniforms were of the cheapest wool, thin and shiny in places. Their boots were dull as black licorice, cracked across the toes, the heels worn down. The truncheons that hung off their belts were another story. Those appeared new, the wood smooth, the leather straps thick and the knots strong. It had to stay securely wrapped around the guard's wrist while punishment was meted out. As one of the guards stepped back, he bent to pick a button up off the ground. The base of his truncheon rose and William noticed a metal plug on the end. Closer inspection revealed a smaller metal plug in the handle. He'd heard of some street thugs who used various means to make simple weapons more effective, deadlier. Nightsticks, clubs, truncheons, cudgels, were drilled and filled with lead or sand. The practice of common crooks now became common place among those who operated within the law. *Interesting.*

Frobisher led the way past the statues of Portland Stone, through the domed entry hall deceptive in its grandeur, into the main wards. The block of cells they walked by reeked of sweat and excrement, and human misery. William gagged and brought his handkerchief to his nose.

The doctor continued on, but one patient stopped William in his tracks. The walls of the man's cage were lined with India rubber and the floor was made of cork. Inside, a barefoot man, his hair matted, his beard alive with lice, lay leg shackled to a cot. What remained of the tatters that were his clothes looked as though the man might have been, not indigent, but a working class fellow. Once.

"Why is this man chained to the bed?"

Frobisher walked back to join William. "Because he's violent—killed an attendant last year."

"How long will he be manacled?"

The doctor stared at William, a quizzical expression on his face, as though the simple question didn't warrant an answer. "Until he dies, of course."

Revolted, William stared at the prisoner and estimated his age to be early forties, not much older than himself. "He's better off dead."

"Oh, in his lucid moments, he has asked for the mercy of death," Frobisher said, unaffected by the miserable sight.

"Why do you deny him? What purpose does it serve to keep him alive?"

"This is a hospital. We can't go about murdering inmates because they wish it. A hundred years ago we used to charge folks one pence admission to see the lunatics. Referred to as 'curiosities,' the hospital made a pretty penny on the tourist trade. Our civilized society doesn't tolerate such activity anymore. They call the practice abuse." Frobisher snorted in disgust. "Lord knows what they'd call killing them."

He fixed on the hopeless wretch on the cot. A man can do worse than die. With every bone in his body, William knew he'd never be tethered like an animal no matter what.

William jumped as the doctor tapped his arm with a cane end. "My other patients are further down."

"Don't touch me with your unclean cane again. You need only tell me where we're to go," William said.

They walked by a cell, or a cage, as William began to think of them, where a woman sat still as stone. The acrid scent of urine wafted over. "Does the staff not attend to the toilet needs of these inmates?"

"Yes, twice daily. Since the patients constantly soil themselves, cleanup would be never ending. So, the administrators limit the task of emptying their waste buckets to morning and evening." Frobisher made the whole process sound so mundane. "She is the lady whose child died by her own hand. She won't speak to me while you're here. Shall we move on?

"Here," he gestured with an open arm at a relatively clean man who toyed with a rat, letting the creature run over his laddering fingers. Between attentions to the rat, the fellow worked on a charcoal drawing. "This is my fire starter. Doesn't look so dangerous now, does he?"

Finally, a patient who aroused his curiosity. *What sort of thrill does a he get from setting fires? Does he feel the same frisson of excitement as when I watched my lover struggle?*

"May I speak with him?" William asked.

"Certainly. Andrew come and talk with this gentleman."

Andrew set aside the drawing pad and came to within arm's reach of the barred door. He stopped abruptly one foot lined up with the other, military fashion. William stood back from the cage not wholly trusting the patient nor his apparent calm. The man scrutinized him and William wondered what was going through his mind.

Andrew arched a brow. "What do you want?"

"How you feel when you see a blaze you've set take hold?"

Andrew grinned and his expression softened. "I like it." He leaned in, his feet didn't move, only the upper half of his body. For the briefest of seconds, his eyes glittered. "In the very beginning, it's not the flame that entrances, it's the sound. The music of the fire. A few sizzling notes to start, then a pop or two, a hiss, then the whoosh when the flame flares."

He closed his eyes and licked his lips. The grin turned to a rapturous smile. "I feel the fire grow, building, higher and higher inside me as it grows hotter and hotter outside."

Andrew's eyes flew open and he focused on a spot over William's shoulder. "When my inferno is at its peak I am blessed with a myriad of shades of blue, red, orange, and yellow."

He didn't spare the doctor a glance, but fixed his gaze back to William. "I know what you really want to hear." The pleasantness of his smile turned smarmy and he rubbed a charcoal blackened finger over his chin. "The answer is yes, the sight makes my knob--" Andrew thrust his hips forward, clamped himself with a hand and gave his groin a squeeze, "Stiffer than an officer on parade."

The madman had William's full attention. If the intent had been to offend his visitor, then the attempt failed. Somehow, William didn't think that had been Andrew's purpose. He had the uncomfortable feeling the lunatic saw a brother-in-arms. "No Chinese whore could do for me what the flames did," Andrew added, with a wink.

Amused by the lack of subtlety, William snickered at the innuendo and let it pass. He wanted to change the direction of the conversation. "China, can I assume you were in the army?"

"Twenty years, Sergeant-Major Norris at your service sir," Andrew said, straightening and tapping soundless, old civilian shoes together, he saluted.

Sergeant-major, hmmm...William didn't have to think on the matter long. A man didn't rise to a senior non-commissioned position like that unless the army was his life's career. It was common knowledge every man of that rank dreamed of doing his minimum twenty-two years and getting selected to be a Yeoman Warder at the Tower. Norris's service was two short. *Court-martial*? –Had to be. But, was it arson? The wheels of William's mind turned on the possibility. It had no bearing on anything other than his simple curiosity.

"If you don't mind me asking, how did you wind up here?" Unable to hide his disgust, William's eyes swept over the interior of the cell.

"China is the birthplace of what is both the bane and greatest inspiration of my humble life, fireworks. The power is in the fire. The fireworks are the ultimate beauty of that force." Andrew stared hard at William. "I suspect you've felt the power."

The question would go unanswered. "Obviously, you were disciplined by the army and sent back. What did you torch?"

"The brothel the inadequate whore worked at..." He paused and put his hands on hips. He gave the impression of a man trying to find the words he needed to rationalize his deeds.

William wondered if Norris was an excellent actor or sincere. In a world devoid of many pleasant pastimes, honing one's dramatic skills might be *de rigueur*.

"I figured I'd get my satisfaction one way or the other," Andrew added.

William thought that sounded pretty close to the truth. "I understand Dr. Frobisher gives you medication for your condition. Does it quell your desire for this...power?"

Andrew didn't respond immediately. His attitude seemed to relax. His proudly puffed out chest sank with the sagging of his shoulders. "The thrill remains. When I see a fire my body hums with excitement. But, the medicine keeps the cravings away. I no longer feel the need to set the blaze."

He winked at William again, "All this talk about flames and what not, has given me a stiffy. And I'm stuck here, without a bit of muslin in reach." He glanced at the silent woman who'd lost her child and sighed.

"Does the medicine do anything else for you?" William saw a new pleasure light in Andrew's eyes.

"Yes, I feel like a lad again." He performed a backflip from his standing position and another that brought him the original spot. "Haven't been able to do that in two decades," he said with a proud note.

The jolly man who did a backflip to amuse his audience disappeared behind a somber expression. "Do you know why the doctor experiments on me?"

William knew, of course but playing along to see what Norris would say, he shook his head.

"I don't protest. I don't care, you see. It matters not if the formula kills me. I have no fear of the fire-and-brimstone of hell. What can Satan do to me in death that compares to what my life is here? I welcome death." Then he walked away, back to his drawing pad. The rat had scurried off.

William had enough of the stench, the madness, the hopelessness. He spun on his heels and hurried toward the main doors that led outside, not stopping until he was past the gates. The guards sniggered as he rushed by. They made sure he heard their mocking comments. If this were Cornwall or Belgravia, or anywhere else, he'd have challenged them. Never once had he run from a fight or declined to defend his honor. The crude bastards enraged him and he hated Frobisher for it. The doctor had brought him here where he couldn't risk a scene. Now, he was forced to swallow his pride and endure the laughter of rabble.

Frobisher strode across the courtyard, his arms pumping, lending impetus to his short legs, the tail of his frock coat flapping. Incensed, William watched and decided the time had come for the doctor to turn over the elixir and the two would part company. As Frobisher grew closer, William's anger mounted, convinced he'd been lured under false pretext to this God awful place, exposed to the worst of human conditions. Even the somewhat lucid Andrew didn't exhibit a "cured" face, merely a somewhat controlled one. William would wager that his changed image resulted as much from cunning as the formula. Only his new found strength interested him.

"Sir, I think you can see the remarkable possibilities of the medicine."

"Possibilities? The man was mad as a March hare.

What it did to him physically, now that is of note."

"I am..." Frobisher caught himself. "We are on the brink of seeing the full potential of this discovery. Men and women who had no hope of leading normal lives might be able to leave the asylum because of our find."

He stalked farther down the path, away from the gates, toward a for-hire coach, apparently unaware of the bone chilling effect his words had.

William's long strides closed the gap between them. "Other than dispensing this so called 'find' to your patients, what do you plan to do with the information? I was explicit when I paid you that I didn't wish this discovery, as you refer to it, to be made known." The madman's newly returned young man's strength impressed William. The potion held the promise of youth he sought. "You will give me all that you have of this medicine. Tell me what you need to complete your experiments here and I will ration that amount to you. The rest is mine."

"It is with profound regret that I must go against your will sir." He grabbed a handful of William's coat sleeve. "This is too important. I'm writing a dissertation documenting how I came to obtain the compound. I'll elaborate on how I took it to the next step, beyond the youth enhancing power."

William pressed his thumb between the bones on the back of the offending hand. Frobisher winced and instantly released the sleeve. The painful message didn't stop his rant. "Dr. Gull and the others will have to accept me into their social circle and their clubs now. This is my reward. After my study is made public, they will seek me out, my opinion, my presence."

He listened to the doctor's feverish ramblings. They weren't all that different than the fire starters. The ex-sergeants were more interesting, he thought dryly. He had to stop the doctor. How would it look, a member of the Lords, a viscount, dabbling with some ancient formula out of a sorcerer's book? It wouldn't stop there. The gossips and rumor mill would speculate why he sought the help of a rogue doctor. Sooner or later, they'd bring up the death of Isabeau. He dredged up the most ingratiating smile he could manage and asked, "Surely you can spare some that I might try?"

"For you, of course."

"Good, where is your office? I'll be by tonight."

"37 Commercial Street. You'll see my shingle. I can't remember the last time I felt this good." Frobisher cackled and rudely gawked at a handsome, middle-aged woman who strolled by. "It's a little early for lunch. What do you say we stop for some tea and biscuits?"

"I have to decline. I've another appointment." Right now, William needed to go home, formulate a plan. He wouldn't have dined with the tedious doctor under any circumstances. Everything was at his office, the elixir, the paperwork, Frobisher's notes. Who knew what else the doctor documented?

"Out of curiosity doctor, can you or do you ever take any of the inmates out, to your office for example?"

"Yes, on occasion."

"I'd like you to clean Andrew up, leave him shackled but bring the man to your office this evening."

"Why?"

"Who pays who, doctor? The giver asks—the taker does."

Frobisher cocked his head to the left and stared hard in William's eyes. "All right but you should know I am not comfortable bringing him outside the safety of the asylum."

"Just do as I instructed."

## Chapter Thirteen

"Burton," William called from the library. The valet appeared at the door before William finished turning back toward the desk.

"Sir?"

Where had he come from? Sometimes, he thought his valet a bit spooky.

"Burton, I need one of my father's dueling pistols and ammunition."

#

It was dark when William, dressed as a common man, stopped the hired carriage three blocks from Frobisher's medical practice.

He entered without knocking. A simple screen of cotton cloth on a metal frame separated the waiting area from the exam area. He went straight through and on into the doctor's personal office. As instructed, Norris was in attendance and seated in an old wooden chair. His feet were free but Frobisher had manacled one wrist to the chair arm. The restraint had neither the strength nor complexity of those used at Bethlehem Hospital. Instead of a sturdy padlock and thick iron bracelets, this was a rough leather wristband with a buckle fastener. William wondered when in private practice the doctor used the device.

Frobisher reclined in a swivel chair behind a stack of open journals on the desk. He poured a glass of wine and handed it to William.

William took the port but didn't drink any. "Are these all the notes?" he asked gesturing to the stack. "Or are there others still out, stored elsewhere, the hospital perhaps?"

"Nothing is at Bethlehem. I keep the majority of my paperwork regarding the history and results of my work locked up. The experiments are too important and I feared the information falling into one of my rival's possession." He patted the closest book. "These are the latest results."

"Where do you store the formula?"

"Those I keep on the top shelf of my exam room cabinet. Again, I feared losing my...our, discovery and that cabinet locks."

"I assume you injected your test cases." William picked up the top sheets of handwritten notes and skimmed the contents.

Frobisher rolled his shoulders back and stood. "I do sir, I use the Pravaz Syringe, keep an ample supply in the same locked cupboard."

Norris tapped William's arm with his free hand. "Care to donate that port you don't happen to be drinking to an old *incurable*?"

"Not advisable," Frobisher said and cast a stern glance at his half-tethered patient.

William handed Norris the glass.

The doctor's lips thinned. "Would you like to see how well and secure your property is stored?"

"Absolutely."

Frobisher took William back to the exam room and removed a ring of keys from a hook on the wall. The scarred wooden cabinet had three locks but only one was in plain sight. The secondary ones lay hidden beneath a thin wooden flap made to blend with the door. Inside were six shelves most full to overflowing with glass bottles of brown and green.

"Do all of these contain the formula?" William asked.

"No. I cannot be sure of the time frame when it might start to lose its potency. Only the top shelf, the front three bottles are filled with the compound. The bottles behind are chloroform and ether. The box to the side holds my hypodermic syringes." Frobisher fingered the ring of keys. "Nothing to worry about, all is well secured." He started to relock the cabinet.

William wrapped his hand around the doctor's wrist and calmly took the metal ring from his hold. "Do me a favor Frobisher, bring Norris in here."

The doctor resisted and pulled against the hold. William tightened his grip. "Bring him here."

Saucer-eyed, Frobisher nodded. "Whatever you wish."

William let go of his wrist and Frobisher darted off.

William took the three bottles with the compound along with the box of needles and set them on the examination table, then changed his mind and put the supply on a nearby counter. The examination table became the focal point of his interest. The wooden slab measured approximately six-feet-by-four-feet and lacked any cushioning material. Rough leather straps were attached to three corners of the utilitarian table. A section in the fourth corner was cutout but the restraint was missing. Frobisher probably used it to secure Norris to the chair. At one end, another strap was run through the a bored out portion. This restraint was made specifically to hold one's head in place. The bond kept the patient from rising up in pain or fighting the procedure. An involuntary wave of revulsion passed through William at the thought of being tied down while the doctor worked, any doctor. But for his purposes, the unpleasant tether was convenient, very convenient.

He returned to the cabinet and removed a bottle of chloroform and a bottle of ether. Uncorking each, he took a quick whiff. Both would achieve his purpose. His exposure to them, however limited, still had to be considered. William heard ether caused vomiting and chloroform caused dizziness. Both had a repulsive smell, pungent and sickeningly sweet like rotted fruit. He decided on chloroform and replacing the stopper, put the ether back on the shelf.

William pulled his handkerchief from his coat pocket and poured three drops of the chloroform onto it. He held the polluted linen behind his back and leaned against the counter as Frobisher led Norris into the room.

Frobisher had tethered his wrists together. The doctor also looped a length of chain around the strap and pulled the patient along like a vicious dog. Both men offended William, the so called civilized doctor more than the lunatic. Frobisher unfastened the restraint then strapped Norris to another chair with it.

Frobisher didn't have a chance to turn around. William shoved the tainted handkerchief under his nose. Within seconds, the doctor collapsed to the floor in a crumpled heap. There hadn't been enough of the chemical to make Frobisher lose consciousness. The intent was to disorient him, render him unable to put up a struggle. It succeeded. William hoisted the man to the table while Norris watched silent and wide-eyed. Although on the small side, getting a man even Frobisher's size onto the table proved no simple task. Maneuvering Frobisher took longer than William anticipated. At one point, he considered more chloroform but decided against the idea. The modest amount of scent he'd already endured made his stomach queasy. In the end, the feeble resistance Frobisher exerted wound up providing a source for William to use as a counter weight and gave him added leverage. He laid the doctor out straight on the table, tied his hands down, then attached the third and last restraint to Frobisher's leg.

William grabbed the handkerchief he'd tossed onto the counter. He measured out a couple more drops on top of the damp spot in the center. Finished, he held the linen square down at his side and stood next to Norris. The lunatic's gaze never wavered.

"Do you still wish to die?" William asked.

The lunatic hesitated only a few seconds before acknowledging with a single nod. Frobisher groaned in the background as William pressed the handkerchief to the base of Norris's nose. He breathed deep and continued to do so about six times before slumping forward. The full weight of his head rested against William's palm.

The odor of the chemical wafted up. A little lightheaded, William threw the cloth into the far corner of the room. He found water left in the pitcher and poured half into the matching bowl. He searched the cupboards above the counter and found a bar of lye soap. After washing his hands repeatedly William withdrew his pistol from the back of the heavy belt he wore. "Better where you're going then where you were." He pressed the barrel to Norris temple and pulled the trigger. "Wish granted."

Norris's body sagged and tipped sideways, his head dropped to his chest like a man in deep sleep.

The doctor grunted and his head lolled to one side. William put the gun back in his belt and went to the table. He grabbed a handful of hair and yanked Frobisher's head back so the doctor faced him. "The lunatic is dead. I killed him. I can kill you or spare you. It depends on your answer. Where are the missing journals?"

Frobisher's eyes bounced in their sockets like a china cup in an old man's hands. No color showed in the doctor's eyes. The pupils had dilated but remained unfocused. William jerked hard on the clump of hair in his hand. A mumbled, "desk" came from the doctor, then "lock...drawer."

He let go of Frobisher's hair and rifled through his pockets until he found a ring of keys. The circlet held skeleton keys of all sizes. William went into the private office and started with the smallest.

The third key he tried opened the bottom drawer. Inside, were two ledgers of meticulous notes regarding the patients, the applications and the results. A separate, but smaller logbook contained the formula's breakdown and dosage information.

He spotted a Gladstone bag on a chair by the door. Larger than his valise, the square-jawed portmanteau would be perfect to hold the information. He dumped everything into the bag. A thorough search of the other ledgers, journals, and notes disclosed only mundane medical observations and theories. Satisfied, he went back into the exam room, loaded the leather case with the needles and bottles.

Frobisher's wits had started to return and he tugged futilely on the restraints. His voice reedy and whiney, he repeated William's words to him. "You said if I told you where to find my journals you'd spare me."

William didn't respond. He laid his hand across the doctor's forehead and held it in place while he secured the head restraint. With one hand, he pulled the leather strap taut then using his forearm as a weight, he secured the buckle.

His prisoner's eyes darted from side to side. They still had that strange bounce William noticed but not as pronounced. A low, keening sound came from deep within Frobisher's chest and he started to cry. He begged for mercy. He swore and promised never to reveal or do anything ever again to offend William. Outside of the odd jiggle to his eyeballs, the doctor seemed to have regained his wits. William idly wondered if the great surge of fear on Frobisher's part affected the potency or duration of the chloroform.

"You swore," the doctor pleaded. "I told you what you wanted to know. You promised to spare me."

"I lied."

Frobisher screamed and screamed again. William looked around in a panic for something to stick in his mouth. The cloth lay in the corner but he didn't want the doctor to sleep through the ordeal. Something bumped his knee. A chewed wooden dowel hung on a thin rope attached to the under corner of the table. William grabbed the dowel and shoved it into Frobisher's mouth just as he opened wide to scream louder. "How many times have you silenced a patient's cry of pain?"

William went to the cabinet and removed all the bottles of ether. "Disloyalty can never be justified, Frobisher. I hired you. I'm a generous man and paid you well for your knowledge, your assistance and your discretion. Failure by you in either of the first two is unfortunate. Failure in the third area is unforgivable and intolerable. You went beyond indiscretion. You had the effrontery to challenge my objection. You forgot you serve me and not your vanity."

He lifted a bottle of ether and drew back. "Vanity has a price and a penalty." He hurled the beaker, smashing it against the far wall. Then, he flung one of the oil lamps. The wall exploded into a fiery curtain and spread fast.

William spun around and threw another bottle of ether at the opposite wall. He leaned down so Frobisher would be certain to hear him over the roar of the growing blaze. "Breathe deep and the smoke will take you before the fire. Or, so I hear."

Flames took the wall's half-timbers first before racing across the room's ceiling beams.

"Now this is a fire that would make Sergeant-Major Norris proud." William said and grabbed the Gladstone and his valise and hurried out the door.

He waited in the shadows of a derelict building a few doors down and watched. The inferno blew out the windows of the examination room. The flames shot through the gaps and licked their way to the windows of the second floor. Loud bangs sounded in succession. William assumed the fire had found the remaining ether.

People came running from all directions. Some came with tankards of ale, some came empty handed. The constables came blowing long, high-pitched emergency calls on their whistles. William made it a point to stay long enough to know for certain the fire brigade wouldn't be able to save the building. By the time they arrived, all they could do was work at containment and hope the neighboring structures didn't burn.

William turned and walked down Commercial Street. There would be carriages for hire where it intersected with Whitechapel Street. The odds of running into one sooner were slim. Most didn't venture into the dangerous area unless they carried a paying customer who insisted.

Noise and laughter from the Ten Bells Pub across the road echoed off the brick buildings and cobblestone street. The public room looked small and judging from the crowd that gathered outside to drink, it was. The men were ruffians, thieves, and laborers, five pence away from being vagrants. The women roused a bit more sympathy in him. From his vantage point, he guessed most to be prostitutes, the rest simple drunkards. The whore's clientele being unpredictable at best, guaranteed some would wind up at the wrong end of a punishing fist, and some, the really unlucky ones--the wrong end of a blade.

Ahead, a man who'd been leaning on the side of a doorway stepped out. Shorter than William, the barrel-chested man had thick arms and thighs thicker than ham legs. On alert, William gave him a quick once over. The fellow kept the palm of his right hand hidden and his fingers cupped around something. Two other meanly dressed men came out of an alley and stood alongside the first. He blocked the walk forcing William to stop, the others made sure going around was impossible. The first man eyed the Gladstone, then his scrutiny shifted to William's plain frock coat.

"Evening guv'nr."

William slowly slipped his hand into his waistband. The stranger's lips twisted into a crooked line nowhere near a smile and something in his right hand flashed. A moment later, a straight razor glinted in the light of the streetlamps, inches from William's face. "I'll have your case or your blood."

William moved too fast for the robber to counter and jammed his father's dueling pistol into the stranger's belly. "Good evening to you...guv'nr."

The robber's eyes popped open like a stomped on toad's. He began to back away, his hands flailing the air at his sides. He hadn't gone three steps when his cohorts ran down the nearby alley, leaving him to fend for himself. The man snapped the razor closed and took off running too, looking over his shoulder every few steps.

William could chase after him. Run him into the ground like a hound on a fox. Then what? Shoot him like a...a what?...Cowboy? He sighed and put the pistol away.

## Chapter Fourteen

Ruddy slowly rolled the coat button over his fingers, stopping to rub the face with his thumb. Why couldn't he find the origin? His best clue, a small piece from a murderer's clothing and no one recognized it. After he left the City of London's Police Department, he met with a rail supervisor and one from the city tram and omnibus systems. Neither had ever seen the button.

He removed a sheet of paper from his personal stationery box. The cheap blank sheets the department provided often smeared certain inks and applications. He removed a soft lead pencil and harder lead one from a cup on his desk. He used a variety of pencils for his ironwork sketches and kept several at the station in case of sudden inspiration. He drew the shape and basics of the button, shaded the background and then used the hard-tipped pencil to fill in the details of the insignia. He'd draw several copies today and tonight and give them to the constables walking a beat near the crime scene. They could show the drawings to local merchants. He held little hope anyone had the information he needed, but it was worth a try.

Archie came from the backroom with a cup of tea giving everyone he passed a chipper hello. He set his tea down and sat at his desk opposite Ruddy. "Jameson wants to see you."

Most conversations with the superintendent had a way of taking a wrench to the day. Ruddy anticipated this talk would be no different. "Did he say why?"

"No. I don't think it's anything too serious. He didn't act peevish when he said to send you in."

Ruddy put his pencil and drawing down. He stood, put

on his suit coat, went to Jameson's door and knocked.

"Come in."

Ruddy poked his head inside.

"All the way Bloodstone."

He entered, but stayed by the door for a quick exit when Jameson was done with him.

"Rudyard, we haven't chatted in a while. Please," he gestured to the chair in front of his desk, "Have a seat. Shall I ring for tea?"

"No thank you, sir, I'm fine." Ruddy sat, stiff and upright like he was still in the military. "You wanted to speak to me."

"Relax Rudyard, I want to hear about your run-in with Napier."

"My run-in..." Ruddy forced a smile but remained ramrod straight. How had Jameson heard about the encounter already? Had to be that yapper Archie. "It wasn't much of a quarrel. Napier is a loud-mouthed sly-boots, and annoying as a carbuncle on the arse. Out of respect to you sir, I'm keeping the worst of my opinion to myself."

"If it gives you any pleasure, his boss Effingham is no better, dull-witted and prickly as a hedgehog. Much as I might enjoy a bout of rough-and-tumble with him, even at my age, I strive to contain my temper with him. He is, after all, a man of rank in the agency closest to the queen. It doesn't do you any good to get involved in fisticuffs with one of his rising stars like Napier."

Jameson was neither dull-witted nor given to bristle over small matters. To his credit, he managed the station by strict adherence to the department's code of ethics. If a man broke the rules, punishment was meted out in equal measure whether the offender was a favorite of his or not. But at the end of the day, when any question or comment came from the Commissioner's Office, he stayed true to the path of least resistance. Didn't matter if he was right, he lacked gumption and avoided complications that might draw negative attention.

For a moment, Ruddy thought how pleasant it would be to resign, how the cool taste of freedom might feel. He'd take his savings and travel to a place where good and evil were clearly designated and politics didn't make a muddle of the two. Old world Europe was steeped in corruption. Africa was a mess, and even if it wasn't a mess, he'd never go back there. South America held no interest for him: too much Spanish influence in the settlements and too many unknowns with the native people, the strange animals, and the dense forests. North America was a different story. America and Canada held promise.

Jameson cleared his throat and the North American daydream vanished. "Will that be all, sir?" Ruddy rose.

"Not quite. What's the status on the Russell Square murder, the one in the museum gardens? Any developments?"

"We haven't much. We have one good piece of evidence. If we could connect it to the source it would probably result in an arrest. What we really need is an opening of some kind in the case: a witness, or another good piece of evidence, or a substantial clue. None of which seems to be coming any time soon."

"Keep at it. Nose to the grindstone and all that. I've every confidence you'll solve this in no time."

Ruddy returned to his desk feeling none of the confidence the superintendent had.

Archie stopped wading through a stack of reports and looked up. "What did Jameson want then?"

Ruddy leaned in. "What do you think you gossipy old woman? He asked about my run-in with Napier."

"He couldn't have been angry. He laughed when I told him."

Ruddy sat back. "He wasn't mad, but he wasn't happy with me either."

"I told everyone you'd have made mince of the

bugger."

"No matter. In the future, just keep that sort of heated exchange with one of the City lads between us."

"Sorry. Let me make it up to you. Meg is making roast beef with potatoes tonight. There's plenty to go around. Come by and join us."

"Thank you for the invite but I've plans. Allegra wants to go to a new restaurant in Belgravia Square. The proprietor allows dancing and has set off a portion for that pleasure."

"Sounds swank. Do you own formal attire?"

"No." In Ruddy's opinion, it was a silly waste of money for a working man. He picked up his sketch pad and continued shading the button drawing. "I already told Allegra I won't go to some hoity-toity place where I'm expected to wear a fancy dinner jacket and whatnot. She assured me it wasn't necessary."

"You dance?" Archie's brows shot up.

"You needn't look so surprised. I've known how to dance since my military days."

Archie smirked and said, "I can see the younger you now, boyish ballroom student to some bored Colonel's wife."

"Don't make me laugh. Colonel's wives don't give dance lessons to non-commissioned officers, not if they had an ounce of wit. No, I learned from a lady named Pansy, a..." He paused, searching for the right word. "What the Americans call, a *soiled dove,* who worked in Natal's most popular whore house."

Archie screwed up his face.

"What? Why the sourpuss look?" With devilish effort to keep a straight face, Ruddy fought to hold back laughing. Arch was such easy prey for his jests. He should know, no soldier worth his salt went to a lady of the night for dance lessons.

"Rudyard," Arch said in a damned good impression of a stern headmaster. "As you know, I'm no prude. I had my rowdy days—"

"You were married at seventeen."

"Still, I had a couple of years where I made short work of a young woman's willingness."

"And your point?"

"I never took you for a fool, but really, to throw away a tart's talents on dance lessons."

"You're so easy to hoodwink. I never took dance lessons from Pansy, but I did avail myself of her main skills every payday. I actually learned to dance from a lovely nurse named Edith Durham."

They were interrupted by one of the constables who'd detained Davey Wilkey. He entered the station and walked straight to Ruddy's desk and stood close to attention like many others. He removed and tucked his helmet under his arm, then wiped a hand over his sweat-flattened hair. "We've had another murder, sir. A lady's body was discovered in the shrubs by the gardener's shed across from the museum."

"Bugger me blind," Archie swore.

In a subtle tilt of his head, the detective behind Archie turned to better hear the conversation. Ruddy put a finger to his lips for Archie to keep his voice down. He turned back to the constable. "I saw you come in so I assume you haven't told Jameson yet."

"No, sir."

"I'll tell him, but we'll go in together. Has the discovery drawn a big crowd?" The last thing they needed was to deal with the press who'd make the situation more lurid than it already was.

"No. My partner and I were cutting through the park and saw a grey bundle we took for a drunken lout. I poked him with my truncheon. When he didn't respond, we pushed the shrubbery aside to rouse the tosspot. That's when we realized we had a dead woman." He pressed his face closer to Ruddy. "Dead in the same way as the other lady found at the museum, judging from the bruises on her throat."

"Bloody hell. How are you keeping folks away?" Ruddy asked.

"My partner covered her with his cape so she blends in with the foliage."

"And the patrons in the tearoom, can they see anything?"

"No, I don't think so. If they had, I'm sure we'd have been contacted by customers. Just opinion, but I don't think she was killed there."

"Why?"

"There's a fresh pattern in the leaves and twigs on the ground. They looked like drag marks to me. I believe she was killed somewhere else and dragged behind the shed."

Drag marks weren't much of a clue, not in the park where children rode wagons, and women walked with prams, along with the numerous other means they could be made.

"Is there a way to follow the markings?" Ruddy asked. A weak clue was better than none at all.

The constable shook his head. "Not really, not for very far anyway. They stop at the stone path."

"Let's see the superintendent," Ruddy said. He, Archie, and the constable went into the office and informed Jameson of the crime.

"Do you think we should call in the press? We can put out a warning to women in the area to be especially careful early in the morning?"

A look of horror crossed Jameson's face, followed by consternation. "Certainly not, Sgt. Holbrook. We don't need to send a ripple of hysteria through the ladies of London. Tales of violent crime are not suited for gentle ears."

"But, what of their safety?"

"What of their safety?"

Ruddy tried to intercede. Holbrook was right. "If we take the lead, sir, we can contain the information better. If this leaks to the press, the newspapers and scandal sheets can run wild with falsehoods. We needn't tell the press all of what we know, or in this case, what we don't know. Once reported, the story alone might frighten the killer and keep him from committing another murder. In the meantime, we will search out and follow every detail of the crimes."

"Sweet Mother of God—you too, Bloodstone? None of you has any idea how difficult the museum curator is to deal with on any normal day. Xavier Weeks is a living example of unpleasant hubris. Men who aren't academics go to the museum because women like it. Scare the women and the men stop coming. Weeks will have a bloody cow. He'll go straight to the Commander, who'll go to the Deputy Commissioner, who'll come high-stepping into my office to give me an earful I don't care to hear."

Jameson pulled a bottle of whiskey from his bottom desk drawer and poured three fingers full into his teacup. "Well, why are you all still here? Go." He waved them off.

"I'd like Northam to come for photographs," Ruddy requested.

"Take men as you see fit. Now go."

As they were leaving the station, Ruddy stopped at the desk sergeant's chair. "Do you have someone you can spare for an hour to run an errand for me?"

"No problem."

"Good. Ask him to go to Mrs. Porter's Hat Shop. I'll write the address down." He jotted the shop information on a scrap of paper from his pocket notebook and handed it to the sergeant. "Have him tell her I'll be late tonight."

#

When they arrived, Ruddy had the reporting constable and his partner send all the patrons and staff from the tearoom away. En route they commandeered rope from a work crew and used it to seal off that part of the park under the guise of investigating an industrial accident. Two additional constables manned the four-corners of the perimeter to secure the scene.

Archie knelt and pulled the constable's cape off the victim and felt her wrist. "Cold as a witch's heart." Keeping her skirt over as much of her as possible, he discretely slid his hand between her legs and felt her inner thigh where body heat was strong. "Cold as well."

"I'd be surprised if it wasn't. From the lividity, I'd say she's been her for hours." Ruddy indicated for Northam to take pictures of her face where the blood had pooled to a bright purple. "Between the lividity and the risk of getting discovered I estimate her time of death in the early hours when the park is empty before the foot traffic increases."

Archie sat back on his heels. "I agree. From this stain on her skirt and the faint odor, I'd say the murderer pleasured himself afterward, like with the Ellis woman. Risky business."

Ruddy knelt on the other side of the body and turned the woman onto her back. He ignored the vacuous stare that so many victims shared but her eyes held what he wanted to see: the pinpoint red splotches of ruptured blood vessels indicative of strangulation. Lividity made any bruises on the neck difficult to decipher, but there were numerous scratch marks. Her hands were red and chapped. Ruddy thought she might be a laundress. He inspected her fingernails. Several were broken and jagged. Ruddy suspected the marks on her neck were where she clawed herself in a desperate attempt to wrest the killer's hands from her throat. He'd seen the same marks in strangulation cases many times.

"Grim business," the constable said.

"Sir—" The young officer pointed to the soil and grass that collected in the heels of the victim's shoes. He'd been right about her being dragged but from where exactly? Ruddy wished he knew.

He wiped the blade and handed it back to the constable then searched her reticule she still clutched. It only contained a few pence, a hanky, and a bone comb. She appeared to be around twenty-five and wore a wedding band. "If we have a morsel of luck, someone, her husband or children, will report her missing and we can identify her."

Northam finished taking pictures and returned to the station. Ruddy and Archie stayed until the body was loaded and sent to the doctor's office who did the autopsies for the agency. The two constables who discovered the body would file their reports for review by the detectives the next morning.

#

"Murder at the museum, read all about it," a boy hawking broadsheets yelled out as Ruddy and Archie neared the station.

"What the..." Ruddy tossed a penny to the boy and snatched two copies from his hands.

They stood on the sidewalk and skimmed the sheets. "This is about the first murder. Thank heavens the press hasn't heard about the latest killing," Ruddy said, knowing a report of the one would put Jameson in a rage.

Archie held the door open for Ruddy as they went inside the station. The two constables who'd detained Davey Wilkey had ended their watch and changed out of uniform. They relaxed by the front desk and chatted with friends still on-duty.

"Here's an interesting tidbit, nothing to do with our victim fortunately," Archie said. "A doctor's office near Whitechapel burned to the ground yesterday." Arch chuckled and went on, "It says he worked with patients at St. Bartholomew's a lot. He signed out one of the loonies last afternoon to conduct an experiment at his office. Both died in the fire."

"From what I hear, death might be a better option than the asylum. Can't say I feel much sympathy for the doctor. He, of all people, should've realized the dangers of handling loonies outside of a secured environment," Ruddy said and reread the more important murder article. At least some of the most important details weren't mentioned. If the papers had known about the semen and the button, they'd have included the information.

Jameson stormed into the lobby area with a handful of rolled copies of the broadsheets. His attention fixed on Ruddy and Archie. "In my office...now." He spotted the two bobbies in their civilian clothes. "You too."

"This won't go well," Archie said, looking from Jameson's back to Ruddy.

"What was your first clue?"

"Well, from his—,"

"Stop. I was being sarcastic."

The two constables trailed after them into the lion's den.

"Close the door." Jameson eyed each of them and aimed the rolled papers their way. "Which one of you talked to the press? Tell me now."

All four denied having anything to do with the press. "Sir, we weren't the only ones who knew. The guard who discovered her might've told or that Davey Wilkey we interrogated. Northam was at the scene and the runner from Paddington Police Station. Frankly, I don't think either of them breathed a word. I'd say most likely it was Wilkey or the guard," Ruddy argued.

"The deed is done so let's figure out what we can do about controlling the situation."

Ruddy took the opportunity to speak his mind. "If you recall, we—"

Archie guessed where he was going with the comment and jumped in, "Sir, things weren't tickety-boo...no worries, before this. We all knew the news was bound to get out—"

The four of them flinched at the sharp crack the papers made smacking against the desk in a rare display of temper by Jameson. "I will not brook your hindsight criticism. Please remember, *sergeant,* you can find yourself back to being a mere constable on patrol with the swipe of my pen."

Jameson wasn't the type of man to recognize he'd insulted the constables in the room. Archie was right, but that, like the insult, wouldn't be acknowledged either. Jameson sank into his chair, laying the papers out over his desk. "Back to my original question, what can we do to control the situation?"

Ruddy tried another approach, a more positive one, hoping Jameson might be more receptive. If not, Ruddy was at a loss as to what could be done, if anything. Two things loved by London readers were scandal and sensationalism.

"Since the story is out and we can't deny the crime occurred. We can control how much information is released while appearing like we are fully co-operating with the newspapers. Don't let reporters set the narrative," Ruddy suggested, which Jameson shrugged off when he'd proposed a similar tact on another case. "Invite the most popular reporters in the city, including the one who authored this article. Drown them in unimportant facts that make no difference to the investigation. Talk, talk, talk. Eventually, they'll stop listening and all they'll remember is the first few bits you told them and print that."

Jameson played with the papers for a long moment, then finally said, "All right. Let's see if that works. All of you can leave now."

"Ruddy," the desk sergeant called and waved him over. When Ruddy reached him, the sergeant and the desk officer pulled him aside.

"That man sitting on the bench came to report his wife missing. We thought it might be worth you talking to him, just in case her disappearance has something to do with the latest victim." The officer tipped his head toward a man on the bench with two small boys and an infant in his arms.

Ruddy read the missing person's report, dread of giving the man the tragic news weighing him down. He wished he was wrong but the man's wife fit the description of their second victim too well to be a coincidence. The worst part of his job—telling someone their loved one was dead.

Ruddy went to the man, the report in hand. The boys, one about four and the other, a toddler about two, played with a button whirligig. They shared the same mass of white-blonde hair as the man. The infant was wrapped in a worn pink blanket. The man laid the baby in a bassinet on the floor as Ruddy neared.

"I'm Detective Inspector Bloodstone. I'd like to talk to you about your missing wife."

The man extended his hand. Ink stained the fingertips. "I am Willem Offerman. My wife, Tess, has not returned home. This is most unusual."

"You're Dutch?" Ruddy recognized the accent immediately but thought to confirm what he knew.

Offerman nodded. "How do you know this? I am always taken for German."

"I fought with the British military in the Zulu Wars. I had the occasion to meet many Boers. Are you a typesetter?" Ruddy pointed to Offerman's fingers. If so, he'd have started his shift early, before his wife left most likely.

"Yes."

"Tell me about your missing wife. What was she wearing the last time you saw her, which was this morning according to the report?"

"She wore a plain, brown wool dress. That's what she wears during the week while she works."

"What sort of work does she do?" With three small children Ruddy wondered how she managed to work as well.

"She takes in laundry. She picks up the dirty clothes, washes and presses them, then returns the basket with those clothes the next day. She does this everyday but Sunday."

Ruddy couldn't imagine taking the children with her or them witnessing the crime. Injury to their mother would've sent them into a wailing, crying panic. "Who watches the children while she runs her errands?"

"A widow who lives upstairs. Do you have news of my wife?"

"Do you know if she travels through the gardens by the museum coming or going with her tasks?"

"Yes. We live close. She likes to pick modest bunches of the flowers in the spring and bring them home. She never took too many. From all your questions, I think you do have news of Tess. Is she injured?"

Ruddy breathed deep and shook his head.

Offerman looked at his boys who were still playing and then turned back to Ruddy. "Is she dead?"

"I'm sorry. A woman, a murder victim, was discovered today in the gardens. It sounds like your wife. If so, she was taken to a local doctor's office. I'll take you there to positively identify the woman."

"There might be a chance you are wrong then?"

"A minute one, I'm afraid. Everything you've told me about Tess fits the lady we found." All except the basket of laundry. Where had that gone? The two murders had what appeared to be a sexual motive, not theft. He and Archie eliminated robbery or theft as motive since both women had money, not much, but enough to take, in their reticules.

Offerman wiped at his tears. They abated briefly but began again. "How can I take care of my children? I must work."

"Perhaps the widow who watched them when Tess conducted her business."

"She's old and my young boys will be too much for her all day. The baby still needs mother's milk...Tess's milk." A steady stream of tears rolled down his cheek.

Ruddy excused himself to speak with Archie. "If the desk sergeant can spare four officers, two if he can't, have them search a three block radius around the park. The victim carried a basket of laundry. If we can locate the basket, we'll know the crime scene."

"The odds of finding a basket of clothes now are slim.

I don't see many folks not making away with them."

"Neither do I really. It's a long shot but worth a try."

"Want me to go with the men?"

"No, if you're amenable I'm hoping you'll watch over the children while I take the husband to the morgue."

"Certainly."

Ruddy returned to Offerman who had composed himself and held the toddler on his knee. "Tess and I loved each other, detective. That is rare in this world. She and the children are all I live for. Better I should've died."

Nothing Ruddy could say made the loss tolerable. The boys needn't see their dead mother. All he could do was offer temporary help with them. "I'll have my partner, Sgt. Holbrook watch the children while I take you to the doctor's office we use as morgue. The sergeant has two small girls and is good with young ones."

Offerman gave a weak nod. "Please, I would be grateful. Will we be gone long?"

"No." Identifying the dead never did take long and was often the same. Hope fades completely from the eyes of the person who the identifying falls to. Denial takes its place. Tears wet their cheeks and chin. Ruddy learned long ago not to allow the person into the room where the body lay. Better to have them identify their loved one through a window or from a distance. Otherwise, too many fell over the body weeping and in their grief fought against relinquishing the position.

At the morgue, Offerman confirmed the second victim was his wife. To Ruddy's surprise, he didn't break down again. He identified her and only said, "Cover her, please." He remained silent as they walked back to the station. There, he thanked Archie and left with the children who happily told him about the sweet the policeman had bought each of them.

"I'm tired. I'm going to go home. I want to kiss my wife and hug my girls tight," Archie said, putting on his coat and hat.

"I'm going to stop by Allegra's and then go on home. I feel a thousand years old." Ruddy put his coat on and they both left.

#

"Sorry, I'm late. We missed your special dinner and dance night," Ruddy said and stepped into Allegra's entry.

"Don't apologize. You have to do your job. Our night out can wait. But speaking of dinner, are you hungry?"

"Ravenous. I haven't eaten since this morning."

Allegra patted the thick cushion on one of her parlor chairs. "Sit. Relax. I don't have a lot in the house but I'm sure I can throw together a plate of eggs and kippers."

"Sounds wonderful." Ruddy carefully folded his jacket and laid it across the arm of another chair, then sank into the one Allegra indicated. He rested his head on the back of it and closed his eyes.

He dreamt he had yellow fever again. He staggered down a dirt road under the merciless African sun. Lost and searching for his company's camp, he fought the dizziness and pain in his stomach that slowed him. A man he didn't know, a Boer on horseback with a blonde-haired boy in the saddle in front him stopped. "Where is my wife, Englishman?"

Jarred awake by Allegra shaking his shoulder, he sat up and rubbed his eyes, taking a moment to shake off the dream. She set the tray of food down on the ottoman and handed him a knife and fork. "You were dreaming. You mumbled something about being dizzy and said, 'help me.' What were you dreaming?"

He shook his head. "Nothing interesting, bits and bobs of a time long ago."

"From your time in Africa?"

He nodded and took a forkful of eggs.

Allegra moved his jacket and pulled the chair next to his. "Tell me about it. How did you get your Victoria

Cross?"

He took a bite of a kipper and thought whether or not to talk about the battle. He'd never spoke of it to anyone other than to Morris, who'd understood, having been in the Crimea.

"I'm a good listener and I think it might help since I suspect your dream was about something that happened," Allegra said.

"What's the point?"

"I needn't be a clairvoyant to guess you were having a bad dream. People don't say *help me* when they're having a good one. I doubt it's the first bad one you've had. There's something to be said for lightening the burden on your soul by sharing a troubling time with a good listener."

After taking a long swallow of beer, he said, "I joined the 24th Regiment, South Wales Borderers in 1871, when I was fourteen. I lied and said I was seventeen so they'd take me."

Allegra's brows dipped. "Why would you do that at such a young age?"

"The army sounded adventurous. I'd get to see exotic foreign lands and whatnot, plus it was one less mouth for my father to feed." He gave her a wry smile. "Eight years later I got my adventure, just not the one I envisioned."

He drank half his beer...remembering the events of the days leading up to the battle. "We crossed the Buffalo River in Zululand. I had come down with yellow fever so I was sent on to the hospital station at Roarke's Drift while my company made camp at the base of Mt. Isandhlwana. The morning of January 22, the Zulus attacked my company there. Heavily outnumbered, our men held their ground in spite of the odds. But within hours the camp was overrun and all but a handful survived. They rode to Roarke's Drift to warn us.

They arrived around 12:30. We were only about one-hundred-thirty strong, most were sick or wounded. I had terrible bouts of dizziness and horrible stomach pain. I was lying in my cot when I heard all the commotion outside, shouts, and men running. I'd suffered feverish imaginings and wasn't sure if I was hallucinating. Then, I heard the Color Sergeant Bourne order the men to fix bayonets. I knew then the noise was a defensive wall being built and manned. On his way to his place on the barricade, one of the men told us, *Zulus, thousands of them.*

"The handful of us who were ambulatory—"

"But you weren't really ambulatory, not if you suffered such terrible light-headedness."

"None of us were in good shape, but we'd die fighting. The natives attacked. You can't imagine the noise. There was a great roar of screams and gunfire. Those of us in the hospital used rifle butts and bayonets and went room to room knocking out hunks of wall to create firing holes.

Suddenly the straw roof was ablaze and burning fast. Zulus who'd broken through our ranks had thrown lit clumps of grass on it. Some of the lads engaged the Zulu snipers, covering us as Williams, Hook, and I helped get the men out who were too sick to walk. We dropped them in front of Surgeon Reynolds building. It took no time at all before the hospital was almost totally engulfed in flame. We made a last effort to reach the rest of the men inside."

Allegra put her hand on the sleeve of his burn scarred forearm. No hair grew over the puckered skin and the injury was sensitive to heat. It still pained him to sit with that side to a fireplace.

"Is that how you got this?" she asked, giving his arm a light squeeze.

"Yes."

"Then what happened?"

"I took a place on a secondary defense wall made of biscuit boxes and overturned wagons. The men from the perimeter retreated to stand with us."

"How could you fight, injured and running a fever?"

The question brought a smile. "Trying to stay alive was a great distraction. Although I had moments where I couldn't see what I was shooting for the black spots in my vision."

She reached up and touched the scar on his neck. "Did you get this in the same battle?"

"Yes. The Zulus kept coming and coming. The hills seemed alive with them. One that came over the wall slammed me to the ground. I took a spear in the throat."

Her eyes widened. "Dear Lord, you're lucky it didn't hit an artery."

"I know." He smiled again at the memory of the warrior's wide eyes when the rifle round Ruddy managed to get off struck.

"Is that why you got the V.C.?"

"No, it was for evacuating the hospital." He laid the plate of half eaten eggs and fish on a side table. "But I should've been at Isandhlwana with my company...with my friends."

"With Yellow Fever? You should've been at the hospital. Your friends would've died with or without you. Had you not been at the hospital, the men you helped would've died instead."

"Someone else might've gotten them out." He should've been at Isandhlwana. Allegra, like most civilians, didn't understand a soldier fights for the man standing next to him in battle first, for his regiment second, and the queen third. No amount of explaining could make people understand that type of loyalty. "Now you know everything."

She pressed forward giving him a lovely view of milky cleavage and a whiff of lavender. "Enough war talk. Will you spend the night? Just because we're not dancing at a restaurant doesn't mean we can't dance in other ways."

"You tempt me but not tonight. I must go somewhere. It has to do with a case."

He finished eating and kissed Allegra goodbye. He originally intended to stay but remembrances of battle faded and thoughts of murder plagued him. He went back to the station to see if anyone found the basket of clothes. No one had. As Archie feared, they'd likely been stolen. Instead of going straight to his flat, he detoured and cut through the museum gardens. He wandered the immediate areas around the where the bodies were discovered trying to get a sense of the killer. "Where did you hide? Where did you lie in wait?" he whispered.

Ornate cast iron street lamps with fluted bases and globe holders lined the walkways of the garden. Ruddy stopped to admire the workmanship on one. Mass produced in ironmongeries around the country, one had to appreciate the small details added to the utilitarian lights.

When he reached the fountain, he sat on the surround, taking in the shadows and the leafy canopy the trees formed. Intuition and instinct, two natural abilities that served him well in the past, failed him now.

Street noise penetrated the foliage. Laughter, and snippets of loud talk, mixed with local pub drunks..typical Londoners. Other than the mysterious button, his only leads were the victim Ellis's male friend, the well-dressed man with bright blue eyes. Londoners..they'd never suspect a well-dressed man with murderous intent. To them, the rich didn't need to kill. They had all the comforts.

"Above suspicion, did you hide at all?"

## Chapter Fifteen

William already read two of Frobisher's journals. This was the last. The others didn't offer much insight on the effects of the formula. They were basic logs. The doctor had used the formula on the *pyromaniac,* Norris, and logged the effects. The term for Norris's compulsion was new to William and he resented it. Resentment came not from his unfamiliarity with the term, but the fact Frobisher knew the word. It troubled him a weasel like the doctor had even that small leg up on him.

Across from him, Catherine sat curled up reading. A short stack of broadsheets on the table beside her—scandal sheets in his opinion.

"Merciful heavens. A woman was murdered a stone's throw from here in the museum gardens," Catherine said in an octave higher than usual voice. "Read about it for yourself."

"I've no interest in the matter." William continued going through the journal. "London is a big city. Murders are bound to occur."

"I'm afraid. It's terrifying to think this happened so close. How can I protect myself?"

He looked up. "I'd suggest you not walk in the gardens in the early hours," he said, knowing his droll answer would aggravate. "Seriously, I don't see why you should worry. You're never alone. There's always a member of the staff with you when you're out and about."

"Your concern for me is less than sterling."

William ignored the comment, reading on in the journal.

"What has you so absorbed?" Catherine stood and

crossed to where he sat. She leaned over his shoulder and peeked at the book. "Looks devilishly boring."

"Please don't stand behind me like that while I read. It's annoying. Besides, there's nothing in these books you'd understand."

She came around, grabbed a tasseled chair pillow and threw it at his head. He dodged right. The pillow missed him but jostled his snifter of brandy before falling to the floor.

"Pick it up," he said in a soft voice.

Hands on her hips, she confronted him, "That was very rude of you. I am not without education. I was a governess."

"Pick up the pillow."

Catherine responded with a fiery stare.

He smiled and asked, "Shall I make you?"

Catherine wisely picked the pillow up. "There." She tossed it back onto the chair she'd taken it from. "You should say you're sorry."

"I would, if I was, but I'm not. Get out now. I don't want you in here sulking and moaning."

The belligerence drained from her face. Eyes softening, she entreated in humble tone, "Let me stay. I won't moan."

William put the last journal down and snatched her wrist before he was out of the chair. He tightened his hold as she pulled against him and pushed her out the door. "I don't care where you go in the house but get out of my sight."

"I'm sorry. Don't make me leave."

He closed the door and locked it, then returned to the journals. He read each entry with special attention to the effects on Norris. The documentation was interesting but would've been more informative if Frobisher had experimented on others beside Norris, men in particular. Individuals had different sensibilities. Why not his patient Norris as well? The formula may not have affected him the same way it did with Norris. William knew men who became drunk on one pint of ale and men who drank six pints with little visible change on them.

The lack of test subjects aside, how the compound changed Norris intrigued William. The alchemist declared it a miracle that made one young again, not in years but in body and ability. According to Frobisher, Norris moved heavy objects with relative ease, objects he struggled with prior to ingesting the formula. Exactly as William hoped, Norris was sexually aroused much of the time and the mention of setting fires exacerbated the state.

"Yes. Yes. Yes." When he and Faith married, their intimacies would go long into the night. Deep-seated fear of any inability to satisfy her as often as she liked was gone now.

Isaac, Catherine's butler knocked and opened the door, stepping just inside. "You called sir?"

William hadn't realized how loud he'd spoken his glee.

"No Isaac, I didn't mean to disturb you." Isaac nodded and left.

Frobisher's notes went on to document excursions with Norris. On several occasions, the doctor took the lunatic out of the hospital to observe how he behaved. The doctor kept manacles hidden by long trousers on Norris's ankles with just enough chain for him to move relatively normal when they were in public.

Frobisher had Norris drink the liquid the first few times but didn't note how much dosage he used. The formula traveled through his system slowly before taking full effect. Too long for the doctor's purpose. The next time he injected the formula into Norris with a hypodermic syringe directly into a vein.

William shuddered with the unpleasant thought of cold fluid injected into him. His best veins were in the back of his hands. He closed his eyes and imagined how the cold would travel up his arm, into his shoulder, his chest and then to his heart before getting pumped through his system. He hated being cold. Everyone suffered in the Cornish winters, himself included. The hot muggy summers were almost as bad. Even in the oppressive summer heat, with the Atlantic waters a short trek, he never swam off the coast. Those waters never warmed sufficiently to his taste.

Cold or not, he wanted to experiment with the formula. He'd get the syringes from Buckle, the pharmacist.

He rang for Isaac.

The butler stood in the doorway awaiting instruction. "Sir?"

"Have my carriage brought to the front."

William packed up the journals in the doctor's Gladstone bag. He'd locked the bottles with the formula in the desk at his townhome. When he finished, he found Catherine in the small parlor embroidering a pillow cover. "I'm leaving now."

She put her sewing down and came to him. "I'm sorry I lost my temper with you. Please don't go. Spend the night. I thought that's what you planned. Cook is making a lovely dinner for you."

"I have business to attend to or I would stay." He'd told her that to appease her when he arrived. He wouldn't have, not really. She always asked him but he never did, always finding a reason to leave.

Anxious to see the effects of the formula, this time he meant it when he said, "I'll spend the night tomorrow."

#

William filled the syringe a quarter of the way with the formula and laid it down on the library's wine table. He'd told Burton that he didn't want to be disturbed and gave the staff the rest of the night off. He poured and drained a glass of whiskey, pacing, eyes fixed on the syringe. Finally, he sat in the chair next to the table and poured another whiskey.

"What the devil am I doing?" he asked, patting the

veins in the back of his left hand. Blue-green ropes of blood popped up. Determined, he held tight to the syringe and pressed the needle into his hand. He hadn't broken the skin before he lost his courage. Unable to complete the injection, he pulled his finger from the plunger. Cowardice was such a pathetic quality. He never thought himself a coward but he'd never stuck a needle into his flesh. "Bloody hell."

At first Frobisher had Norris drink the fluid. William went to the kitchen for a spoon. He hesitated over which to use, a teaspoon or soup spoon and chose the way of caution. Back in the library he filled a teaspoon from a beaker. One sip and he spit the bitter liquid into the fireplace. Nothing in memory compared. Another large swallow of whiskey couldn't erase the taste. How the doctor managed to get any down the throat of Norris was a mystery. He must've tied him to the cot and forced it after the first time. No man, lunatic or sane, would drink the foul stuff voluntarily.

William poured a third whiskey and mustered his courage. He patted his veins up again, stuck the needle in but the vein rolled and he pulled the needle out. Desperate to get it done and over with, he jabbed the hypodermic into his thigh and pushed the formula from the syringe while his bravery held. He sank into the wine table chair and waited for the burst of vigor he anticipated.

#

"Is the shine-boy around?" Ruddy asked, looking at his muddy boots. He'd made a mess of them the night before revisiting the crime scenes.

"Saw him a few minutes ago by the cells with the night patrol boys. They're having a cup of tea before heading home," Archie said.

Ruddy went to the cellblock area and found the youngster. "When you're finished, come round to my desk."

"I'm just done now, Mr. Bloodstone."

The boy followed him back into the investigator's room and set up with his various brushes, rags, and wax polish. Ruddy propped one foot onto the wooden box and turned to Archie. "I've a new theory for us to consider," he said.

"Go on."

"We're spending today interviewing every workman in the immediate vicinity of the murders. I went back to where the bodies were found last night—"

"What're you doing lurking around there?"

"I wasn't lurking. I wanted to get a sense of what happened. As I sat there it occurred to me our assumption the killer lay in wait for the right opportunity to strike...a tedious action even for a murderer. I don't think he hid. I think he might've been someone the victims saw all the time and paid no attention to."

Archie took a swallow of tea as he absorbed Ruddy's idea. "What do you mean by paid no attention to?"

"Someone the victims saw and paid no notice, like a common worker who was part of the landscape. In turn, they were women he saw regularly. Once he planned his attack, he just needed a time with no one else around."

"Are you disregarding the well-dressed man the Ellis woman mentioned?"

The shine boy stopped. "Why'd you stop, boy?" Ruddy asked.

"Sorry, I need to add more wax to the toe." He dabbed more polish and began buffing again.

"I'm not throwing out any viable suspect but nothing has come of the mysterious swell. Nor does a person fitting that description have any obvious connection with the second victim," Ruddy explained.

The shine boy stopped again. "What's wrong with you today?" Ruddy asked, seeing him looking up.

"Nothing sir. Switch feet."

Ruddy propped his other foot onto the shine box. "I don't care how long it takes but we're going to comprise a list of the area workers, names, where they live, the hours they arrive and leave. We'll interview their families and friends. If they're an odd fish, sooner or later someone will tell us."

"People love to point a finger," Archie added with a grin.

"A pence isn't it?" Ruddy verified after the boy finished. The boy nodded and Ruddy felt around in his waistcoat pocket for change. "You did a nice job. Here," he said and handed him a tuppence.

He and Archie left as the boy was packing up.

\#

Out of sight of the station the reporter gave the boy a florin. "Anything new on the murder?"

"Yes, there's been a second near the museum too."

## Chapter Sixteen

The desk sergeant, who also served as Jameson's secretary, came over to Ruddy and Archie. "The superintendent wants to see you in his office, immediately."

"Do you know why?" Ruddy asked.

The sergeant shook his head and walked back toward the front desk where a crowd of civilians waited to file reports or post bail for loved ones.

"What's this about, I wonder," Archie said and brushed the crumbs from his breakfast jam butty off his shirt.

"Probably still in a dither about our lack of progress on the murders. He knows we've little leads, not that it matters to him." Ruddy checked the front of his shirt for biscuit crumbs as well. He never ate jammy tarts or powdered confections at work. Anything that might cause a stain on his clothing, he avoided.

They entered Jameson's office and closed the door. In a chair in front of the superintendent sat Detective Inspector Lewis Waters. Waters wore baggy, grease stained trousers, a faded plaid shirt, old hard-worn boots, and a herringbone apple cap. He managed to not look silly in the cap, which Ruddy had no inclination to own or wear. Waters had his father's stevedore build and was inches shorter, barrel-chested, and broader all-around than Ruddy. He investigated suspicious fires, bombings, and anarchists groups as they were often behind the bombs. Ruddy liked him and respected his courage in dismantling and handling unexploded bombs. A job Ruddy wouldn't do for twice his salary.

"Sit," Jameson told them and pointed to the two empty chairs in front of his desk. "Are you aware of the fire at a doctor's office near Whitechapel?"

Ruddy and Archie nodded.

"Two bodies were found in the rubble."

"The doctor and some looney he worked with according to the paper," Archie said.

"At first I figured it for a murder-suicide," Waters said. "Patient kills doctor, then takes his life in a blaze of glory. Hard to tell for certain as the bodies were so badly burned."

"Now we're also considering this might be a double homicide." Jameson turned to Waters. "I'll let you explain."

"The looney was an inmate at St. Bartholomew's named Andrew Norris. We talked to the guards at the hospital. They said he was mad as a March hare but never exhibited suicidal tendencies. I'll admit to you that he was also a fire bug—"

Ruddy heard enough. "You're having me on, right? A lunatic fire bug coincidentally dies in a fire with a doctor who didn't have the sense god gave a squirrel. The doctor ran around with a crazy man and paid the ultimate price. End of investigation as far as I see."

Lewis held up his hand. "Please let me finish."

Ruddy spread his hands in an open gesture conceding to Waters although he doubted Waters could convince him the case merited further investigation.

"I went through Norris's letters. He wrote to his sister and mother, but never asked to have the guards post them. No one at the hospital knows where they live or even if they live. Nothing in them talks of setting fires."

"Please. Even a daft bugger isn't going to tell his mother how aroused he gets setting fires." Ruddy struggled to keep his temper in check with the ridiculous talk. He wasn't being deliberately arbitrary but had little patience for the direction of this investigative turn.

"From what I was told at the hospital, many of the loonies write letters to God. Norris followed the same pattern and wrote to him too. Nowhere in them does he discuss a desire to start more fires. He talks of the pleasure the ones he set gave him but not of new ones."

"Could easily have been an accident," Ruddy countered.

Waters shrugged and said, "Could be but the position of the bodies indicates neither man tried to get out. That points me in the direction of homicide."

"Understandable." Ruddy turned to Jameson. "Why are Archie and I here, Superintendent?"

"You two are taking the case over."

Ruddy looked from Jameson to Waters to Archie and back to Jameson. He thought Jameson and Waters as daft as the dead man for continuing an investigation on such a thin suspicion. "They died in a suspicious fire. That's his bailiwick." He indicated Waters. "Arch and I are working on the museum homicides. The newspapers only know of the one, thankfully, but you know how the press will dog us until we solve it. Lord help us if they learn of the other."

"Lewis and I would prefer he stay on the arson case but the Commander has requested he be reassigned to a Markist group making trouble in the East End. The government needs to know what the devils have planned." His brows notched up slightly. "It's not as though you two have a lot of suspects to go through."

"As a matter of fact, sir, we have a list of workmen in the area the time of the murders. We plan to interview their family and neighbors."

"A goodly list of suspects?"

Ruddy shifted in his chair. "Not exactly."

"I thought as much. Lewis will give you his notes and who to contact at the hospital." Jameson raised his hand cutting off Ruddy before he could comment. "Interview the guards again and anyone else who might give us more insight in the doctor's activities and madman's behavior. They might remember some information they forgot to mention the first time." He rose and stirred the kindling on a small wood stove in the office. The dying fire flared to life and he put his tea kettle on. "All of you may leave now," he said with his back to them.

Like reluctant ducks, Ruddy and Archie followed Waters to his desk to get the case file and his information.

"Sorry about this," Waters said as he gathered the paperwork, "But I had no say in the matter."

"We know," Archie said.

A copy of the Illustrated London News sat on Waters desk. The front page had a picture and story of a Marxist organized mini riot that occurred the previous day. Waters choice of clothing fit perfect. He'd look just like one of them if he carried a makeshift club.

The job of double agent held no appeal for Ruddy. It seemed a pain to him, the creating of a credible personal history, always careful of slipping up in conversation. Then there was the chore of remembering what lies you told and to whom. He preferred no frills investigative work. Everyone knew he was a detective. He asked questions. He sought answers and his job was to get them, one way or another. Far cleaner than having to mix and mingle with low life rabble-rousers.

"What story do you give these anarchist groups?" Ruddy asked, genuinely curious.

"I'm a day worker on the docks."

Ruddy thought it a clever cover. Waters had knowledge of the job from his father.

"Do you like doing this—this spy business?" Ruddy prodded.

"Yes and no. Jailing the criminals I like, but I must keep emotional distance with some, which is difficult at times. It's easy to grow close to some and that complicates performing the job expected of me."

Ruddy didn't think he'd suffer empathy with any radical cause, but he'd never been in Waters shoes.

Waters handed Archie a short pile of paperwork with his personal notes on top.

"Sorry Lewis, but I'm still mystified why you put much store in the writings of a madman. It's obvious what happened and to delve deeper is like a dog chasing his tail," Archie said.

"I've done enough arson investigations to know the types of men who set fires. Norris would've documented, in some way, what he'd like to do to the doctor or what he planned at the first opportunity. The ego of such men demands it. Like their fires, it must be fed."

Archie tucked the paperwork under his arm. "If you say so."

"What next? Do you want to start on Lewis's list or ours?" Archie asked when he and Ruddy reached their desks.

"Those hospital guards aren't going anywhere. Let's at least work on part of our list."

#

When the day started, the last thing Ruddy wanted to do was dance. But after the depressing dead end where he and Archie found themselves, it sounded inviting. An evening of dining and dancing with Allegra would keep the problems with the case at bay. They'd interviewed a good third of the families and friends of the workmen on their list. None of the men had stood out to him when first contacted, which was, itself, unusual for Ruddy. He generally could fix on a man or two who raised his suspicions. Their families were less forthcoming with information than the men themselves.

Ruddy changed into a new charcoal grey suit. He added a new grey and black striped four-in-hand silk tie and tiger's eye stud. The tiger's eye went well with his dark waistcoat. His tailor had suggested the stone.

"Oh my, don't you look handsome Mr. Bloodstone." Mrs. Goodge smiled girlishly as she eyed him heading toward the front door. She often teased about setting her cap for him if she were young again.

"Thank you, Mrs. Goodge. You're looking quite fine yourself this evening."

"Listen to you, smooth as silk against the skin."

He chuckled. No one ever called him smooth.

"Are you seeing that nice Mrs. Porter?" Mrs. Goodge asked.

"I am. We're going dancing. I hope she approves of my attire as much as you do. I hear the place she wishes to go is pretty fancy."

"Fancy is as fancy does. You'll be the handsomest man in the room."

"Ah, my sweet Mrs. Goodge." Ruddy bent and kissed her hand, which sent her scurrying off toward the kitchen giggling.

#

The door opened and Allegra greeted him with a kiss on the lips. She wore a pretty deep blue dress that exposed her creamy, white shoulders and hugged her breasts nicely.

"Don't you look dapper," she said as he came inside.

"Thank you, but you'll be the belle of the room tonight."

"I've not seen this suit before. How many suits do you have?"

"Six, counting this. Nice suits are an extravagance of mine."

She handed him her lace shawl and he draped it over her shoulders.

"Not to be impertinent but isn't that rather a lot of suits for a policeman? I can't think of any men who own so many, let alone on a civil servant's salary."

He wasn't sure how to interpret the question. It almost sounded like an accusation of corruption. If it came from anyone else, he'd think it rude, but Allegra wasn't the sort to offer insult so indirectly.

"I have five older brothers. Growing up, not one shirt

or pair of trousers came my way that wasn't worn by one of them first. I spent eight years in the queen's service wearing the cheapest, itchiest, coarsest wool available. I promised myself when I left the military I would never wear such god awful material again. I can't tell you how good it feels to not scratch my way through the day until my thighs bleed."

Allegra pinned on a light blue hat that had been sitting on an entry table. "Since you're such a fashionable man, tell me what do you think of my new hat?"

"Like the lady who wears it, lovely."

"Thank you. Do you think I used too many flowers?"

Why do women ask men such things? He always suspected the question a trap. The only safe answer was to say it's pleasing and change the subject.

"I'm afraid it is too showy. Be honest, what do you think?" She looked as sincere as could be when she said, *be honest.* But he knew the phrase from a woman was rarely meant to be taken at face value.

"Allegra, I'm not good at judging ladies fashion. Ladies hats are like wine to me. It tastes good or it doesn't. Hats are either pretty or they're not. Yours is a pretty one."

He breathed a sigh of relief as she smiled and moved for the door.

#

Their meal was excellent and he enjoyed the dancing more than he expected.

"Rudyard, I was thinking how nice it would be to go to Brighton for a couple of days. We could take long romantic walks in the moonlight, take in the fresh sea air. Can we go?" she asked as he helped her with her shawl.

"I'm afraid I can't, not while I'm working this case."

"Maybe down the road then."

"Maybe."

Outside, he stepped to the curb to hail a carriage. Down the street a newsboy with the evening editions shouted, "Second lady found murdered at the museum."

"Damnation." How could the press know? "Here boy." Ruddy waved him over and gave him a coin. "I'll take one."

"What's wrong?" Allegra slipped her arm through his as he skimmed the story. The article was slim on details but had the basics of Mrs. Offerman's murder. "Is this one of your investigations?"

"Yes. The men at the scene and the victim's husband are the only ones who knew of it. Well, until now. I don't know how the deuce the press is getting the information. I can't imagine it's one of us." He shook his head with glum anticipation at what the morning would bring after Jameson saw the paper.

"Do you need to go to the station? Do something to mitigate the damage?" Allegra fiddled with his tie, pretending to straighten the knot.

"There's no way to fix the uproar the story will cause. Besides, I planned on spending the whole evening with you and I'm keeping to my plan." He folded the paper, put it inside his coat pocket, and hailed a waiting carriage.

"Rudyard, I understand this story is a nasty distraction. We'll have other nights," she said as the carriage pulled up.

"My only distraction will be you." He gave her bum a squeeze as she climbed into the carriage...and did a good job of getting through yards of dress judging from her little jump. He slipped his watch from his waistcoat pocket and snuck a peek. In exactly eleven hours, he'd be on the wrong end of a verbal flogging.

## Chapter Seventeen

Ruddy and Archie shut the door to Jameson's office and walked in silence back to their desks.

"How does my arse look?" Ruddy asked, turning his back to Archie.

"Looks like it always does. Why?"

"I wasn't sure I had any left after the chewing we just got."

Archie sank into his chair and sipped on his now cold tea. "I don't know what he expects us to do about a leak. We're not the ones doing it so why dump the finding out on us?"

"Better him than the Commissioner. He's the next to lay blame on our doorstep." Ruddy pulled the drawing of the button from his case file. "We need a lead on this case something fierce. Although an arrest on the arson case might appease Jameson for a short time. We'd work a bit of good press from that."

"What do you want to do first, today?"

Ruddy stood and put on his hat. "Let's finish interviewing the people on our list. Then, let's have a chinwag with Mr. Marsden about his source."

#

Ruddy and Archie flashed their badges to the front desk clerk at the London Gazette. "We want to speak with Geoffrey Marsden," Ruddy told him.

The clerk's head shifted slightly with a quick glance to a desk in the corner of the room. "Give me a moment and I'll see if he's here."

Ruddy put a hand on the man's shoulder halting him mid stand. "Too late."

A narrow-faced, prissy looking man in a light blue floral cravat and light blue waistcoat tried to hide the nameplate on his desk as they approached. Ruddy always thought cravats too dandified, which added to his predetermined dislike of the reporter.

"Don't bother moving the nameplate. We know who you are," Archie said and leaned over to take the nameplate out of the reporter's hand. He set it in the same place Marsden had it.

"I know who you are," Marsden said. "I've seen you coming and going from the station. Too lofty to speak with any of the press. What do you want, Inspector?"

Archie gave Ruddy a light jab to the ribs. When Ruddy turned, Archie tipped his head toward the others in the room. Everyone's eyes were on the three of them.

"Let's take a walk," Ruddy told Marsden.

"I'd prefer to talk here."

"I don't. You can voluntarily take a walk with us or you can leave in manacles," Ruddy said flat voiced.

Marsden leaned back in his chair. "In manacles? Don't make me laugh. On what charge?"

Ruddy smiled. "As Mr. Lytton said, *the pen is mightier than the sword.* You're not the only creative person among us."

"You'll never find a charge that will hold me for long."

"Long enough to make you miserable. The special cell for drunkards you might find especially foul," Archie said.

"What'll it be?" Ruddy asked.

"Fine. I'll go with you but don't think I won't tell the superintendent of this abuse."

"I'm sure he'd *love* to talk with you too."

Marsden rose and put on a frock coat worn at the cuffs. Ruddy noticed.

Outside, Archie and Ruddy walked him into an alley concealed from most of the foot traffic behind a closed factory.

"Is this about my stories on the murders in the museum gardens?" Marsden asked, confronting Ruddy.

"Yes. Tell us who your source is."

Marsden stuck a mulish, defiant chin out. "I won't. I can't give up a source and expect anyone else to ever confide in me. Besides, there's nothing wrong with what I wrote. People have a right to know if a place is dangerous, particularly the ladies."

Ruddy didn't have a solid defense against Marsden's statement. He'd argued the same point with Jameson. "We've every intention of releasing the information to the public at the right time," he lied.

"When is the right time? When a third woman is murdered? A fourth? Not only does the public have a right to know about the killings, they have a right to know how well they're being investigated. What steps you're taking."

"That they don't have a right to. They only need know the cases are being handled as a high priority and every investigative avenue is being pursued. To tell the public all the details is to also tell the murderer. Or, don't you think he'd follow his own sordid story?"

"A chance I'd be willing to take if it meant more safety for everyone in the area."

Again, Ruddy agreed with the logic. The powers that be did not. He stepped closer to Marsden, close enough for his breath to ruffle the remaining thin strands of the reporter's hair.

"We don't have time to argue. Who's your source?"

"Give me an exclusive, not all the details but a general overview of what you're doing."

"Superintendent Jameson would have to approve that and he'll never agree. He doesn't like reporters and you in particular."

"You two could talk him into it."

Archie nodded, his expression serious, a wiggle up and down gave spirited life to his brows. "Have you ever written one positive story about the constabulary or even about one of the officers?"

Marsden didn't respond.

"No, you haven't," Archie answered for him. "Could we talk to him? Yes. Will we? No." He winked at Marsden and added, "It's called reciprocity, mate, reciprocity."

From Marsden's stormy expression, Ruddy guessed he'd love to punch Archie in the face. Ruddy wished he would. Fisticuffs, however short-lived by Archie's trouncing of Marsden, offered an amusing break to the day's monotony of interviews with no results.

"We're wasting time. Who's your source?" Ruddy asked.

"Again, I won't tell you."

"Oh, you will. Maybe not today but very soon. We'll make it our mission to discover the truth." He and Archie left Marsden fuming in the alley.

#

At the station Ruddy sought out Ernest Young. Of all the men assigned to Holborn Station, he had the most mundane and common face. Of medium height and weight, with medium brown hair, no facial hair, and no memorable features, he'd blend in with anyone on the street.

"Constable Young," Ruddy waved him over. "Come with me."

Ruddy sat on the edge of his desk, joined by Young and Archie who had gone for a cup of tea. "I want you to follow somebody. Have you ever seen a reporter named Geoffrey Marsden: short, plump, with thinning ginger hair and a skinny mustache that looks like it was painted on? He tends to loiter around the station when we're busy with what might be a big story. I wish I had a photograph of him but I don't."

Young shook his head. "Sorry, sir. The description doesn't bring anyone to mind. Should I know him?"

"No. But he's the man you're going to follow. Stay out of sight as much as you can. He's not stupid. You're to wear regular clothes, but uniform or not, if he suspects he's being watched, he won't do what we want him to do."

Ruddy wrote down the address of the paper Marsden worked for and that he could be seen from the street through a front window. "I want you to wake up with him and go to bed with him—"

Young stiffened. "Sir?"

"Not go to bed literally, Young. In other words while he is up and about, I want you with him. Whoever he meets with, try to get us a name or at least a description along with time and place."

"Is he the one running the department to ground about those murders?"

"Yes. He's got a source close to us and we're going to find out who, even if it's one of our own. Although, I truly hope it isn't" If it was, Jameson would see the man's career with the department finished, whether or not he had a family to support.

"When do I start?"

"Get your street clothes on and get over to his office. I want eyes on him as soon as possible."

Young nodded and went off to change.

"What if following him doesn't work?" Archie asked.

Ruddy came around and sat at his desk. "Then we release false information, a false lead. We put the story around the station. If it gets to Marsden, then it's one of our boys. If not, then at least we've narrowed the field through elimination.

*Journal Entry*
*June, 1888*

*For the first time in ages, insomnia hasn't troubled me. I stayed awake long as I could, waiting to feel the results of the elixir. Before I realized it, exhaustion came over me and I slept in the chair. I slept like a dead man for a mere five hours and then awoke as energized as if it was for ten. I wanted to ride, to have the cool morning air in my face. At daybreak I saddled Major and galloped the length of the path around the Serpentine, twice. At that hour, I had the park to myself, save for the occasional lamplighter making his rounds extinguishing the lights.*

*What a change in my sexual stamina. A couple of weeks ago, I was often too tired to make love to Catherine. This morning I gave it to her three times. Three, and we hadn't had breakfast yet.*

## Chapter Eighteen

"Do you think I might stay with you until this murderer is caught?" Catherine asked from across the table. She made it sound like she asked him to pass the butter.

"We've had this discussion. I said no. I told you, stay out of the museum gardens in the early morning and you'll be fine." For a woman who claimed a better than usual intellect for her gender, she failed to grasp his serious objections and continued to badger him over sharing his townhome with her.

He'd read the financial pages of the morning London Times while she ate in the dining room. When she finished and was ready for a cup of tea with him, her butler came to the library and William joined her. Had he known this subject was going to be broached, he'd have left and gone home earlier.

"I won't be moved on this, so quit making excuses and pressing me to move you into my place. I will not do it. You have a house filled with staff. How on this green earth is a killer going to manage to kill you without one of your staff discovering him first? He isn't."

"There are times I believe you couldn't care less if something terrible happened to me." Catherine followed the comment with a pouty face he'd seen too often of late.

The temptation to say, *times like now you mean*, played at the tip of his tongue. That honesty would only drive the conversation into a subject he hadn't patience for at any time.

She continued to press the issue into the tedious subject. "Do you think you could ever love me?"

"You are my mistress. I provide you with anything

you need and more. Am I not generous with you?" Tight-lipped, she nodded. Not what she wanted to hear but he knew that. "Love is not part of our bargain."

"What if I told you I love you?"

"I'd say you're a fool. Love involves a possible future together, long range and nuanced with different emotions. We have the present...the here and now. Our time together is based on carnal symbiosis and an affection that allows us to tolerate one another."

She stared at him, showing no reaction to his analysis of their relationship. She blinked and he almost missed the slight flare of her nostrils. Some bolt of insight had come to her. "Are you in love with someone else?"

"Since that's none of your business, I won't bother to answer your inappropriate question." He'd never tell her about Faith. The two women were as different as night and day. One would be the mother of his children. One was a brief source of amusement until he married and cut her from his life.

"If you did fall in love and marry, would you still keep me? I mean not in Cornwall, obviously, but for when you're in town."

He'd had enough of this. A kind lie would bring a speedy end to the barrage of questions. That and the distraction of him spending money on her. "Of course," he said with a emotionless smile. "Now get your gloves and hat. I'm taking you shopping."

#

As they strolled down Oxford Street, he paused in front of Lambert's jewelry store briefly, so not to draw Catherine's attention. A cameo of the three muses was displayed on a blue velvet cloth in the window. Magnificent and unique, Faith would love it. He'd come back to buy it when he wasn't with Catherine, who'd no doubt assume the purchase for her. When she found out different, she'd turn sulky and petulant and back to posing a string of questions.

They continued on and stopped when Catherine saw a lady's emporium she wanted to go into. William wanted to return to Lambert's and have them put the cameo away until he returned. With Catherine busy in the shop, he'd be able to dash back to the jewelers. "I'll catch up to you. There's a tobacconist I like just down the road who carries my favorite cigars."

He'd made numerous purchases at Lambert's and they were delighted to set the piece aside for him. When he came back to the shop Catherine entered, he stopped and watched her through the window. She stood by a crib swaddled in a lace-trimmed canopy and ribbon-trimmed rails. She fingered the lacey material with palpable yearning in her eyes.

A yearning mistress was a dangerous mistress. Only one had ever gotten pregnant. He gave her a very generous sum of money and she genially agreed to live in France until the baby arrived. Yearning wasn't in the lady's nature and she had no argument against giving the child up. After another generous donation to the local convent, the nuns agreed to raise the baby. He didn't believe he'd be so lucky with Catherine if she became pregnant. He couldn't have a bastard running around. How could he tell Faith and her parents? He couldn't subject them to scurrilous gossip. He should've learned after the previous accidental baby and been more careful. For all he knew, Catherine might already be pregnant. Had her breasts felt a bit larger lately? He couldn't recall.

He stepped away from the store's picture window and thought how to solve the problem. He needed a permanent solution. One came to him and he hurried back to Lambert's, where he bought a gold bracelet with a heart charm. He'd give it to Catherine tonight. She'd love it.

\#

"It's beautiful," Catherine said, offering him her wrist. He obliged her and locked the clasp.

"I've a special evening planned," he said, when she

released him from a long hug. Still in his arms, she leaned back eager to hear the plan.

"I'm taking you to the Museum's teashop. It's a miniature version of the Royal Pavilion in Brighton. You'll like it. Cut-crystal lamps light the tables and elaborate crystal chandeliers hang overhead. Didn't you buy a new dress last week?"

She nodded. "Yes." And as expected she asked, "Shall I wear it?"

She'd never refused him any type of sexual activity, but he needed her in the gardens, where she feared going into. He added a compliment to guarantee her willing obedience, "Yes, I want to show you off."

#

They didn't eat, but she understood they'd only share champagne. He ordered a bottle of Moet et Chandon Imperial, a favorite of the Duke of Wellington in his day. William kept Catherine's glass filled while he took the occasional sip. Outside the daylight turned to the grey and lavender of early evening. To kill time, he ordered strawberries and cream for her in spite of his aversion. Thankfully, a harpist played Debussy in the background, which helped dull the sound of Catherine and the other patrons eating. The serving of the strawberry dish surprised her and she ate slowly, taking great caution to make as little noise as possible.

Half a bottle of champagne remained after she finished the dessert. William kept pouring, making pleasant chitchat. When she began to slur her speech and the lowlight of dusk had finally faded, he checked his watch. It was late enough for foot traffic in the gardens to be at a minimum, especially with the negative press about the murders. The lamps that bordered the path would be sufficient to accomplish his plan without being too bright. Shadows and filtered light was all that he needed.

The time was right.

"This is a lovely evening. Let's go for a stroll."

She looped her arm through his and he pulled her close as they walked by beds of flowers, each bed featuring a different flower type. Just past the staircase to the museum entrance and where the stone path through another garden started, he stopped and turned her so she faced him. He brought her hand with the bracelet to his lips and kissed the inside of her wrist.

"You make me feel romantic," he told her, getting a broad smile in response. On this, their last night together, he'd give her the words she longed to hear. "This judgmental society of ours will never grant me the luxury of loving my mistress. But, I do care for you. I care for you in a way I've never cared for another woman."

"You've no idea how I treasure what's between us. I know you cannot marry me, but there's so much more we can share."

He'd been right about her ambition and yearning to tie him to her. She'd wield a child of theirs like a weapon. The desire to strangle her before she uttered another word surged. *Be patient. Soon*, he thought. *Soon.*

"I want you here and now. I don't want to wait until we return to your home," he said. "Come."

He led her away from the path. They found a shadowed patch where verdant shrubbery shielded them from the prying eyes of anyone passing.

"Here. I'll have you here. The lushness of the garden is nothing compared to your lush body." He dropped to one knee and began to pull her down.

"What of my new dress? It'll be ruined."

"I'll buy you a dozen more." He tugged on her wrists easing her down to her knees. Then he gently laid her down. Like the ideal lover, he brushed her cheeks with the back of his fingers and kissed them, then her forehead and finally her lips.

"I love you, William. I can't help myself, I do," she

said as he raised his lips ever so slightly from hers.

"I know." He kissed again. "I know."

He pushed her skirt and sateen petticoat up and made love to her. When she neared her point of release, he pulled Isabeau's scarf from his pocket and slipped it around her throat. She was too far gone to object, not that she would in her passion. He tightened the silk, tighter than ever before when she'd let him use the scarf. Her eyes flew open. She beat on his arms and desperately clawed at the silk wrap. She tried to wrest him off of her but lacked the strength. Within minutes, it was over. Diminutive Isabeau had fought longer and with more strength than Catherine. William fleetingly wondered why.

William stood and straightened his clothing. He didn't bother with her skirt and petticoats. Let the police believe it was another victim sexually assaulted before she was murdered. He wasn't certain if they had a way of telling when the actual death occurred. He relied on the similarities to the other killings to lead the detectives to believe it was the same man.

The heart charm on her bracelet glittered in the moonlight. He reached down and removed it. He'd get another box from Lambert's and give it to Faith. She'd certainly love it too.

#

Ruddy woke with a start. No memory of having dreamed lingered. The only dreams he ever remembered were the dark ones that took him back to the war.

He swung his feet to the floor, yawned, and scratched.

The loud banging that brought him awake continued. "Mr. Bloodstone. Mr. Bloodstone, wake up."

*Mrs. Goodge.* "Coming," he called out loud so she'd hear and went to the door.

"Mr. Bloodstone, open the door, please."

He opened it but bent to only expose his top half to her. She didn't need to see him in his underwear. "What's wrong?"

"There's an officer in the vestibule. He said he had to speak to you on an urgent police matter."

A glance at the front window showed early light peeking through but no sun yet. Yawning again, he asked, "What time is it?"

"Half-six." The early hour meant nothing to her. Mrs. Goodge rose at first light and began her morning routine, making breakfast for the boarders.

"Please show him to the parlor, and if you would, give him a cup of tea while I dress."

"Kettle's already hot." She bustled off downstairs.

Ruddy closed the door and went into the bathroom to cleanup. He splashed water on his face and brushed his teeth, grimacing as he did. The only tooth powder he had contained clove, which he disliked. He intended to get a different brand from the chemist the day before and forgot. The clove—cinnamon powder ruined his sense of taste for an hour after he used it. With no time to shave, he quickly dressed. He had a bad feeling the urgent police business involved another murder.

## Chapter Nineteen

"C.O." Archie showed Ruddy the embroidered handkerchief. "At least it's something, not much of a clue to her identity, but a start. From the state of rigor mortis, this one appears to have been killed late last night. Odd."

"Anything else in her reticule?" Ruddy asked.

"Just a few ladies things: a comb, an enamel box with mint candies, and two guineas and one gold sovereign."

The amount raised eyebrows in all the officers within earshot, including Ruddy. The last was more money than any woman he personally knew carried. It was more than many men or women earned in a month. Robbery couldn't have been the motive. No everyday street criminal would leave that kind of money behind.

Ruddy knelt by the body, turning Catherine's head right and left. "I don't think this is our man's work. I suspect this is a killer who wants us to believe it's the same man. Look at the bruises on her throat. The others had finger marks, they were manually strangled. You could tell how he choked her. This one's neck lacks those marks. Instead the only bruising is here in the front, like some kind of ligature was used. A knot might've left this."

"There's usually a band of bruising around the neck with a ligature."

"Yes, but we might not be looking at the typical rope-style type. I wonder if something like a belt wasn't used, something wide enough not to dig into the skin like a cord. Although I imagine a belt would make some kind of mark as well. Autopsy will tell us more."

Archie squatted on the other side of the body.

"Doesn't mean a different killer. Maybe he just changed his pattern."

"I doubt it. People stick with what they're comfortable with and our former victims were a different style death and a different style lady. You knew they were working women, their clothing simple and inexpensive. The dress is too expensive for the average woman."

Archie turned a hand over and ran his thumb over her palm. "Soft. If she worked, it wasn't with her hands."

Every working woman he knew had telltale signs on their fingers or hands. Even Allegra had rough fingers from working with straw for bonnets. "What jobs could this woman have held? Governess? Lady's companion? Actress? None of which pays enough for her to walk around with that much money."

Ruddy went on comparing the inconsistences in this murder from those before, "Also, there's no sign the killer spent himself on her clothing like the others. Again, we won't know until after the autopsy, but from the scent, I'd say this victim had sex. Maybe willingly, maybe not, but her partner completed the act the normal way."

One of the constables standing guard over the scene laughed low and whispered to a second constable who also snickered. Ruddy heard the first repeat, "the normal way," a comment which they both found oddly amusing.

"What's so funny about that?" he asked. He looked back and forth between the two. "Well?"

"The *normal way* sir? Many of us younger folks try other positions," the first constable said. "*The Kama Sutra* doesn't offend us."

Ruddy bristled. He didn't need any mystic foreign book to give him ideas. He'd describe himself as modern in all ways. Being older than them didn't make him a codger and it hadn't stopped him from trying this and that in bed. "How old are you?"

"Twenty, sir," the first one said.

"Twenty-one, sir," the second one said.

"You young lads..so adventuresome...an inspiration to us all."

Ruddy had told the desk sergeant to send Northam to the scene as soon as he arrived for duty. The station photographer arrived while Ruddy and Archie interviewed the gardener who discovered the body. When Northam finished and was packing up his equipment, Ruddy asked, "How long with it take to develop the photographs?"

"I can have them to you within two hours, sir."

"Good. I want more than one copy though. Make three or four of the best picture you have of the body and victim's face."

He turned from Northam. "You two," he said in a stern voice to the young bobbies who'd bragged of their bedroom gymnastics. "Come here."

They stopped their jabbering and exchanged a worried look with each other before joining him.

"Sir," the twenty-year-old said.

"In two hours go to the station and pick up a couple of photographs of the victim. Show them to everyone in this vicinity: shopkeepers, pub staff and customers, housemaids, footmen, everyone who lives and works near here."

Both bobbies sagged and sighed with the boring order. The assignment took them off their regular patch much of the day. There'd be no cups of tea in the backrooms of shops, idling chit-chatting with employees and owners. No free meals. No flirting with the shop girls.

"Is there a problem, gentlemen?" Ruddy asked, burying his amusement.

"No sir," they said in unison.

"In the meantime, stay here until they come for the body," another dull assignment that Ruddy enjoyed giving. This wasn't their patch, any other time, the constables who walked it daily would do the job of minding the body. The regular beat men were older than the two bobbies and had heard their bragging. They, Archie, and Ruddy enjoyed a laugh as the four walked away.

#

Everhard's residence was a fashionable Georgian style, white, colonnaded across the front with an elegant Palladian door. The architecture an homage to Classical Greek structures. A flower box graced each side of the walk. The decorative wrought iron along the tops was mediocre at best, in Ruddy's opinion. The welded joints were poorly done and wouldn't last in the damp climate. A man with as much money as the viscount should've demanded better work. Maybe he didn't know the workmanship wasn't well done.

Ruddy rapped on the door, curious as to why Everhard installed a life-size, brass fox head as a knocker. Then again, he'd learned early on in the department that many of the English wealthy were an odd bunch. He didn't know any rich Welshmen, so he had no comparison.

The butler answered, stiff-backed with a stoic expression. He scrutinized Ruddy and Archie with what Ruddy could only call uppity butler disdain. "May I help you?"

"Is Viscount Everhard in? We need to speak with him," Ruddy said.

"Who may I say is calling?"

Ruddy handed a business card to the butler, who read it and still shut the door in their faces.

"Boot-faced bugger," Archie said, putting away his card, which the butler had ignored.

"I don't expect Everhard to be warm and overly polite. In my experience, the nobility never is," Ruddy said, studying the flower boxes, thinking what he'd have done differently.

After several minutes, the door opened again and the butler showed them to the library. A dark-haired man who looked about thirty, casually but well-dressed sat by a fireplace of carved stone. The morning paper lay folded on a table next to him. Shelves of leather-bound books lined the walls with recessed paneling in between. Across from him was a mahogany desk nearly half the size of Ruddy's bathroom with paperwork stacked to the side. A thick, floral patterned Aubusson rug covered much of the floor.

"My Lord," the butler said. "Inspector Bloodstone and—" He didn't spare Archie a look but gestured in Archie's general direction. "His associate."

"He has a name and a title," Ruddy told him. "Detective Sergeant Holbrook."

The butler tipped his head and turned to Everhard. "Will you be needing anything, my Lord?"

"No. You may go." He stepped back, allowing Ruddy and Archie to come further into the room. When the butler closed the door, the viscount remained seated. He eyed Ruddy like he would filth under his nails. "What business can you possibly have with me?"

Up close Everhard showed the signs of a man nearer forty than thirty: fine lines around the mouth, a slight sagging of muscles along the chin, and the beginnings of drooping eyelids.

Ruddy held out the photograph of the latest victim's face alone. "Do you know this woman?"

"Of course, she's my mistress. "Why? Has something happened?"

"She's been murdered."

Everhard sprang up from his chair, a stricken look on his face. "No. It can't be." With his back to them, head hung, he gripped the mantel. "Dear sweet Catherine, my poor darling."

The worst part of a detective's job was giving death notifications, telling a family a loved one is dead, the victim of a crime. All asked the same questions wanting to know more. What happened? Did they have any suspects? Everhard's failure to ask the questions that normally came between the denial and the disconsolate acceptance struck Ruddy as odd. Rehearsed came to mind.

"You haven't asked how she died or where we found her," Ruddy said. "Aren't you curious?"

Everhard pivoted and gave him his best *I'm a powerful man* glare. "Of course. I may not have loved her, but I cared for her. I didn't ask because I thought you'd refuse to offer details."

*Maybe, maybe not.* Ruddy couldn't tell from his manner-of-fact tone if that was true. Hard to believe a *powerful man* like the viscount wouldn't demand details.

"We'll tell you what we can," Ruddy said. "She was found strangled in the museum gardens early this morning." This was the part that always turned ugly. "We believe you're the last person to have seen her alive." He silently counted and waited for the explosion sure to come.

At two, the viscount railed, "Are you suggesting I'm a suspect? My God man, if this is some kind of sordid joke, I'll have your jobs."

Ruddy wished he had a guinea for every time he'd heard that threat. He'd have enough money to go someplace warm for the holidays. Italy perhaps, although he found Italians rather too excitable when they talked.

Archie stepped up and stood shoulder to shoulder with Ruddy. "It's not a joke. The waiter at the museum's garden restaurant recognized her as the lady with you last evening.

Let's start with the simplest question. What's the lady's name?"

"Catherine Owensmouth. We were at the restaurant, shared a bottle of champagne and left."

Archie glanced up from his notes. "What time did you leave?"

"Around ten."

"Where did you go afterward?" Archie asked, jotting down the answers in a notebook he carried on interviews. Between the two of them, he was the better note taker.

"Were you two together all night?" Ruddy asked for the record, thinking he already knew the answer. A man and his mistress, where else would she be?

"No. We were coming here but quarreled as we reached my door. She became quite angry and stormed off."

"Stormed off?" The answer didn't shock Ruddy but it did surprise him. What sort of man lets a lady go anywhere, even in the fashionable part of London, alone? "She was alone at night but you didn't go after her?"

Anger flared in Everhard's eyes again. "No."

*Blue eyes.* The Ellis victim's roommate's description of the man she was seeing popped into Ruddy's head. *Deep blue eyes, dark hair, a proper gent.*

"Did you see where she stormed off to?"

"She jumped in an empty hansom and went the direction of her house. I didn't follow because I assumed she was going there."

"Where does she live?" Ruddy asked.

"I rented a townhouse for her near Russell Square. Number thirty-seven Bedford Avenue to be exact."

A stickler for a man honoring his duty to protect the women in his life, Archie's tight expression gave away his obvious disapproval of Everhard. "What did you quarrel over?"

Everhard stuck a defiant chin up so he literally looked down his nose at Archie. "Why is it important? The matter was personal business between she and I and nothing to do with this case. Obviously, she was killed by the same fiend who murdered the other two women. You should be working to find the real perpetrator instead of troubling me with these questions."

Ruddy wanted to see how Everhard would react and said, "We believe she might've have been killed by someone other than the murderer of the other two."

Everhard took a half step back. For the first time since they arrived, he dropped the haughty, put upon posture. A reaction Ruddy found very interesting.

"Why? What's different?" Everhard asked in a tone that almost sounded like sincere concern.

"We're not at liberty to say," Archie said. "Putting together the events of the night she was killed is part of our investigation. Your quarrel drove her to dash off without an escort. We'd like to know if it was serious enough to make her do something else foolish, like taking a stroll to ease her anger," he explained. "Again, what was the quarrel over?"

The superior demeanor returned. "I was severing our relationship. She became distraught and claimed she loved me and begged me not to leave her." He looked from Archie to Ruddy and back to Archie. "As they're expensive to keep, you're not in a position to know, but a mistress declaring love is not unusual. It's a bargaining chip, a means to obtain better compensation for the loss of a benefactor. I explained she wouldn't be without a patron. A friend from my club is in the market for another mistress. He'd gladly enjoy her companionship."

"Then what?" Archie didn't look up from taking notes.

"I told you. As soon as we arrived here, she left. I believe we're—"

"Did you have sexual relations with her at some point last evening?" Ruddy suddenly asked, knowing it'd catch Everhard off guard.

"You overstep your authority Inspector. How dare you ask me such a personal question? I want you both out of my home."

Ruddy enjoyed pricking the skin of men like the viscount. It was so easy. "You can answer the question here or at the station, viscount. We speculate she had sex not long before her death. The autopsy will no doubt confirm our belief."

"Why does it matter?"

"If she had consensual sex, if it wasn't with you, then who?"

"Yes, we were intimate yesterday. Now, if I've answered enough of your questions, I'd like to go about my daily business. The butler will see you to the door."

"Don't bother. We can find our way," Ruddy said. Outside, on the sidewalk, he turned in time to see the curtain on the library window move back to the middle. "What's your impression of the viscount?"

"Same as every other toff we've met...hoity-toity attitude with an annoying need to show the world how much better they are than us. Why do you ask?"

As they continued on out of sight, Ruddy asked, "Think he's capable of murder?"

"I suppose. You've something you're mulling regarding him. What?"

"The description we have of a possible suspect, which admittedly is thin as a frog's hair, fits him. Ellis's roommate said Ellis described the man she was seeing as a proper gent with deep blue eyes and dark hair. Everhard is all that and by remarkable coincidence, his mistress lived spitting distance to the museum gardens."

"What's his motive? Men discarding mistresses happens every day. They manage to do so without killing them."

Not ready to let Everhard off the suspicion hook, Ruddy said, "Doesn't mean they won't or don't or never have."

Archie chuckled. "You really dislike him for such a short encounter. You act like he insulted your mum."

Ruddy didn't have a ready response. He really couldn't qualify his visceral reaction to Everhard, other than a feeling about the man that made the hair on his neck rise.

A terrier type dog with wiry hair on his ears that stuck straight up ran past and sat down on the sidewalk in front of them.

"Look at this poor little guy. He's all ribs and backbone. I don't think he's eaten in a week." Ruddy stopped to pet the dog. "He must be a stray. If he isn't, then whoever owns him needs a sound beating for starving the lad."

Ruddy went up to a green grocer adding cabbage to a crate. "Is this anyone's dog that you know of?"

The grocer shook his head. "No, he started coming round with another dog last week. A carriage ran over his mate. This one's stayed around begging at the shops."

"Thank you." Ruddy patted his chest and called the dog. The terrier leapt into his arms. "There's a butcher shop a few doors down, I'm going to buy some scraps for my hungry friend here. You should take him home," he suggested to Archie as they headed for the butcher.

"Me? Why?"

"He'd be a good playmate for your lame cat once they got over their dislike of one another."

"Oh no, I've enough of a menagerie. Besides Muffin, Meg has half dozen chickens now for fresh eggs and a rooster to encourage the hens. I hate that rooster. My girls now have Gemma and Marigold, two rabbits they rescued from the butcher's cleaver. That's quite enough for me. Why don't you keep him?"

The last thing Ruddy needed was a dog. Who'd watch him while he was away at work? But he couldn't leave him to starve on the streets. He grew up with dogs and always liked them. They had a sheepdog to watch the few sheep his parents grazed on their property. His dad loved the little terrier who played in the barn all day and was an expert ratter. Mrs. Goodge's corgi died the previous year, maybe she could take care of this dog while he was at work.

"Well, are you keeping him?" Archie asked.

The dog seemed happy to be cradled in the crook of Ruddy's arm. "I imagine so. It's the only way he'll survive. After we feed him, I'll get a crate with straw from the green grocer. I'll put it by my desk and he can sleep there until I go home."

"He's something in his eye. It's watery and he's constantly blinking."

Ruddy used his handkerchief and gently wiped fuzz from the watery eye, which helped with the blinking, but didn't stop it completely. "I'll rinse it when we get to the station."

"Got an idea for a name?"

"I'm going to call him Winky."

Archie chuckled. "That name will get you a fight or two."

"Probably," Ruddy said and smiled.

## Chapter Twenty

At the station, Ruddy set the crate on the floor next to his desk. He filled a teacup with water and put that in the corner as Winky nestled in the straw and fell asleep.

"Who's that with the Deputy?" Archie asked.

Ruddy looked up as Eustace Higgins, the Deputy Commissioner, or Useless as the men privately called him, and a short, bald man left Jameson's office. The stranger's jowly cheeks gave him a hangdog expression. He whipped out a handkerchief and dragged it over his sweaty forehead, then shook it with a flourish.

The appearance of Higgins rarely resulted from a social visit. Ruddy shuffled the paperwork on his desk and hoped if he looked busy they wouldn't approach and ask questions about the museum murders. He breathed a sigh of relief when they left the building.

Jameson stepped from his office. "Bloodstone, Holbrook, get in here."

Ruddy glanced over to a forlorn looking Archie and gave a gloomy sigh.

Archie barely had the door to the office closed before Jameson resorted to finger pointing. "Do you know who that was with Higgins?"

"No, should we?" Ruddy wished he hadn't asked as soon as the words left his lips.

"The most unpleasant, Xavier Weeks, Curator of the British Museum, and man of influence. At the moment, his influence is aimed at his disappointment with you two. Not to mention the Commissioner's.

Ruddy thought how tempting it was to bring the file and dump the paperwork on Jameson's desk and tell him, *you work it, if you think you can do better*. He smiled so the superintendent couldn't see and decided this battle wasn't worth fighting. Nothing would change. "Sir, we want to solve this as much, if not more, than Weeks and the Commissioner. But, we're not magicians. We can't create evidence and leads out of the air."

Jameson gave a heavy sigh. "I know. I'm confident you're doing your best." He lit the pipe he kept on his desk. Smoke briefly obscured his face, then dissipated, and he propped his feet up on a drawer he'd pulled out. "Use...Eustace insists I admonish you both. Consider yourselves admonished."

Ruddy never heard Jameson refer to the Higgins as anything but by his title or his surname. None of the men, himself included, thought Jameson knew their salty version of the D.C.'s name. He'd have to let them in on this cheery tidbit.

Jameson who'd been relaxing back with his eyes closed cracked one open. "Holbrook, the middle decanter on the side bureau is whiskey. Pour me a bit, would you."

Archie did and set the glass on his desk.

Jameson took a swallow, leaned back again and said, "Why are you two still here? Go. Solve this case and get Higgins out of my hair."

"I thought you'd surely have a sharp comment about Weeks and the D.C.," Archie said as they closed Jameson's door.

"No point. Besides, all in all things went well today." Ruddy put his arm around Archie's shoulder. "Why let a dunderhead like Weeks and his minion Higgins spoil the day?"

"What's got Bloody-Ruddy in such a good mood?" Freddie Coopersmith, the detective who sat behind Archie, asked when he and Ruddy got to their desks.

Only the other detectives called him Bloody-Ruddy. The foot patrol constables never did.

"He got to be a thorn in the paw of a member of the nobility, and he's acquired a mutt who took a shine to him."

Ruddy reached down to scratch Winky behind the ears. Winky tipped his head up, enjoying the attention. He arched when Ruddy moved to his withers scratching more vigorously, his bony backbone becoming more pronounced.

"Speaking of shines, has anyone seen that boy who comes around?" Ruddy asked.

"When we came in, he was sitting in a doorway across the road," Archie said.

Ruddy went out onto the curb and yelled to the boy, who was still there, to come over. The boy grabbed his shoeshine box and wove his way through the traffic to where Ruddy stood.

"Come with me." Ruddy didn't wait to see if the youngster followed and headed inside the station. "What's your name boy?" he asked as the boy started to open a polish tin.

"Seamus."

"I'm not looking for a shine, Seamus. I want you to run an errand for me." He handed the boy a sixpence. "Go down to the butcher and get some meat scraps and a marrow bone or two. Don't let him give you all fat. Tell him they're for me. He shouldn't charge you more than three pence. You keep the change."

Seamus bent to pet the dog then stopped when Winky sat up. "Does he bite?"

"Don't know. He hasn't bitten me, but he likes me. Have you ever kicked a pup?" Ruddy asked.

"No," Seamus said wide-eyed.

"Well, he should like you too." Winky wagged his tail as the boy patted his head.

"So, what nobleman's feathers did you ruffle?" Coopersmith asked, smiling.

"The Viscount Foxleigh, William Everhard," Archie told him.

The detective looked puzzled like he was trying to place who the viscount was exactly. "Is that the Cornish fellow who's been waffling on in Parliament about the state of the city's hospitals?"

Ruddy fluffed the straw in Winky's crate while the boy stroked the pup's back. "I believe so."

"Be careful of those Cornish chaps, even the rich ones are only a couple generations away from being pirates," Coopersmith warned with another smile.

"That's enough petting, Seamus. Now be off with you. This little fellow is hungry and he might swallow your hand if he doesn't eat something soon."

Ruddy and Archie had a good laugh as Seamus jerked his hand back and dashed for the door.

"There's another skinny mutt, only two-legged," Archie said, watching the boy. "The three pence change is more than he's probably made all week."

"I know."

After the boy returned, Ruddy gave Winky a marrow bone to tide him over and sent an elated Seamus home with his extra pence. Then he fashioned a makeshift collar and leash out of rope they used to tie the evidence boxes. He took the file with the crime scene photographs, the pup's crate, and walked home.

#

"Mrs. Goodge," Ruddy called out from the boarding house foyer.

Mrs. Goodge came from the dining room, wiping her hands on her apron, her face pink from kitchen heat. Winky barked and jumped up high. She managed to catch him in her apron. "What a dear but so thin. There's not a spare ounce on the poor baby. Is he yours?"

"He is now. His name is Winky and I'd be much obliged if you'd fry up some of these for him. I'll bring more food tomorrow." He handed her the butcher paper with the scraps.

Winky climbed higher on her ample chest to lick her neck. "Settle down, lad." She eased him away with his incessant canine kisses. "Will you be taking him to work with you? If not, I'll be happy to watch him during the day." In a serious voice like his mother had so often used, she warned, "A pup has to have outside time."

"He does. I hoped you'd offer."

She sniffed Winky, wrinkled her nose, and then gave him back to Ruddy. "He needs a bath as well. He'll have a proper wash tomorrow in the yard. Once we get some weight on him, I'll fish out my boy Tim's old jumpers for when winter comes."

Tim was her beloved late corgi, short-legged, long-bodied, and fairly barrel chested. Ruddy doubted his sweaters would fit, but knowing Mrs. Goodge, she'd knit new ones.

While Mrs. Goodge cooked the scraps, Ruddy walked Winky around the back garden, letting him get used to the smells. Ruddy and another male tenant had put up a wooden fence the year before. Tall enough so a dog couldn't be able to jump it, but short enough for Mrs. Goodge to lean over the top and chat with the neighbor ladies.

Ruddy didn't want to go out to eat and leave Winky alone this first night. Mrs. Goodge was happy to bring him a plate of sausages and mash with onion gravy and peas along with the fried scraps. The food smelled wonderful. All Ruddy had the whole day was a jam butty for breakfast and one for lunch. He wasn't sure who dug into his meal faster, he or Winky. He soaked a hunk of the soda bread in the gravy and tossed it to the pup, who caught it midair.

He placed the empty tray outside his door and went through the flat opening all the windows. He kept them closed during the day to keep out the garden's flying bugs but opened them at night for the occasional breeze. The heat of the house gathered in his top floor flat. It was a great relief in the winter but a brutal annoyance in the summer.

With a full meal finally in him, Winky nestled in the crate and slept while Ruddy went over the photographs again. He had a table lamp and a stand lamp, one on each side of his old and most comfortable chair. He studied Northam's pictures feeling, he was missing an important clue.

When nothing jumped out at him, he stubbornly refused to give up. Every suspect leaves something of himself behind. It might be minute but something was always left. His job was to find that piece. Ruddy went to his desk and pulled his sketch and soft pencils from the drawer. He'd recreate what he saw onto another page. Somewhere between the camera's eye and the artist's eye, might be a new clue.

He drew the women so they lay side by side. What he and Archie suspected became crystal clear. Owensmouth was not just an anomaly, but a big one by comparison. Only her sex, the manner of death, and the location of the crime scene were similar to the others. Drawing the women, copying the tiniest details the way he did with his wrought iron floral designs, revealed layer by layer the differences. No murderer changed his methods or preferred victim this much.

He tossed the sketch pad onto a wine-colored foot rest. He couldn't care less that piece didn't match the tapestry chair. Comfort mattered more to him than a good looking room, like Everhard's library, which was impressive. Ruddy would give him that. But it didn't look comfortable.

Ruddy checked that Winky still slept. His dinner tray hadn't been moved yet. He'd save Mrs. Goodge the trip and brought it with him down to the kitchen. She kept a small barrel of beer in the mudroom, which she gave her tenants who drank beer at dinner. Ruddy pulled a tankard from the cupboards, filled it nearly to the top and returned to his rooms.

He considered how unhinged Jameson would get when

Ruddy told him it looked like there were two killers. The longer he could hold off saying anything, the better. Once the Jameson knew, then he'd be obligated to tell Higgins. Higgins would turn the investigation into a circus. Ruddy had no problem keeping the information a secret for a bit. Archie, on the other hand, might not be so amenable. Arch was honest to a fault...except for the occasional kind lie to spare someone's feelings. A lie told to a suspect disturbed him, even if it produced much needed information or a confession. The thought of not coming forward might strike him as prevaricating.

On second thought, Ruddy changed his mind. He might as well tell Jameson right away rather than have the ensuing storm hanging over his head. If only he had a strong suspect for the second killer: a name, a description, a specific motive, he'd avoid the threats from Weeks, vis-a-vis Higgins with his non-productive badgering. What really irritated was the fact that Higgins, who never solved or even worked an important case in his career, had the audacity to dole out criticism. The man couldn't find his arse with a mirror and four hands.

#

The meeting with Jameson went better than Ruddy or Archie expected. Ruddy had brought the photographs and his drawing with the three victims side by side to the Superintendent's office. Jameson asked a few questions but saw the logic for a two killer theory.

"Rudyard if you feel this theory has merit, then by all means pursue the case from the possibility more than one man might be involved." He handed the pictures and the drawing back to Ruddy. "Keep me informed."

As Ruddy and Archie left the office, Effingham and Napier from the City Police Department came through the front door.

"Bloody hell," Archie said. "What do you think brings them here?"

"I have a bad feeling it's going to involve us," Ruddy said, resigned to the likelihood it was more than a feeling. Napier's smug smile hinted he was right.

Ruddy and Archie weren't seated long at their desks when Jameson stepped out of his office and called, "Bloodstone-Holbrook, come in here, please," then stepped back inside.

Both Effingham and Napier were seated in front of Jameson's desk. Grey-haired and skeletal thin with a well-trimmed beard, Effingham's frock coat hung loosely over his narrow shoulders and chest. The word breakable came to mind whenever Ruddy saw him.

Unlike Effingham, the beardless Napier filled out his suit coat, and as usual, had his hair parted in the middle and slicked down with Macassar Oil. He appeared casual and at ease. Legs crossed, fingers steepled under his chin, he still wore that smug smirk. Ruddy willed him to tip the chair back the way he'd seen him do at his desk and fantasized kicking the chair all the way over. Disciplinary action was worth the satisfaction. Too bad Napier was too clever to act so disrespectful in the presence of the two supervisors.

He and Arch weren't asked to sit, which Ruddy hoped was as a good sign it'd be a short meeting.

"You've something to tell Inspector Bloodstone and Holbrook," Jameson said, directing the statement to Effingham.

"I do. Without informing our bureau, you took the liberty to speak with the Viscount Everhard, liberty that's not your place to take."

"How do you figure?" Ruddy said flatly, not quite keeping insolence at bay. "His mistress was murdered here, in our jurisdiction. We have witnesses who can testify they saw them together the night of her murder. We'd be remiss if we didn't question him."

"I know that, Inspector," Effingham continued. "It's the manner you conducted the questioning—"

"Are we expected to baby him because he has a title in front of his name?"

"The viscount isn't some costermonger like you generally interview and is incensed to be treated as such."

The cool-headed Archie chimed in, "He was treated politely and appropriately."

Effingham cranked up the superior attitude a notch, "Apparently, he doesn't agree."

Ruddy had had enough. "Fine. If we need to speak with him again, we'll handle him ever so gently, like a baby bunny."

"Don't get impertinent with me Bloodstone."

Effingham's withering look might work on his subordinates but Ruddy didn't give a fig...A sentiment on the tip of his tongue to give voice to.

"It's been my experience that people offended by basic questions are people who have something to hide," Ruddy snapped back.

"Exactly what I mean when I say you and your..." Effingham looked over at Archie and then to Ruddy again, "...your partner, have no idea how to conduct an interview with the upper classes."

"Fine, let me rephrase our position so not to sound impertinent. Next time, if there is a next time, we'll handle it with velvet gloves." Ruddy turned to Jameson. "Are we done here, sir?"

"No, you are not," Effingham answered. "From now on, you two will notify us if you need to interview the viscount again. Then, Napier here will accompany you to make certain the contact is handled properly."

Ruddy turned to Jameson again, seeking confirmation of the horrible order. He'd rather walk through one of Hell's own portals than go anywhere with the toady, Napier.

Jameson responded with a tiny nod and a half-hearted shoulder shrug. The wordless message loud and clear: he'd have to comply.

"Now we're finished, Bloodstone," Effingham said, "Unless your boss has something to add." He offered the superintendent a smile as though they were battle buddies. "Don't want to step on your toes, Jameson."

"You and Archie are free to leave," Jameson told Ruddy.

The two walked in stoic silence to their desks in case Napier and Effingham came out of the Chief's office.

Effingham and Napier did leave Jameson's office shortly after Ruddy and Archie. As they made their way to the door of the station, Napier lifted two fingers to his brow in mock salute to Ruddy.

"I'll teach you a proper salute, you fawning weasel. And when I'm done, I'll stick your head in a horse trough." He said it loud enough to bring an appreciative smile to Archie and Freddie. Freddie, like most of the detectives, felt no sense of camaraderie with the officers from the city agency.

On his way out, Napier nearly collided with Constable Young. Young who had no idea who Napier was sternly told him, "Have a care."

Napier's offended look was worth buying Young a beer at the end of shift.

Young came straight to Ruddy and Archie. "I believe I know who the leak is," he said to Ruddy. "I can't be certain as I didn't hear the conversation, but it looks to be true. It's not a copper but I warn you, you probably won't like hearing who I think it is."

"The fact it's not one of our own is a great relief. Who is it?"

"The shoeshine boy. Late yesterday afternoon I saw him enter the newspaper office and speak briefly with the reporter Marsden. He wasn't in there long enough to give anyone a shine. He left Marsden with a big smile on his face. Whatever the lad told him, he ripped the paper in his typewriter out and began a new sheet."

"Interesting. That's right around the time I sent him for meat scraps. Right around the time we discussed the viscount." All the times he and Archie spoke openly in front of Seamus, they never really paid attention to him. "You go back to your post watching Marsden. I'm going to fetch the lad and see what he's been up to."

Young left going one way while Ruddy spotted the boy across the street sitting in a doorway offering a shine to passersby. Ruddy hurried over and took him roughly by the arm. "Grab your shine box. You're coming with me."

At the station, Ruddy sat the boy on a chair between his and Archie's desk. Ruddy stood in front of the boy, leaning against the side of his desk. "I'm in no mood for tall tales." If he'd ever had a worse morning, the memory escaped him. "What did you tell the reporter?"

"Nothing."

"Don't lie. You told him something. You were seen and whatever you said pleased him. What was it?"

Seamus's scared gaze shifted from Ruddy to Archie and back. "He gave me a florin to tell him what you said about those ladies what were murdered."

"And you repeated everything we said, didn't you?"

Seamus nodded.

"We trusted you and you betrayed that trust. For shame."

"He gave me a florin." The boy bowed his head and made like he was crying. Ruddy lifted his head up by his hair. His eyes were watery but no tears fell.

"Do not cry. You're not in the least sorry for what you did you're just sorry you got caught."

Seamus blinked to clear his eyes, smiled as sneaky a smile as there ever was and insolently said, "Crying gets me an apple from the fruit vendor, sometimes even a peach."

"It's going to get you a cuff on the ear from me," Ruddy told him and sat in his desk chair. "You're a blabber. That means you can't come here anymore to shine our shoes.

You realize that?"

Trying to look innocent and wide-eyed, Seamus countered, "I can keep silent as a stone for a tuppence."

"Listen to you, trying to extort me."

"What? Ex...?"

"Extorting, means you want money to keep from blabbing, which you shouldn't do to begin with."

"Where's your mother?" Archie asked.

"The Workhouse mostly."

"And your dad?"

"Haven't got no dad."

The boy said it with such nonchalance as though not having a father was normal. It probably was in his part of London. Ruddy thought of his childhood. His father wasn't an affectionate man, but there was always food on the table. He and his sisters and brothers never had to beg for an apple. They always had a roof over their heads and his dad was home every evening to say goodnight to his children.

Ruddy dug in his waistcoat and gave the boy a half crown. "Here, stay away until I tell you can return, that's *if* I decide to let you return. If you ever talk to the reporter again, I'll know, and you'll never be allowed back."

Seamus clamped his small hand around the coin like it was gold and for now, for him and his mother, it was. She wouldn't make that much in two weeks long hours of labor at the Workhouse.

"Let's get Marsden in here," Ruddy said, "now."

#

He and Archie told Jameson about Marsden paying Seamus to spy for him. An incensed Jameson ordered Marsden's editor and owner of the paper brought in along with the reporter. Ruddy and Archie took a uniformed constable with them for effect. For months, rabble-rousers around the city had been especially vocal in their criticism of the police. This way any citizen watching could see the newsmen were involved in a police matter and not being unjustly harassed. Ruddy questioned if the press could be unjustly harassed. As far as he was concerned, they were a flock of pot stirring instigators.

Ruddy and Archie returned quickly with both the editor and Marsden in tow and ushered them straight away into Jameson's office. They also yanked the story Marsden was working on regarding the interview of Everhard from the typewriter.

"This is Geoffrey Marsden." Ruddy pushed the reporter into a chair in front of Jameson's desk as Archie did the same to the editor. "This is his editor, Orlando Humphrey and the story they were going to press with." He tossed the sheet of paper on the chief's desk.

"I understand you bribed the shine boy to spy for you and give you information on our murder investigation." Humphrey opened his mouth to respond but Jameson continued. "First you print a sensationalized story of our investigations into the murders by the museum. Now you've decided to make public our interview of Viscount Everhard. Details of the crimes, details only the police should be aware of and reported by you are an invitation for a copycat murder."

Humphrey's turn to cut off Jameson. "Rubbish—there haven't been any yet." He tilted his head like a dog hearing a strange noise. "Or, are you saying the last murder was done by a different killer?"

Surprise flashed across Jameson's face, which he quickly covered. Neither Jameson, Ruddy, nor Archie had thought Humphrey might key on the theory a new suspect was involved.

Ruddy jumped in and clarified before the editor could ask more pointed questions. "Nobody's saying that, Humphrey. He said it is an invitation, not was one."

"Sounds like it," Humphrey said.

"Our interview of the viscount was for general information about the last hours of victim three's life.

Nothing more. Nothing less. The mere mention in your paper of the interview casts a shadow over Everhard's reputation. Kill the story," Jameson ordered.

The superintendent cared little for the viscount's reputation. His goal was to keep the story under wraps, while the possibility of a second killer was investigated further. There was nothing they could do about the reporting of the murders. The damage was done on that matter. Now, he sought containment of the facts.

"You've no right to order my story buried." Marsden started to rise but Ruddy put a heavy hand on his shoulder forcing him down.

"Mr. Marsden, we can do this the easy way or the hard way." Jameson looked up at Ruddy. "Isn't the paper printed in one of the older buildings in the neighborhood?"

"It is."

"It's my understanding many of those older places are fire traps. Do we know when the local fire captain inspected the building last?"

Ruddy smiled, amused by the turn of the conversation. "Can't say for sure, sir but I imagine it's well overdue."

"For everyone's safety in the area, let's get the building looked at," Jameson said straight-faced.

"I know what you're doing. This is your backdoor way to get me to co-operate," Humphrey leaned forward and tapped hard on Jameson's desk with his finger. "I won't stand for it. An inspection will close us down for days, weeks even if the captain orders repairs."

"Sit back, Mr. Humphrey." He waited until the editor complied and then went on, "You're right. Fire hazards can shut down most businesses so I'm going to ask you again to pull the story. Think before you answer."

"You can't let them bully you. Stand firm," Marsden pleaded with Humphrey, then confronted Ruddy, "A viscount who's had two mistresses die within months of each other...we'd be fools not to run with the story."

Ruddy, who'd been leaning half-propped with a shoulder against the wall, half-listening with a cynical ear, suddenly straightened. "Two? What happened to the other one?"

"Why should I tell you? All you bleeders have done since we got here is make demands and threaten to have the fire department shut us down," Marsden shot back.

"You can tell us now, or we can find out from a reporter from the *Times* or another paper. It would be easier to hear the story from you," Ruddy said. "Just a reminder, but if you are closed down, the length of time can vary. How much money do you have saved, Marsden?"

"Bastard."

Ruddy shrugged. "I've been called worse. Now, are you going to tell us about the other mistress or not?"

Marsden looked to sour-faced Humphrey who gave a slight nod.

"This past spring, near his land in Cornwall, they were out riding at dawn. She got off her mount and was walking along the cliffs when the ground gave way. She fell to her death. That's the story anyway. No one other than the viscount actually witnessed the accident."

"How do you know?" Ruddy asked.

"I inquired. It adds a bit more color to the story—beautiful mistress falls to her death. I mean, think about it. She dismounts and is walking along but she doesn't hold onto the reins. Why let go of the horse?"

A good question. Ruddy couldn't think why she or the viscount would let the horse wander about the moor unless he held her reins. No one probably thought to ask. He wondered if by some slim chance the local constables made more than a cursory accidental report. He doubted it. He'd send an inquiry anyway.

The horse question was a minor oddity for sure. More important, the misfortune of Everhard's two women, especially so close together wasn't coincidence. Not one

Ruddy bought into, even if the queen and the rest of the Ton refused to believe otherwise.

He appealed to Jameson. "If Everhard thinks we suspect him in the slightest, he will move heaven and earth to stop us from further investigation. They can't print anything referring to the viscount. We have to be free from his interference and political influence."

"Inspector Bloodstone is right. I can't order you not to print the story but you know the consequences," Jameson told Humphrey.

"Where's the quid pro quo?" Humphrey asked as Marsden groaned in the background. "I don't appreciate your threat. Investigating crime is your business and reporting the news and what's happening in the city is mine. You're asking me, no coercing me, into doing something that hurts my business. I deserve some kind of recompense in exchange."

Ruddy had an idea what recompense Humphrey might want. Marsden had asked for an exclusive when first approached about reporting the stories. Humphrey would no doubt seek the same or close to it.

"What do you think is fair?" Jameson asked.

"An exclusive."

Ruddy would've loved to blurt out *I knew it.*

"An exclusive," Jameson repeated. "What exactly do you consider exclusive?"

"When you get the suspect into custody, we get the full story, gory details and all. We'd like a crack at interviewing the suspect too."

"Yes and no. Yes, I'll have Bloodstone and Holbrook provide you with how the investigation progressed and what led to the arrest. Yes, I'll have him give you some, not all, of the details not generally revealed to the public. No to the interview. I don't want the suspect using it as a opportunity to try his case in the court of public opinion."

"What can he say? He's a killer?" Marsden asked,

looking puzzled.

"You never know. I just rather not open that door for him." Jameson turned to Ruddy and Archie. "Is this agreement acceptable to you both?"

Ruddy couldn't see any way around co-operating with Marsden, a prospect he didn't relish in the least. Between the possibility of having to work with Napier and having to work with Marsden, he felt like going out and lying in the road. If he was lucky, a loaded beer wagon would come along to give him a quick, merciful end.

Archie nodded.

"Fine," Ruddy said, depressed already.

## Chapter Twenty-One

Glad to be on the train and en route home, William entered the First Class car. The train stopped overnight in Southampton and left early the next day. It arrived in to Cornwall late, but he didn't care. The day after tomorrow, he'd speak to Faith's father about marriage. Both her parents would be over the moon pleased to have a viscount for a son-in-law. Dennis was only landed gentry. Far from poor, the Goddard's wealth was decent when combined with the large tract of inherited land. Their financial comfort didn't come close to William's. The Everhard's could buy the Goddards several times over with wealth to spare.

As he took his seat, he immediately recognized Emeralda Sanborn sitting three rows up with friends. The dark-haired beauty had been the longtime mistress to the late Earl of Stowe. The powerful earl's death ended much of her influence. But the cunning Sanborn had made sure her circle of friends included other, even more prominent women. She lunched regularly with Lily Langtree, a lady with a well-known and very close association with Edward, the Prince of Wales. Sanborn's shopping sprees with Jennie Jerome, the American wife of Lord Randolph Churchill were notorious for the amounts spent.

A good deal of laughter came from her group. William didn't care to gossip himself, but wasn't adverse to hearing a juicy bit. He tried to pick up pieces of the conversation but it was too difficult to hear anything amusing or better yet, useful.

He mulled over changing seats when the earl's ex-mistress glanced over, looked him up and down, and smiled, which he returned. William first knew of her from the talk at his club. Then, they'd been formerly introduced at Royal Ascot, where she wore an enormous hat covered in red feathers. The last time he'd seen her was two years ago and they never had the opportunity to speak. People whispered the old earl had grown obsessed with her. No one saw the beauty past teatime. Friends at Boodles said he kept her prisoner at night. William thought it likely true. It'd account for her wild spending when she was let off leash during the sunlight hours.

Once the train left the station, the smoking car opened. He hurried there before other First Class passengers crowded the carriage. He sat at a small, leather-topped wine table next to the long bar. The position gave him a good view of the door and who came and went. The clacking of the train's wheels from the partially open window above his seat drowned out the talking of men nearby. Away from the more loathsome smells of the city, he relaxed and let the night breeze waft over him.

Sanborn's throaty, sultry laughter filled the carriage's entrance, sounding as he remembered. He caught her eye and she came over.

William stood to greet her. "Miss Sanborn, how propitious to run into you here. It's been a too long since we spoke. Allow me to reintroduce myself."

"I remember you, Viscount Everhard."

"Please call me William." He kissed her gloved fingers. Once her friends had moved to the rear of the car, he took advantage of their temporary privacy. "This is rather forward but I hoped you might join me for a sherry."

She sucked on her lower lip and looked up through sooty lashes, pretending a shyness she probably hadn't possessed since she wore braids. "I would love to join you. However, I have agreed to play cards with my friends until we arrive in Southampton. Does your invitation still stand once we have disembarked?"

"Of course."

"Where are you staying?"

"The White Swan. Where are you booked?"

She dropped the façade of innocence. A crooked smile replaced it. "I am too." She laid one hand on his chest and drew it down to his belly. "I look forward to our meeting, but please call me Esmeralda."

He bent and kissed her fingers again. Eye level with her ample bosom, he thought of different ways he'd enjoy toying with them later. "Tonight then."

\#

At the White Swan, William booked a separate room for Burton, which he didn't often do. He preferred to stay in a two-bedroom suite, keeping the valet close.

"I won't need you anymore this evening. The night is yours to enjoy," he told Burton who finished setting William's clothes out for the next day.

"Very well, sir. I take it you'll undress yourself?"

"I hope not."

"Good evening, sir." Burton's lips twitched with a suppressed smile and he took his leave.

Not for the first time, William wondered if he sought female companionship on his off time. The man had served him for twenty-five years since his previous valet up and died. In all that time, there was precious little William knew about Burton's private hours. The valet might even prefer the company of men. A criminal offense he'd surely keep clandestine. If men or boys were his preference, William wouldn't have cared. The man was dear to him. He'd spent more time with the valet than he ever did with his father.

Alone in his hotel room, William removed the hypodermic and vials of Frobisher's elixir from his Gladstone bag. He'd need to fortify himself. If the other rumors about Esmeralda were true, she had an insatiable sexual appetite. According to the gossips, she made regular trips to Paris where she indulged in all manner of debauchery with young male prostitutes.

He'd read and reread all of Frobisher's journals. The documentation showed the doctor used various amounts on his subjects. Early on William had stopped trying to understand the math and concentrated on the observed changes in the subjects. From that, he guessed at what the right dosage might be and hoped he was correct. He was happy with the amount so far. He slept more sound, had more energy, and made love two or three times a night with ease. Catherine had been pleasantly surprised by his new found lust.

He'd never found the courage to inject himself in the hand again. He rolled the left sleeve of his shirt to above the elbow and made a fist. Veins, green and ropy, popped up on the crook of his arm. He slapped them until they formed a bigger target. Then he injected himself just below the previous pinpoint bruise from the last injection. He rolled the sleeve down and refastened the cuff link. The concoction took effect fast. If cells could spark, then he'd swear that's what happened, seeming to burst with new life. He remained seated and closed his eyes while the liquid coursed through him.

Esmeralda came earlier than expected. He opened the door in his shirtsleeves and smoking a Montecristo. The smoke swirled around her like fog. Her hair fell in curly waves over her shoulders. He wasn't sure how she achieved the effect, but the top layer lifted in glossy wisps. Briefly entranced, he thought she was a close to ethereal as a flesh and blood woman could look. The perfect spirit to haunt the Cornish moors.

"Come in." William stepped aside.

Two steps inside, she spun and kissed him. Hard. Like a man does a woman. "I'll take one of those," she said, breaking off the kiss. "In fact, I'll take this one." She took the cigar from his fingers.

He didn't protest. However, the idea of a woman smoking didn't set well with him. It reminded him of the whores in Whitechapel. She brought the cigar to her lips and sucked on it like she would his manhood. The eroticism of the sight both aroused and disgusted him. Why it disgusted him, he had no explanation. Faith drank coffee. That was acceptable, not especially feminine, but not beyond the pale.

"I'd like a brandy to go with this." Esmeralda blew on the lit end of the Montecristo. "Watch." Her chest expanded as she inhaled.

*Inhaled.* So unfeminine. He suppressed his disgust.

She held the smoke in her mouth for the span of several heartbeats before letting it out in a slow, steady stream. Inhaling simultaneously as she did, the smoke flowed upward into her nose. "They call that French inhaling"

"Fascinating. Here." He handed her the brandy and replenished his own. "Learn that in a Parisian whore house?"

"I learned it from a Parisian...among other things."

Esmeralda set both their brandies on a side table. She turned and stood with her back to him...a silent directive for him to undo the buttons of her dress. He did and the gown fell to the floor. She turned. She wore no underpinnings except for her lacy garter belt and silk stockings. A rush of lust stirred at the sight of the pink nipple peaked on her pale breasts and the thatch of black between her legs.

She urged him with the flat of her hand down onto a chunky upholstered chair. Picking up both of their snifters, she handed him his and sat on his lap, alternately sipping the Courvoisier and puffing.

Between both, she kissed him, tasting of smoke and cognac. For all her beauty, she was at heart common as a dockside tavern wench and would probably fight like one.

"We should be something special tonight." She wriggled her bottom against his erection.

"I'm listening."

"Stowe was a doddering old man, sweet but not robust, not exciting. I want excitement." She downed her cognac in one gulp and tossed the cigar nub into William's wash basin.

Fine quality didn't take the heat out of the liquor. He merely sipped, as one was supposed to when drinking good brandy and it still burned all the way down his throat.

"Inflame me." She nipped at his neck. "Surprise me." She swung her legs around and straddled him. "Let's play. I can be a shepherdess looking for my lost flock and you can be a marauder, a Visigoth or something."

He smiled knowing he could do anything he wanted with her and to her. He suspected a steely nature, manipulative and hardened by experience lived beneath the flirtatious shell.

Once she realized the game had turned deadly, she'd put up a good fight, certainly better than Catherine.

"Are you traveling with your lady's maid?"

"No. I dismissed her when Stowe died. I want my privacy."

"Good. Where is your room?"

"The end of the hall, why?"

"We'll move to it. My valet is in the next room. I wouldn't want him to mistake the sounds of ecstasy for needing help," he said, smiling.

Esmeralda stepped into her dress and William buttoned it just enough for her to keep it on until they reached her room. He opened the door and checked no one was in the corridor to see them.

"You go first," he instructed. "I'll follow in a moment."

She licked his cheek and dashed down the hall to her room. He waited for her to enter before closing the door. He pulled the scarf from his bag, uncertain if he'd use it or not. Erotic excitement rushed through him at the thought of how her struggle would feel. He drew the silk over his palm and then tucked it into his trouser pocket.

After checking the corridor once more, he hurried to

her room, found the door unlocked and stepped inside. Esmeralda had the dress off again and greeted him in only garters and stockings.

"I'm ready to play," she said and slipped her arms around his neck. "You choose the game."

"Why don't you be the lost lamb and I'll surprise you with who I am." He led her to the bed and pulled the scarf from his pocket, then striped off his clothes.

"Stand here." He pulled her to him so she stood between his legs as he sat on the edge of the mattress. "Take your garter belt and stockings off. Slowly."

She did. Naked, she straddled him again. He rolled her over and made love to her twice. While inside her the third time, he slid the scarf around her neck. She proved him right and fought like a lioness protecting her cub.

#

The train for Cornwall departed early and a little after sunrise Burton knocked. William slept naked and stood behind the door to let Burton inside.

"I'm going to have a quick bath and then I'll be ready to leave." He retired to bathe in private with no thought about the leavings from Esmeralda's visit.

While in the tub, he remembered the tray with the dirty brandy snifters, the top of one stained with the remnants of her waxy lipstick.

As he rose to dry off, a loud commotion in the hall and a louder knock on the outer door brought Burton to the bathroom door. "Sir, there are two policemen here to speak with you. I told them they might come in while you finished."

William's first reaction was to berate the valet for granting them entry without seeking permission first. He contained his panicked anger, which would only bring suspicion down on him.

"Thank you, Burton." William came out barefoot, wearing only his trousers and undershirt. The two constables were in uniform, which meant they there doing legwork for the detectives. From their youthful appearance, both were new to the force. He doubted one had begun to shave yet. Some of his initial apprehension eased. The simpletons wouldn't be hard to convince of whatever story he told.

"Gentlemen, you've caught me at an inopportune moment. But, I have a brief time till I leave for my train. How can I help you?" William ran a towel over his wet hair and let it hang around his neck afterward.

"A woman named Esmeralda Sanborn was found murdered in her room at the end of the hall—"

William broke in, "Good Lord." He sank into the chair he'd shared with her the night before. He spread his hands out in a gesture of disbelief. "How could this happen here? This is the best hotel in Southampton. Riffraff are not tolerated either inside or on the grounds, let alone someone of a criminal nature."

"It remains to be seen whether the perpetrator was a murderous stranger or an associate of hers, or even a staff member," the constable who had something of a beard said.

"It's incomprehensible that anyone other than a murderous stranger is responsible," William countered, having fun with the cat and mouse conversation.

"It's too early for that kind of speculation. We're asking everyone on this floor if they heard anything out of the ordinary or saw anyone or anything of a suspicious nature."

Beardless added, "Your valet said he hadn't. A lady friend of the victim's said you had a short private conversation with her while on the train." He walked over to the brandy tray with the dirty glasses and examined both snifters.

A rush of possible explanations for the lipstick on the one came into William's head. All sounded dodgy and weak, but he'd try the simplest when the constable asked his inevitable question. It didn't take long.

"Did you plan a social evening together once you both left the train?"

"No."

"Are you sure?" He turned the snifter so William could see the lipstick mark.

"Quite. The glass was left filthy by the maid. I used the clean one. I intend to inform the head of staff when I checkout. I had two glasses of brandy, read some Parliamentary reports I brought with me from London. Then, I went to bed. You do know I'm the Viscount Everhard and a member of the House of Lords?"

"We know," beardless said, matter of fact.

"I'm sorry to hear about Miss Sanborn's tragedy but unless you have further questions, I really must get ready. I have the early train to Cornwall."

"We have nothing more at this time. Will you be at your Cornish estate and available if the detectives have any other questions?"

"Yes. I bid you good day, gentlemen. My valet will see you out." William turned his back to the constables and returned to the bathroom and closed the door.

Satisfied he carried off the proper amount of surprise over the murder, he stared at the overall more youthful appearance of his face, thought about Esmeralda briefly, and then put her from his mind. When he came from the bathroom, Burton silently busied himself packing the clothes from the night before. William had no recent memory of the valet not chatting with him as he worked.

"Is everything all right, Burton?"

"Of course, sir. Did you want me to take the dirty snifter to the desk man and register our dissatisfaction?"

"Yes."

Burton stared him for a long moment before picking up the offending glass. "You do realize the housemaid will lose her employment here."

"And well she should."

Loyal to the bone, if Burton guessed the lipstick stain story for the lie it was, he'd carry the knowledge to the grave. William wasn't worried.

Burton paused in the doorway and turned. William cut off any question the valet might be tempted to ask. "Hurry back please. I don't want to miss the train."

*Journal Entry*
*The White Swan Hotel-July, 1888*
*How could I be such a careless fool? I can ill afford to be so again. I must be diligent about any evidence. Although, I doubt I'll be in the same position in the future. After last night, I'll never take the elixir again. As good as it makes me feel, it clearly affects my mood and desires in unwanted ways. Isabeau's death was an accident. She loved the feel of the scarf around her neck, my taking her to the brink. Catherine's death wasn't what I sought from the start of our relationship. She forced the necessary act, when she became a threat to my happiness with Faith. Esmeralda I have no explanation for what possessed me other than it is the effects of the elixir. I never expected to enjoy the struggles for life by any of them. I thought the alchemist's potion magical at first. Now I suspect it is a curse that's made a monster of me.*

## Chapter Twenty-Two

By the time he was home, the effects of the elixir had worn off and William felt himself again. He came down early for  breakfast toast and tea, saving his appetite for the ploughman's he asked his cook to pack. Faith's birthday was in two days. He daydreamed about her waking, hoping he remembered and bought her some candies or flowers. Instead, he'd take her on a picnic today and give her the beautiful cameo of the three muses. She'd be thrilled. It was but a preliminary gift before he received permission to marry her. That reaction would pale in comparison to her joy at the two carat, pear-shaped diamond engagement ring he bought before he left London.

A noisy disturbance came from the area of his front door followed by the sound of hurried footsteps getting closer. Faith rushed through the dining room door, his ancient butler puffing along right behind her.

William quickly stood.

She lay a hand to her chest and waited to catch her breath before she spoke. "Thank goodness, you're home. I wasn't certain when you were leaving London."

"Sir—"

"It's all right. You may go," he told his butler, and ordered a pot of coffee from the footman. His attention turned once more to Faith. "Please, sit." He indicated the chair the footman pulled out from the table. "Dare I hope this excitement stems from my return?"

She took a second longer to answer than he liked. "Well, of course, that's part of my excitement."

He didn't care for the awkward smile she'd given or

the answer. Wary, he asked, "What's got you at sixes and sevens?"

"Mother will have my head if she finds out, but I know I can trust you."

She withdrew a letter from her skirt pocket and clutched it to her breast. She dropped into a chair to his left and used her feet in a most indecorous way to scoot closer. Something else her mother would have her head for if she saw. "I have to share my joy with someone or I fear I shall explode."

In her letters home, she'd spoken of opening a little bookstore in Chicago. Her news probably involved that. She'd get her shop but obviously here, in Cornwall. He'd have some of his book dealers in London ship enough boxes to make her happy.

"You must promise not to say a word to my mother, although I don't see how it really matters. In a few weeks, the formal announcement will be made."

Confused, William repeated, "Formal announcement?"

"My betrothal announcement."

"How did you know?"

"Know what?"

"About the engagement."

Faith looked momentarily puzzled and then said, "Don't be silly, William. Of course, I knew. Devlin and I were unofficially engaged before I left Chicago. We had to wait until he came over to make it official. This letter is from him." She waved it back and forth before bringing it to her chest. "He's sailing from New York Sunday next. Mother plans to hold the party in two weeks to make the announcement. I'm excited beyond words."

He wanted to deny he'd heard her correctly, wished he didn't know anything she'd just told him. He sat powerless and silent for a long moment afraid words or questions would confirm his worst fear. Forcing himself to do it, he asked, "Who's Devlin?"

"We met at a dinner party thrown by my cousins." She smiled at him the way she had a dozen times since her return, a spirited, bright smile he believed meant only for him. "I don't know how to describe the night other than magical. From the moment we were introduced, I knew we'd always be together."

*Magical.* Never had he considered raising a hand to her. Never, until this moment.

No part of him would accept she'd really marry another. She'd been so adoring when they worked on her riding astride. In spite of his aversion to eating with people, he soldiered through the meals together. They'd regularly eaten lunch in his gardens and sometimes off a blanket by the creek that ran across his fields. She loved him, of that he was certain. She couldn't mean what she said. "You're planning to marry some American...some colonial cowboy? You can't. Don't be ridiculous."

"He's not a cowboy, silly. He's a well-respected architect. Almost every building burned down in the fire of '71. I'm sure they heard about the fire in London but I don't think we did out here. Daddy doesn't remember hearing of it at the time. Anyway, Devlin is one of the primary architects helping to develop the fashionable area on the waterfront. He knows everyone who's anyone in the city. He's going to build us a lovely home on the lake and promised to find a good property for my bookshop."

She had to know how silly the idea was. He couldn't imagine why Dennis and Amelia indulged her. "For God's sake, Faith, he's in trade. How could you give him a second look, let alone your hand in marriage?"

"His *trade* as you referred to it, is a well-respected one. He's well-respected. It was the remarkable architect, Christopher Wren, who gave London their beautiful St. Paul's, or have you forgotten about him?"

"London had been a great commercial center for over

a thousand years when he built the cathedral and a city of great culture for hundreds. America barely has a century under her belt. What is Chicago but a cultural wasteland? Nor is he building a grand cathedral."

"It's not London, yet. But it will be beautiful one day and Devlin will be part of that future." She forgot herself and shot forward to hug him in a tight embrace. "Please, just be happy for me," she said and leaned back.

As though eviscerated, a terrible emptiness came over him. "The riding lessons were a surprise for him weren't they?"

She nodded.

A pretense. Everything they'd done together, was a pretense. "I thought you were trying to find a way to spend time with..." he trailed off.

"You? That goes without saying. I enjoy your company, William, you know that, but yes, the surprise was intended for Devlin." The footman returned with the small pot of coffee and poured her a cup adding hot milk, the way she liked it.

"You loved me. You always did. I assumed we would marry."

"From the time I was a young girl, I fantasized about marrying you. I loved you even when I was in braids and you were one of the most eligible, sought after bachelors. I still love you with all my heart. You're my dear William, my dearest friend in the world."

"Your *friend*. Let me correct that: your *dear friend*." She claimed to have loved him for years, yet had no hesitation in betraying him and her alleged love. "At what point did you decide to forsake me?"

She reached over and laid her hand on his. "Forsake you? You make it sound like I planned it. I didn't. I told you, the love between Devlin and I was instant and magical."

Sighing, she drew her hand back. "Oh William, I counted the days and the hours till I could come home. I went to bed every night hoping when I returned you'd see I'd become a woman and fall in love with me.

"Last year on my birthday, I told my aunt I intended to leave for New York and sail to England at the end of the month. Once I turned eighteen, I felt my parents wouldn't object to you courting me. I planned my pursuit of you down to the last detail."

An hour ago, ten minutes ago, he'd have been flattered and amused to hear how she set her cap for him. He'd probably have told her no elaborate scheme was needed. His heart was hers from the moment they met again on the road. Ten minutes and a lifetime ago. Out of morbid curiosity he asked, "Tell me more of this pursuit, this plan, which you threw away."

"I didn't throw it away. I'm not so cavalier or fickle," Faith said with a note of defiance.

"If you say so. Please go on."

"Father sent me more allowance than necessary and I saved most of it. I kept track of all the latest Parisian fashions. My plan was to bedazzle you. I'd wear dresses of your favorite color, the finest French scents, pinch my cheeks and bite my lips raw until you noticed their rosiness."

William laughed at the irony. Faith smiled misinterpreting his amusement and that made him laugh harder. Perversely, he wanted her to go on, the revelation intrigued him.

"My aunt suggested I postpone my departure for a couple of weeks. She needed to make household arrangements prior to chaperoning me to New York. I agreed but by the time we were to sail, an early winter storm blanketed the city in snow. The Cunard line cancelled passenger sailings and only allowed cargo ships across the Atlantic. So, we returned to Chicago." She looked down and stroked the letter then lifted her gaze to meet his. "When we got back, my cousins threw the party where I met Devlin shortly thereafter. I never planned to fall in love with anyone else, anyone but you, never thought it possible. Devlin was completely unexpected."

She stood to leave and William walked her to the door. She paused in the entry. "Please be happy for me."

He wanted to fill her ears with the vilest words and accusations. He wanted her to cry, to hurt, more than he wanted his next breath. "Why wouldn't I?"

"You would tell me if something troubled you?" Faith's excitement had apparently wound down enough for her to *divine* the dark tone of his mood. She couldn't guess at its depth.

"Go home. Go home to your wedding plans," he told her, controlling his anger, knowing he'd make sure the marriage to her American wouldn't come about. He'd see Dennis that afternoon. He'd make it impossible for her father to turn him down. Not that an enticement was necessary when the choice was between a viscount and an architect. English property laws were clear. Only his oldest son would inherit the estate when Dennis passed away. He worried for his youngest boy. William would solve the problem. A tract of excellent Everhard land butted up against the Goddard's. A gift of the land guaranteed the younger son a living.

She kissed him on the cheek and walked away, the letter clutched to her bosom.

#

London

Winky was a quick learner. Ruddy only had to show him hand signals four or five times. With simple gestures, Winky knew to heel, sit, stay, come, belly crawl, and how to dance. His dancing delighted all the ladies in Ruddy's boarding house. Ruddy would motion with his finger and Winky would stand on his hind legs and spin in a circle then dance backward. He was rewarded with small bites of sausage Ruddy kept wrapped in his pocket.

He was still a ruffian with other little critters that crossed his path, especially squirrels. Relentless in his torment of them, Mrs. Goodge, who had a squirrel haven of a walnut tree in her garden said she had trouble controlling him. *He's an incorrigible terror, Mr. Bloodstone, barking and running around the tree until I fear he'll drop over with a burst heart.*

Ruddy told her he'd try to break him of the habit but he'd thought the chance less than slim. Dogs will be dogs and they chase squirrels. That's the way of things. He decided the park was as good a place to start as anywhere else. Kensington Gardens had an abundance of squirrels. They held little fear of humans as people fed them along with the pigeons and so they ran around carefree. That safety didn't hold true for other parts of the city where they'd likely find themselves on a butcher's spit.

Ruddy kept Winky on a long leash and headed for the area with the most squirrels.

"Hello again," a female voice said as they passed the fountain.

He turned. Standing there was the tall, blue-eyed blonde from a couple of months back. "Hello. I'm surprised you remember me." And he was.

"You saved my nephew's boat. I take care of George on Sundays while my sister handles the correspondence for a local solicitor. We visit here often. I wondered if we'd see you again. Where's your wife today?"

"My wife?"

She glanced over to see George was fine and then said, "Last time you left the gardens with a dark-haired woman. She called you by name."

"I'm not married."

"Sorry, engaged then?"

"Not engaged either." She started to smile and then stopped when he added, "The lady is a woman I've been seeing socially."

"Oh."

He was flattered by the disappointment in her voice.

The blonde was interested. That much he surmised and under different conditions, he'd invite her to dinner. But, he wasn't good at juggling women. Years earlier, he'd tried seeing three women at the same time. All he got out of the experience was slapped by all three and called a bounder, a cad, and a despicable villain. An overreaction if you asked him, he wasn't promised to any of them. How they found out about each other remained a mystery, but he avoided embroiling himself in that type of situation again.

"I'm sorry, I never learned your name and I should've after you rescued George's sailboat."

"Rudyard Bloodstone." He tipped his hat.

"I'm Evangeline Bannister. It's quite warm today. Perhaps you'd like to join George and I for a lemonade."

"Your offer is tempting but I don't think it's a good idea."

"Because of your lady friend?"

"Yes. She'd be hurt."

"I understand."

He couldn't help it, he had to ask, and hoped she did. "Do you live close?"

"Not far, a few blocks. What about you?"

"Walking distance." They stared at each other for a long, awkward moment. Ruddy fumbled around mentally for something else to say and came up empty. "Well, I best be on my way. I'm working with Winky here on controlling himself around squirrels."

"He's precious. What a charmer with his wiry hair going every direction." She bent and scratched behind his ears.

"Thank you from both of us. Anyway, maybe I'll see you here again."

"I'm here every Sunday," she said, straightening.

Winky growled and jerked hard on his leash. A cat sat just out of his reach, licking its paws, taunting him. "No." Ruddy forced him to stop pulling and wait for permission to walk. "Maybe we'll meet again."

He walked Winky down the path, regretting how dull his response had been.

## Chapter Twenty-Three

Ruddy stepped back and eyeballed his ironwork, making sure the last ornamental curl was the same dimension as the opposite one. A growling Winky laid at the base of the walnut tree, head skyward, waiting for a squirrel to dare come down the trunk.

At the park, he'd been as Mrs. Goodge described: incorrigible, hell bent on terrorizing squirrels, cats, and birds of every sort. In a show of canine defiance, he'd decided commands were to be obeyed anywhere but the park. His madcap chases startled several ladies who hadn't seen him coming. Fortunately, his funny appearance earned him quick forgiveness from the women. Ruddy, on the other hand, was chastised for his bad parenting.

Sweat ran into Ruddy's eyes, down his face, and along his back from working around the forge. Satisfied with the curl, he splashed water from the bucket he cooled the iron in on his face. It wasn't cold but cool enough to be refreshing. Then he cupped his hands and splashed a palm full of the water over the back of his neck. He didn't feel like making a trip inside for a towel and instead ran his arm over his face, wiping the excess water away on his shirt sleeve.

Winky broke from his vigil. Barking, he ran toward the side gate. "Nice job on the bench," Archie said as he came into the garden, quickly closing the gate so the dog wouldn't escape. He bent to give Winky a pat on the head.

Hair raised, Winky barked and jumped away.

"Winky, come."

He growled and gave one more warning bark then went and sat by Ruddy's feet.

"It's all right to pet him now," Ruddy told Archie.

"Just don't move your hand toward his head too fast, he doesn't know your intent yet."

"No worries." Archie bent and offered his hand for Winky to sniff. Winky approved and allowed Archie to scratch behind his ears.

"You're free," Ruddy said. Winky dashed back to the tree and resumed squirrel watch. "Want a drink? There's a barrel of ale in the kitchen."

"Sounds good."

Ruddy returned after a minute with two tankards. He led Archie to a dilapidated wooden bench that wobbled under their weight when they sat. "I'm glad you're here. The desk sergeant had the Tintagel constable's report delivered to me. I read the bare bones account of Everhard's mistress's alleged accident and death. I don't like it. The viscount's statement doesn't ring true, to me."

"I imagine the constable didn't want to ask too many questions. Foxleigh estate probably employs a lot of the villagers. The local police aren't going to stir that pot too much and aggravate the viscount."

Ruddy nodded. He'd assumed the same. He didn't have the same qualms about questioning the details of the accident. He and Archie faced a bigger problem. They'd found nothing major to point to as truly suspect, nothing to justify interrogating Everhard.

"What reads wrong?" Archie asked.

"The horse, for a few reasons. First, who goes riding at the break of dawn over such rugged landscape when a rider can barely see? Maybe an expert horseman or horsewoman, but this was a coddled mistress. She's not likely to have had the upbringing and training one of our well-to-do country ladies receives from an early age. Second, no one with their wits about them is going to ride along the edge of the cliff—"

Archie raised his hand to halt him. "Hold on. How do you know that? You never lived by the sea."

"Not the sea but in the shadow of the Brecon Beacons. I know a thing or two about how treacherous riding along cliffs is. You don't go cantering down the ragged edge of one. If she remained on her horse when she went over, the horse would've gone too. The report states when Everhard rode into the village for help, he was ponying her horse. I hate to admit but Marsden's right. She handed the reins to Everhard while she walked the edge, which doesn't make sense either. Those craggy bluffs breakaway all the time. I think he'd have stopped her from doing something so dangerous."

Archie sipped his beer, looking like he was on the cusp of believing. "Is there a different theory behind her death? I know you formulated one while dissecting the viscount's story. It better be something good if you want to talk to him again."

"I'm working on it."

"You've also got to convince Napier there's good reason as well."

"Bloody Napier, I've been trying to work out a way to avoid getting him involved if we can talk to Everhard. We won't get anything useful from the interrogation if he's there. He'll make a muddle of it."

Without stoking, the fire in the forge began to die. Ruddy got up and threw water from the bucket on the embers, killing the fire completely. The sizzle of the doused fire woke Winky, who'd fallen asleep. He woke in time to see a squirrel run along the fence rail to safety, ignoring his barking pursuer.

Ruddy sat on the old bench again and took a large swallow beer. The more he thought about leaving Napier out of things, the more he felt drumming up the ire of Jameson, Effingham, and Napier worth the risk.

"Before you go around insinuating Everhard is a devilish liar, consider the possibility it really was an accident but not the way he told everyone," Archie suggested.

Ruddy had considered the possibility and discarded it. If it was an accident, how did it happen and why lie? "Your turn to come up with a theory."

"Perhaps they were arguing. They both might've dismounted and got into a heated quarrel. She's flapping around the way women do. Not paying attention, she took a faulty step and the ground gave way."

"Doesn't explain the lie, but you know what does? Them having the argument you propose and him pushing her. Whether intended or not, in his anger, he shoves her off the cliff. For my money, I'd go with intended, if that's what happened. It's the best reason for a lie."

"Ripe with interesting potential as your suspicions are, we don't have enough to even talk to him, let alone interrogate him. If Everhard is still in London, we're cooked geese when it comes to leaving Napier in the dark. If he's gone home, Jameson absolutely won't let us go to Cornwall in secret." Archie finished his beer and set his empty tankard on the bench. "Too bad we can't lure Everhard here."

"Not a good idea. It'd be impossible to exclude Napier. Besides, Everhard isn't going to talk to us alone again. It's an ugly thought but what if we're right and there are two killers? A case against Everhard doesn't solve the other murders."

## Chapter Twenty-Four

William looked up from his financial logs surprised as Faith stormed into the library.

"You bastard," she said, approaching his desk. "How dare you ruin my engagement and future marriage to Devlin? How could you? I thought you were my friend—"

"I believe the term you used was *dear friend.*"

"I hate you. You convinced father to have me break my engagement and marry you instead. Did you ever stop to think I might not want to marry you? I'm not the young girl sweet on you and infatuated with the idea of our marrying anymore. I love Devlin, not you, not in the way I love him. I'll never love you in that way, not now, not ever."

William moved from behind the desk to stand in front of her. "I saved you from a terrible decision. You don't see it at the moment, but you will once we're married. You are a young girl yet. Away from home and in an unusual environment, it's easy to attach more meaning to a simple attraction than normal."

She slapped him. "Do not presume to tell me my own mind or heart." She slapped him again. "I hate you." She raised her hand to strike him again but he grabbed her wrist, hard.

"Don't make me retaliate in kind."

Her shoulders eased down slightly and he let go of her hand.

"Interesting how you're more than willing to hit me." She backed away and began to circle him. "What else are you willing to do?" Is that what happened to your last two mistresses? They aggravated you and you created a way for them to suffer deadly accidents? Oh, I know all about

218

Isabeau and Catherine. Mother told me how sad it was, both women in such a short time."

From down the hall, a staff member shut the door Faith must've left open when she barged into his house. How she tempted him to shock her with the truth. Let her know exactly what he was capable of. Naturally, she'd threaten to tell people. That would be her first response but he'd remind her of his position and the respect the villagers had for him. He'd claim complete surprise at her bizarre accusation. She'd be the one not believed. Her behavior would be explained away as a form of female hysteria. She'd be sent to a sanitarium by her parents to get over her nervous condition. When he continued to offer marriage, he'd be seen as magnanimous, a man of great kindness and forgiveness.

"It doesn't matter what you will or won't do. What I won't do is marry you. I don't care what you offer my father."

"That's where you're wrong, darling. You *will* marry me. You *will* have my children and you *will* present a happy face to the world."

She shook her head and said, "You can't make me happy. I am not intimidated by your wealth or station. If my family tries to force me into marrying you, I'll run away. I'll find a way to get to Chicago and back to the one man I do love."

He loved her and she returned his love with cruelty. In turn, she'd see how cruel he could be, if forced. "You sound pathetic and desperate. The news was a lot to take in," he said as her circling brought her in front of him again. "Clearly, you're overwrought. Wait here while I get my coat and I'll see you home."

"And I'll see you in hell." Her skirts rustling as she whipped around, she knocked over a vase when a fold ballooned out. She ignored the shattered porcelain vase that was his mother's favorite pattern and continued through the

French doors to the gardens.

Limited and slowed by her clothing, he was only steps behind her when she stopped by the century old dolphin fountain.

"I won't have you following me and pretending to my family you're a good man. You're not. You're horrid, and selfish, and mean." She turned to confront him. "You were my friend and now you're the person I hate most in the world." She turned back.

He snagged her by the arm and spun her around. "Listen to yourself acting like a child having a tantrum. The more you speak, the more a fool you make of yourself and show what a silly girl you are."

"Let go of me." She yanked her arm from his grasp and moved out of reach, taking a step backward. Her foot caught on the hem of her skirt. She tumbled over the fountain's surround into the water, striking her head on the body of a small dolphin. Red colored the water. Hip-high, the water was deep enough to submerge her, the weight of the dress pulling against her as she tried to rise.

Struggling, she pushed up so her head broke the surface, blinked and held a hand out to him. "Help me."

He sat on the edge of the marble surround. "Why? You betrayed my love."

Her head went back under. She fought the water, arms flaying. She managed to grasp the marble edge where he sat and her head broke the surface again. "Help me...please, William."

He looked around, seeing no one, he pressed a light hand to her chest. "You should've loved me," he said, pushing her under once more. She batted at him, trying to knock his hand away. Not very different than the struggle Isabeau, Catherine, and Emeralda made. Her eyes were as wide with fear as theirs. Where tiny flecks of hemorrhaging streaked the whites of their eyes, tiny air bubbles rushed out of Faith. It took less time for her to stop than it did for the others. The water apparently worked faster than the scarf. An interesting detail, he thought.

From behind him came the sound of running feet. William quickly pulled Faith's lifeless body partially from the water. Holding her in one arm, he swept the wet hair from her face with his other hand, calling her name like a man in a panic.

"I was too late," he said as Burton waded into the water. Burton helped raise her more so William could lift her completely out of the water and lower her to the ground.

"Are you sure she's not breathing?" Burton asked. "If she is, even faintly, lay her on her side. She'll cough up the water."

William felt the side of her neck, then her wrist for the non-existent pulse. Burton climbed out of the fountain and hovered over her. William shook his head but slid his arm around her shoulders.

"She left a few minutes ago, saying she wanted to cut through the gardens. I said goodbye and turned back to my financial record. A few moments passed when I heard noise from the area of the fountain. I went out to investigate and found her submerged and bleeding. I was too late."

He brought her close, held her tight. "My beautiful Faith. I loved her so," he said, burying his face into the crook of her neck.

Burton touched a sympathetic hand to his shoulder. "I'll send for Mr. Goddard sir."

#

William had never seen a man so openly devastated by the death of a loved one. Goddard cried like a baby as two of his estate men loaded Faith's body in a wagon to take her home. He fleetingly wondered if he and Faith had married and she died first, would he mourn her as much.

William led him to the library.

"This will break her mother's heart," Dennis said.

All the years of his life suddenly caught up to him plus

some. He'd aged twenty years in the hour since he'd arrived. "There's nothing I can say to ease her pain. How can I, when there's nothing to ease mine."

Dennis's eyes welled with tears again. He stood in the very spot in the library where Faith had told William she hated him before storming out. *Storming to her death.*

"Here." William handed his friend a drink of strong scotch. "Such a tragedy, a kinder, lovelier heart than hers can't be found. I'll never love another the way I loved her. She's the only woman I ever considered marrying." He poured himself a drink and hoped his voice held a convincing amount of grief.

"Dear Lord, I don't have enough time to tell Devlin what happened. He's already on his way here. I felt bad enough having to tell him the engagement was off. Poor fellow, he was coming for a marriage and he's ending with a funeral." Dennis bent his head and covering his eyes, began to weep again. "Forgive me. I have to leave now and tell her mother our darling daughter is dead."

After he left, William went to where he kept his journal in the bookcase. The book was bound in red Moroccan leather and always placed on a shelf with several similarly bound books. He didn't worry at first when he couldn't find it. He searched his Gladstone, emptying it of stationary and pens, and turned it over, giving it a vigorous shake. He rifled through his desk drawers on the off chance he absent-mindedly put it there by mistake. The panic began to set in when he couldn't find it there. One by one, he pulled every book with red binding from the bookcase shelves. None were his personal journal. He'd swear on his life, he put it back on the shelf.

"Burton, gather the staff, everyone, and tell them to go to the parlor."

The servants stood in two lines in the parlor and whispered among themselves. William had never demanded they all come together even for the few parties and social gatherings he gave. Any instructions for planned special events were relayed to the staff by the butler and the head of housekeeping.

"Quiet," William told them. They immediately ceased their whispers. "An important book of mine has gone missing. The most important book I own. I am going to personally search each of your rooms. You're to stay here until I've finished." He went down the line and looked in the eyes of each of them. "Heaven help the thief." He turned to Burton. "You'll assist me."

"Sorry sir," Burton offered when they came up empty. William nodded. He'd dismissed the rest of the staff. As always, Burton remained waiting until he was dismissed as well. "You may go," William said.

Alone now, William sat at his desk and went step by step over what he did after making the last entry. He wrote about Sanborn and how she fought. Then what? To the best of his recollection, he packed the journal in his Gladstone the morning of his departure. Or had he? Had he left it on the lamp table in his hotel room or on the train?

Increasingly alarmed, he dropped into his desk chair, considering what anyone finding the journal might do. If someone turned it into Lost and Found, he'd have been notified. If they kept it, then they meant to blackmail him. No one had asked for money and he dismissed the idea. If they read the last few entries, they'd take the book to the police, who'd have come to arrest him by now. *Where the devil could it be? A book doesn't just up and walk away.*

Every morning after William had his shirt and trousers on, Burton tied his tie or cravat, and then helped William into his jacket. While dressing, the two always talked about what was on the schedule that day and evening. William never refrained from giving his honest opinion of different business associates and guests. Burton's remarks were tempered but not overly diplomatic at times. That morning, he was silent. Nor did he look up once while fixing William's tie.

"I won't need my jacket until later," William said, but Burton still slid it off the wooden hanger. "Burton..." The butler took his clothes brush to the jacket and turned to help William put it on. "Burton, I'm talking to you."

Burton finally looked up. "I'm sorry, sir. My mind was elsewhere. What did you want me to do?"

"I said I don't want my jacket yet. What's got you so preoccupied?"

"I regret having to bring this up at this time, what with Miss Goddard's funeral tomorrow and all. But, do you remember my elderly aunt who lives in Uxbridge?"

"Yes." William watched him in the mirror. How haggard he looked, like he hadn't slept.

William sympathized, if that was the cause. For two nights after the journal went missing, sleep eluded him. He'd searched every possible place with no luck. He finally came to the conclusion he had left it in the hotel or on the train and someone threw it out. That night he slept like the dead.

"Oh dear, your aunt is all right I hope."

Burton rehung William's jacket. "Actually, she isn't. My uncle says she's fading fast. I'd like to see her one last time, if you can spare me a few days. There's a train leaving this afternoon."

"Of course. Please give her my well wishes when you see her."

"Thank you, sir."

#

London

Burton approached the desk sergeant. "I understand that an Inspector Bloodstone is investigating the museum murders."

"He is."

"I'd like to speak with him."

"What about exactly? He's very busy."

"I have something to show him."

## Chapter Twenty-Five

Ruddy and Archie took Burton and the book into an unoccupied interview room where they wouldn't be disturbed. The desk sergeant brought the valet a cup of tea, while Ruddy and Archie sat side by side and read Everhard's journal. The reading didn't take as long as Ruddy expected. Thick as an accounts ledger book and almost at capacity with entries, he figured they'd be awhile wading through it all. But the valet had conveniently placed strips of paper in the book, marking where Everhard documented his crimes. In case the valet missed anything important, Ruddy planned to read the journal thoroughly after Everhard was in custody.

Archie sat back, an incredulous look on his face. "Good Lord," he said. He'd obviously finished the same section Ruddy did a moment before. The entry documented the murder of Dr. Frobisher and Andrew Norris. "If a flying pig landed in this room and said the same as is written here, I couldn't be more gob smacked."

"Not much astonishes me. But I'd never have suspected Everhard of killing Norris and Frobisher and setting the fire."

Ruddy turned to Burton. The valet was as pale as the china cup he drank from. He had a faraway look in his eyes that Ruddy knew well—a look carved in his memory. The few men who'd escaped the massacre at Isandhlwana had the same shock and horror in their eyes. They'd ridden to Roarke's Drift to warn them thousands of Zulu warriors were heading their way. Like all the able-bodied, they manned the barricade, fighting when the attack came. It was after the battle, after the Zulus retreated, and they spoke of

Isandhlwana, of the barbarity they witnessed that the haunting look returned.

Ruddy feared the man would retreat into himself given too much time to think. He and Arch had to get their questions answered in case that happened.

"Mr. Burton, this elixir the viscount speaks of, do you have any idea what is in it?" Ruddy asked.

Burton finished his tea and set the cup down. "No. Whatever it was, it made him feel like a young man again. He talked of having the energy and stamina of a man half his age. Evil business if you ask me. The man I know would never have done these horrible things otherwise."

Ruddy didn't share the same sentiment. People don't change overnight. This wicked side of the man always existed within him.

"Were you ever with him when he met with Dr. Frobisher?" Archie asked.

"No. Had I met the fiend, I'd have tried to save Lord Everhard from dealing with the beastly man."

Only Burton believed talking would do any good with the arrogant Everhard. Ruddy thought if it would put the valet's mind at rest, he'd say as much. But on some level, the man's heart remained loyal to his master. He'd never accept the brutal truth.

"When we're done here, we'll drop in at Ingram's Chemist Shop. Let's find out more about this stuff," Arch said.

Ruddy nodded and he and Archie continued reading.

"I assume the viscount doesn't suspect you took this?" Ruddy asked a short time later, closing the book.

The valet shook his head. "He knows it's missing. He doesn't know who or what to suspect."

Archie went to the door, held up Burton's empty cup, and signaled the sergeant to bring another tea. "Out of curiosity, where did you hide it?" he asked, sitting down again. "The viscount must've been in a bit of panic."

Ruddy smiled. Little details like that always intrigued his partner. Truth be told, he was curious as well.

"The viscount was frantic. He sent a footman to the train station to inquire if the book had been turned in, either in Southampton or at the Tintagel station Lost and Found."

Considering the volatile information contained in the book, Ruddy couldn't see Everhard just giving up. The information would get him hanged. "What did he do then, since it wasn't at either place?"

"He stopped talking about the loss. He'd done all in his power, looked everywhere, and questioned the entire household. He waited for someone to demand money for the return. When nothing happened, he seemed to relax a bit."

"You never answered. Where did you hide it?"

"I knew he'd search everyone's personal belongings. And, he did. He went through all the staff's rooms, their dressers, and every nook and cranny in the house. But I'd immediately hidden the book after taking it. There's an unused stall in the stable with holes in the walls from a temperamental horse who liked to kick anyone and anything. I broke out enough of the wood around the original hole to secrete the journal inside."

The sergeant came into the room with the fresh cup of tea and set it in front of Burton. The valet didn't strike Ruddy as a snoop. He couldn't see the man rooting through his employer's personal papers without cause. Ruddy waited until the sergeant left to ask, "What made you read his personal journal? Have you always done so?"

Affronted, the man's brows shot up. "No. But, I became suspicious when he lied to the Southampton police about entertaining an actress who'd been murdered. He'd been with her the previous night in his hotel room. I thought why would he lie unless...well unless?" Burton turned his attention to a distant spot on the wall.

Ruddy gave him a minute to compose his thoughts, then said, "Go on, Mr. Burton."

"I knew he'd taken to carrying his journal with him everywhere, which he never did in the past. Then, when he murdered Miss Goddard, I knew I had to do something. I believed he might use the journal like a personal diary not just an accounting of his daily life on the estate. Why else would he be so attached to it all of a sudden?"

"But you took it before he murdered Miss Goddard?" Archie confirmed.

"Yes. When he was out with the gamekeeper the day we returned to Foxleigh, I stole the book. I spent the entire night reading it."

"You said you witnessed him kill Goddard. Tell us exactly what you saw," Ruddy said.

Archie sat pen in hand ready to take notes. Of the two of them, he was the better at writing down what was said. He wrote faster and had no trouble reading his own shorthand. Ruddy wrote as fast as Archie when taking statements, but couldn't read it back with any accuracy.

"It was the middle of the day so the staff was busy in other parts of the house doing their work. I'd gone upstairs to the viscount's bedroom to put the shoes I just polished away and to lay out his evening clothes. I was still there when I heard shouting from the library. I recognized Lady Faith's voice—"

"Lady Faith?" Ruddy assumed he referred to Goddard but clarified for reporting purposes.

"Faith Goddard is the neighbor girl. I should say, young woman. She'd grown into a lovely young woman," he said with a resigned sadness.

"Go on."

"I hesitated to go down. Clearly, she and the viscount were arguing and I didn't want to embarrass either. I remained upstairs. The argument continued outside in the garden. I went to the window. I didn't dare open it. They would've heard and as I said, I didn't want to embarrass them. She was terribly angry, yelling at him, her face flushed red. He grabbed her arm but she jerked out of his grasp, lost her balance and fell backward into the fountain. I saw her go under, then break the surface and reach for him. He just sat there on the surround and she went under again. I am ashamed to say I froze, unable to actually believe he wouldn't help. She broke the surface once more and once more reached out to him. That's when he pushed her under again."

"You actually saw him push her?" Archie asked.

Burton nodded. "He held his hand against her chest. The poor child, arms and legs thrashing, she struggled and fought to no avail. I finally shook off my shock. I ran down the stairs and out to the fountain. He pretended he needed me to aid in saving her. We lifted her from the water but she wasn't breathing. He lied and said he heard what he thought was a scream and ran out to the garden but claimed he was too late. He had no idea I saw what he did." The valet bowed his head and covered his eyes with his hand. His shoulders trembled and tear landed on the table in front of him. He pulled a handkerchief from his coat pocket and wiped at his eyes but the flow continued and more tears fell.

"She was such a sweet girl. Her family and the viscount's are longtime friends. I've known her all her life," he said, looking up. "Worse, I loved William like a son."

The use of Everhard's given name by a servant was very rare. A slip of the tongue. Ruddy guessed Burton considered Everhard so much a son that William was how he thought of him in private.

Burton continued, "I was a young footman for the family when he was born. I watched him grow into a wise and capable man. I've been his valet for twenty-five years and now I've betrayed him." He dabbed at his eyes. "I'm sorry. I don't mean to cry..." He quietly blew his nose on a corner of the snowy handkerchief. "But I'm so ashamed I did this to him."

Ruddy and Archie let him cry. They'd been in this

situation with weeping victims, witnesses, and on occasion, suspects, many times. Best to let them work through the emotions of the moment. After a time, Burton finished and they resumed questioning him.

"Mr. Burton, we will arrest Viscount Everhard. We need more of your help to do this safely," Ruddy said.

"Of course."

Ruddy slid a blank sheet of paper and one of his sketching pencils he brought with him across the table. "We'll need you to draw a room by room schematic of the house with all the doors he can use to escape. We also need one of the garden area, the out buildings, stable, the gamekeeper's cottage, and any place the viscount can hide.

"I imagine the viscount has guns." Ruddy couldn't imagine him not having them. Every land owner and farmer he knew of, including his father, whose plot of land was tiny by comparison to most, had at least a shotgun available. Livestock brought vermin, two-legged and four-legged. A gun worked wonders with both. "List where he keeps them, how many, and what kind he has, please."

"I only know what he keeps in the case in the library," Burton said.

"Write it down. We want to know what we're facing should he choose not to surrender," Archie explained.

After Burton listed the shotguns and rifles William kept handy, Ruddy asked, but didn't really expect the valet to know, "Are they loaded?"

"All. The viscount had a poacher sneaking around his stable not long ago. He grabbed a shotgun to confront the man, but in the time it took him to load the weapon, the intruder ran off. From then on, he had the guns ready to fire."

"Can you keep the staff out of the way when we make the arrest in case he becomes combative?" Archie asked.

"Yes, most of them. The butler is a problem. He's the one who will open the door to you and let you in. He'll want to announce you to the viscount."

Everyone in England was aware of the class structures within the upper class and their servants. Who did what was specific. What Ruddy didn't know was whether that job designation was ever altered except by permission of the lord or lady. As far as he knew, certain positions, like valet and butler, were fiercely guarded by the servant in that post. Ruddy had been given to understand they were devilishly territorial. "Can't you answer the door?"

"Perhaps."

Out of the corner of his eye, Ruddy saw Archie stiffen at what he no doubt interpreted as resistance. He had small patience for any argument. "Perhaps won't do. We can't let anyone on the staff know what is about to transpire and we don't want any of them at risk. Doesn't the butler ever get sick or take a day off? There must be a day he isn't available."

"Yes, but the senior footman takes over his duties on those occasions."

"Find a way to prevent that, at least for the time we're due to arrive."

"How will I know you're coming?"

"What train are you taking back?" Ruddy asked.

"The first train tomorrow leaving London for Tintagel. That's at 10:00 in the morning. It stops briefly in Southampton but continues on after an hour, stopping once more in Exeter for another hour."

We'll catch the first train out tomorrow, if possible. What time does the train arrive in Tintagel?"

"Five o'clock. Foxleigh is twenty minutes east of the station."

"It will likely take us an hour to set up for the arrest. We'll commandeer a paddy wagon and an extra man from the local constabulary as driver. Plan on our being at your door around 6:00."

Ruddy had to consider the possibility Jameson would

order them to include Napier, which would delay them. They'd have to take the afternoon train. He'd try to sell Jameson on the exigent circumstances. There was no time to explain everything to Napier and vis-à-vis, Effingham. "If for some reason we are detained here in London, we'll get word to you before you board the train."

"If we have to reach you before then, where are you staying?" Archie asked.

"I have a room at the Black Raven Inn on Old Marylebone Road, near Paddington Station."

Burton tucked his damp handkerchief away, rose, buttoned his coat after smoothing it down, and donned his hat. Looking every bit the dignified valet and not the man who broke down in tears, he declined Ruddy's offer to escort him out and left.

#

"Exigent circumstances, yes I agree," Jameson said.

"You agree. We don't have time to hunt down either Napier or Effingham." On the outside, Ruddy presented a stoic, professional face. Inside, he was dancing a jig. When he found out, Napier would explode like an overcooked egg from anger. Effingham, he wasn't sure how the Chief Inspector would respond but he was sure it wouldn't be with gracious understanding.

Archie made no attempt to hide his pleasure, smirking like Alice's philosophical Cheshire Cat.

"Will Effingham complain to the palace?" Ruddy asked Jameson, concerned how well he'd buck up under pressure from the crown.

"I expect he will."

Ruddy worried now that excluding Napier might not be a good idea. "You don't think the queen will personally intercede on behalf of the viscount, do you?"

"She'll inquire about what happened, not from Effingham but through the Home Secretary, who'll ask me for an explanation. I'll present things in a way that justifies our actions. Henry Matthews is a sensible fellow. He'll convince the queen we affected the arrest the best way possible."

"You're sure you're fine with us acting on our own?" Archie asked, his tentative tone hinting at his uncertainty.

Ruddy leaned in and jabbed Archie in the ribs, who in turn gave him a puzzled look.

"You know me, Holbrook," Jameson said. "I don't give a toss for Effingham and his high-handed attitude. I've given my permission."

Ruddy didn't buy that for a minute. The assertion begged the question: then why did you order us to work with Napier a few days ago when Effingham tramped in here complaining? Best not to bring the challenge up or Jameson might lose his courage and back down.

"Make your rail arrangements. Take Northam with you for additional manpower. I do not see Everhard going with you without a fight of some kind. Wire me when you have him in custody. On second thought, wire me tomorrow night with a status update, no matter what it is," Jameson said.

"Yes sir," they both said and left the office.

Archie pulled Ruddy aside. "What was that poke in the ribs for?"

"To get you to stop being a dolt and asking Jameson a question like that. You can't give him the opportunity to rethink his decision. You know he'll collapse and knuckle under to Effingham's order. Do *you* want to drag Napier along with us?"

"Heaven's no."

"Then leave off the topic. Lock up the journal while I find Northam and tell him the news."

On his way to find the constable, Ruddy went back and forth mentally trying to decide if Northam should bring his photography equipment. He couldn't see the need other than a picture or two of the fountain. If they found the scarf he referred to in the journal, they'd bring that with them. Anything belonging to the mistresses wasn't of use. A jury would accept it as natural for bits and bobs of their property to be on the premises.

Northam was out on patrol. Ruddy and Archie waited at the front desk for him to return at the end of shift.

"Should I bring my camera gear?" Northam asked after Ruddy explained the plan.

"I've thought on it and I think not," Ruddy told him. "I expect Everhard to give us trouble and I'd rather you be free to help rather than burdened with equipment."

"It's times like this, I wish the department gave us side arms," Archie commented.

Apparently confused, Northam argued, "Why fight us? We have his personal accounting of the murders. He has no choice but to face a trial."

"Wouldn't you fight if you were facing the gallows at the end of that trial? I would. He has nothing to lose. If he escapes somehow, he can hide out on the Continent forever."

Northam looked more serious than usual, although, Ruddy had never seen him without a serious expression. When dealing with him in the past, Ruddy sometimes wondered what in the young man's life made him so somber.

"What do you think he'll do to keep us from taking him?" Northam asked, the frown leaving his face.

"Whatever he thinks he has to. There's nothing more dangerous than a man with nothing to lose. Just be prepared."

## Chapter Twenty-Six

Tintagel, Cornwall

The ticket master at the Tintagel station directed the three of them to the one-desk storefront that served as the village post and constable's office. The same man often served as both postman and constable in small hamlets like Tintagel. The train arrived on schedule at 5:00 p.m. The walk to the town's high street was short. They were at the office by 5:15. A shingle in the window read: *Office closed for tea break, will reopen in one hour.* Ruddy and Archie conferred. They had no intention of waiting for the man's return.

Their arrival hadn't gone unnoticed by the villagers. The green grocer whose shop neighbored the post office found a reason to rearrange the outside display of cabbages. Across the road, the edge of a second floor curtain moved and a woman behind it peered out. The curtain quickly moved back when she saw Ruddy looking.

If Tintagel was anything like his home village, only the ladies took tea breaks. The men found more substantial refreshment. Ruddy looked down the almost deserted street and saw the pub sign, The Goat and Pony, at the end of the block. "Northam, see the sign with the picture of the goat and pony? Go down there and see if the postman is inside. If he isn't the constable as well, ask where we might find him."

Northam put his helmet on and ran his finger along his jawline adjusting the chinstrap. He'd taken it off on the train to enjoy the cool breeze from the carriage's open window. Other officers might consider it being out of uniform, a

Rules and Regulation violation. Ruddy would've done the same. More than the itchy wool of his police uniform in the days when he worked a foot beat, he disliked wearing his helmet the most. On a summer's day, sweat rolled down his neck and drenched his uniform shirt through to his undershirt. As equipment pieces go, no matter who issued them, they were universally unpleasant. Uncomfortable as the police helmets were, they didn't compare to the misery of wearing the army issue one in the African sun—the heat of which burned hot as the hinges of Hades or so it felt. Heat exhaustion was a common problem among the men in his company.

"What makes you think he'll be there?" Northam asked, standing at attention.

"Experience."

"Right. Do I tell him why we're here? Might make him more inclined to co-operate."

"No. You're in uniform. He'll figure we're on official business," Ruddy said. He and Archie wore suits like they did every day on duty. Once they showed the constable their detective badges, he'd realize they were there on an important matter. "That's all he needs to know unless he is both constable and postman. In that case, tell him we'll give him the details once he's joined us." Ruddy gave Northam a stern look. "And stop standing at attention when you talk to me."

Northam walked at a brisk pace down the cobblestone street, a hand on his truncheon to keep it from bouncing off his thigh. Minutes later Ruddy saw him emerge from the pub with a ginger-bearded man whose blue uniform coat hung unbuttoned and open, exposing his undershirt. No surprise. Policies and procedures were lax in the villages and towns away from London. The further away, the more lax.

"Afternoon gentlemen, I'm Rob Pender," the constable said and stuck out his hand. "Who might you be then?"

Ruddy shook Pender's hand and then pulled his coat back to show his badge. "Detective Inspector Rudyard Bloodstone." He let go of his coat and gestured to Archie. "This is Detective Sergeant Archibald Holbrook." Archie shook hands with Pender.

"This is Constable Northam." Northam followed suit and extended his hand. Three quick pumps and Pender drew his hand away then half-turned his head and burped. When he turned back to Ruddy, Northam made a failed attempt to wave away the beer and sausage odor the burp left behind.

Pender fished a grey handkerchief from his trouser pocket. "I'm normally off duty at midday," he said, mopping his face. He gave the linen a shake before sticking it back in his trouser pocket. "What's the trouble then?" Before Ruddy could speak Pender said, "Peelers from London. We don't see your lot out this far very often, never in fact. Am I right in guessing there's serious mischief afoot and you'll be requiring my assistance?"

A crowd of onlookers began to form on the sidewalk across the road. "You'd be guessing right," Ruddy told him. "Is there a place we can talk other than the street?"

"Aye, me catchpit is around the corner."

"Catchpit?" Archie whispered to Ruddy, like he'd know the term.

Ruddy shook his head, bewildered by the expression as much as Archie. "I've no idea what he means? Why would I?"

"You're Welsh. You both speak some weird dialect handed down from the Celts. I figured you'd have some word in your language that was similar."

"Well, we don't. To be clear, Welsh people are not the same as Cornish."

"To those of us pure English, all your lot: Welsh-Scottish- Cornish are interchangeable," Archie retorted with an annoying smirk.

Pender ignored the banter about ancestry. "I've got no

wife to tidy up after me. It's my habit to drop things hither and dither, wherever convenient. My cottage tends to always be in a tip so I refer to it as my catchpit.

Pender stopped in front of an old wooden oak door black with age. He unlocked it with a rusty skeleton key and opened it, stepping inside. Ruddy, Archie, and Northam followed him into the dark room. When Pender lit a lamp, the term catchpit made sense. Dirty clothes were scattered over the furniture. Wrinkled and stained, they looked dirty to Ruddy anyway. Plates with the remnants of past meals were stacked on a table next to an overstuffed chair. A mouse scurried along the baseboard toward another room Ruddy didn't care to see.

Pender cleared clothes from the arm of the chair and sat. "So what brings you here, to the end of the world, Detective Inspector Bloodstone?"

Ruddy explained the murders and that Everhard was the killer. They had the proof in his own words. He explained they'd come to arrest him and would require the village paddy wagon and one of Pender's men to drive it.

"One of my men." Pender chuckled.

Not a good sign. Laughter following a request never was. Ruddy waited for an answer he wasn't going to like.

"There is only two us. This is my day to work. I deliver the mail and handle any fisticuffs and whatnot that happen. We do have a paddy wagon. She's old and the lock on the door doesn't work well due to rust from the salt air. But if one of you rides on the rear bumper to keep watch, it should be sufficient to hold the prisoner until you get to the train station."

All the way from London, Ruddy worried there wouldn't be a wagon available. In that case, they could resort to a delivery wagon but it wouldn't be nearly as secure. "Good. We'd like to leave as soon as possible."

"You say you have proof he's a murderer. That's not the man I know. That's not the man any of us knows. Once you have him in custody, I'll take the back roads to the station. Word travels fast. Folks aren't going to take kindly to London Peelers snatching one of their own and the viscount is one of us."

"We know that," Archie said, his patience slipping. "We realize his is the most important family in the area—"

Pender pressed forward, his weight shifting. "You've no idea how deep our attachment to the Everhard family goes—"

Pender turned to Ruddy and lifted his finger toward Ruddy's chest. Ruddy grabbed it. "Don't." He let the finger go and Pender moved his hand to the top of his thigh.

"Let me tell you something of the man," Pender said. "One year everyone's crops failed. Food was scarce. The holidays meant the children would get an extra ration of milk. The old viscount came to the village on Christmas Eve and handed out baskets with a chicken and turnips and flour for bread, and sweets for the children to every family. The current viscount has carried on the tradition. We are all more than fond of the Everhard family. You come here—"

Ruddy put his hand up. "Enough." He grasped hold of Pender's uniform jacket and pulled him up. Keeping his hold, he informed him, "I don't care if the entire village thinks Everhard walks on water. There are four dead women who'd argue that chicken and veggies in exchange for justice is a poor trade. Now, are you going to hitch the horses to the paddy wagon and drive us? Or, do we appropriate it and drive ourselves? I don't care which you choose. But, it will be done. *Now.*"

Pender wrapped his hand around Ruddy's and attempted to get free. Ruddy brushed his hand aside but let go of the coat.

"I'll get the horses harnessed. The wagon is in back next to the stable," Pender said. Looking unhappy but resigned, he turned toward the room the mouse scurried off to minutes earlier.

"Come on," Ruddy said to Archie and Northam. The three fell in line behind Pender.

"Do you trust him after his glowing description of Everhard?" Archie asked Ruddy after Pender went to bring out the first horse.

"No."

Northam looked confused. "Why are we involving him, then?"

"Better we know where he is when we're dealing with Everhard."

Northam frowned deeper, looking more confused. "I don't understand."

"Where are you from?" Ruddy asked.

"London sir. Shoreditch, to be exact."

"Have you ever been this far from London?"

He shook his head.

"This far out, the folks feel little connection to London and anything to do with it, including the government. To them, we represent the government. Most will never leave the shire. They'll likely never go farther than a day's ride. Their connection is to the people in their village and shire. That's what they know and understand. It's the same where I'm from in Wales. Pender is a Cornish man first and a policeman second. Everhard is a fellow Cornish man. That's why I want to know where Pender is."

#

Like Burton said, Foxleigh was twenty minutes from the village. Archie and Northam rode on the back bumper where the guards stand during transportation. Ruddy sat in front, next to Pender. On the way, Pender remained quiet. Ruddy wasn't sure if that was a good or bad thing. He went with a bad thing.

"Stay with the horses and wagon," he ordered Pender, who had jumped down from the seat.

On the walkway leading to the front door and out of Pender's earshot, Ruddy told Northam, "Remember, as soon as we enter the room Everhard is in, you're to fan out to the left. Archie will go right. I'll take the center position."

"Yes, sir."

Like at his London home, Everhard had a huge doorknocker, big as a small child's head. Ruddy knocked, hoping Burton had managed to act as butler and be the one to let them inside.

The door opened and Burton stepped aside without addressing them. "The viscount is in the library. I'll lead the way."

"And the staff? Where are they?" Archie asked.

"All in the kitchen and dining room preparing for dinner, except the upstairs maid who is in the village. This is her afternoon off."

The three policemen nodded. "As I recall, you said the gun case was in the library," Ruddy said.

"Yes." He led them down a long corridor with paintings by Reynolds and Gainsborough and other famous dead artists on the walls. The marble floors were covered with expensive Turkish carpets that muffled the sound of their footsteps.

If there'd been more time, Ruddy would have asked how Burton got the butler out of the way.

The library door was open. Burton stepped aside as he entered. "Police are here to see you sir."

"What? This is in intolerable. It's harassment, pure and simple. Do not show them in. I'll have—"

"We're already in," Ruddy said as the three came into the room and fanned out as instructed.

Everhard rose ramrod straight from the chair where he'd been reading and moved behind his desk. "This is an outrage. Invading my home. The queen will hear of this. You'll all be looking for new employment when she does. Burton, show them out."

The move to the desk put Everhard farther from the gun case. It might be a good sign or it might not. Ruddy couldn't be sure if the viscount would ultimately co-operate...an off chance at best.

"I'm sure you can pay a jailhouse runner to take a message to the queen." Ruddy inched closer.

His attention fixed on Ruddy; Everhard didn't even glance in the direction of the doors. "Jailhouse runner? What the devil are you talking about?"

"We're placing you under arrest for the murder of Isabeau Lavergne, Catherine Owensmouth, Esmeralda Sanborn, Faith Goddard, Eric Frobisher, and Andrew Norris."

He hid his shock well. Only his eyes widened slightly at the mention of each victim. Where was the drama? The lack of it struck Ruddy as too odd for a man of Everhard's temperament.

"You're insane to accuse me. If anyone will need a jailhouse runner, it will be you three. I'll see the lot of you in Newgate for attempting this false arrest," Everhard threatened, lowering his right hand toward the center drawer, out of sight.

Whatever Everhard intended, Ruddy prepared for the possibility the man stored something he could use as a weapon, a letter opener, knife, even a handgun in the drawer. Many wealthy men often did.

"False arrest? No viscount, we have our proof. We have your journal." He crept forward a fraction more, shifting his weight, ready to rush Everhard in case he pulled a weapon.

Everhard turned his menacing glare from Ruddy to Burton. "You—you stole my journal and turned it over to them?"

How pathetic the cold-hearted bastard sounded.

Everhard glanced from Burton to the desk and back. The action so quick, Ruddy would have missed it if he blinked. But, he didn't. Everhard gave his intent away with the subtle action.

Ruddy dodged the book Everhard hurled. In a matter of seconds Everhard seized the gun from inside the drawer. Ruddy yelled, "Get down," and hoped Archie and Northam did.

Everhard fired a single round as Ruddy rushed past the desk and within arm's reach of him. Everhard turned and dashed for the French doors. He twisted and fired over his shoulder. The desperate shot went wide and high.

Ruddy stopped and hurried back to the gun case. The doors were locked. Archie and a saucer-eyed Northam stood by as he used his elbow to shatter the glass and reach in to unlock the case. He kept a rifle and tossed Archie and Northam a shotgun each.

"Burton's hit," Archie said, taking the shotgun.

Ruddy looked over. Burton was crumpled on the floor, hand to his chest, blood spreading and soaking his shirt. Ruddy had seen enough gunshot wounds to the chest to know Burton had little chance of surviving. He hesitated, not wanting to leave the valet.

Burton looked up and waved him off.

Ruddy dropped a handful of shotgun shells in Archie's hand. "Split this between you." The Martini-Henry rifle he had was a single shot, breech-load, a familiar weapon to him. He carried one while in the military. But in that moment, Ruddy longed for one of the new repeating rifles they were using in America. He emptied what was left in an ammo box for the rifle and shoved the rounds into his pants pocket. "Let's go."

Northam didn't budge.

"What are you waiting for?"

"I've never fired a gun, sir."

Precious moments were wasting while Everhard was getting away. Ruddy didn't have time to instruct the constable. "It's like snapping a picture with your camera. Point at the subject and instead of pressing a button, pull the trigger," he said, running out after Everhard.

In the fading sunlight, Ruddy could just make out Everhard's figure passing through the shadows of the garden's trees. Everhard briefly slowed and the light glinted off the metal barrel of his gun as he spun toward them. Ruddy yelled "down," to Archie and Northam and took cover behind a statue of an ancient goddess of some sort. Everhard fired a shot that hit the edge of the fountain. From his crouched position Ruddy took aim, but Everhard suddenly turned before he got a shot off.

Everhard bore left toward the moor and the cliffs. Ruddy was gaining on him, but Everhard was surprisingly fast. Faster than Ruddy would've guessed for a man of his age. In his journal, Everhard had alluded to recapturing the strength and speed he had in his youth after taking the elixir.

Ruddy thought it more a case of Everhard believing the elixir responsible and that belief drove him to temporarily overcome weaknesses.

The moor was covered in animal holes and divots from horses. The treacherous depressions tripped Ruddy up several times. He lost his balance and almost went down but managed to stagger along until he regained his footing. A stitch in his side troubled him too. He'd chased dozens of suspects and never had this problem. He cursed the nagging pain for starting now of all times.

Everhard was now only yards away from the cliff's edge. If he made it down to the water, he'd have a good chance of stealing a boat. The cliffs contained all types of nooks and crannies where a man could hide for hours. Any search Ruddy ordered wouldn't start until first light. Everhard could be halfway down the coast by then.

At the edge, Everhard stopped and turned again. The moor offered little cover, only a few trees scattered here and there. Ruddy shielded himself behind a crooked oak tree. He glanced back checking to see that Archie and Northam had seen Everhard turn and took what cover they could find.

Ruddy knelt and tipped his head to peer around the

tree. Everhard stood with his gun up, sweeping the moor, ready to shoot. Ruddy raised his rifle and sighted in on Everhard. The long shadow cast by the tree shifted and what sun remained bathed Ruddy in light. He swore under his breath and ducked back.

Everhard fired in Ruddy's direction. The round fell short. Ruddy thought it would at that distance unless Everhard got very lucky. Ruddy knew army officers who carried the same Webley sidearm as Everhard and knew its range and where accuracy began to suffer.

Ruddy leaned out past the trunk again and fired a shot. Even if it missed, he might get Everhard to return fire. He'd already spent three rounds with two left. If nothing else, he'd burn up another in the exchange. The ploy worked and Everhard shot. The round ricocheted off a boulder and struck the ground off to the right.

Ruddy crawled on his belly until he estimated he was still out of range but close enough for Everhard to hear him over the crashing waves.

"You can't win, Everhard. Wherever you go, we'll find you," he lied. Truthfully, a man with the viscount's resources might escape to almost anywhere with little trouble. "Give up. Have some dignity. Don't shame your noble family." Ruddy wasn't confident in the argument, but it was all that came to him in the moment.

"Surrender and give myself over to face the noose. You must take me for a fool."

Everhard wasn't the sort of man who'd tolerate a personal attack or insult and Ruddy used that pride. "No viscount, not a fool. I take you for a man who couldn't gain sexual satisfaction the normal way anymore—a man who needed to kill to prove he was still a man," Ruddy taunted.

"Liar. Women sought me out. No woman was left unsatisfied by me. They're the ones who took our lovemaking to another level. They liked for me to choke them. They enjoyed the fright it gave them. They insisted I participate. I'd never done anything like that on my own."

"Faith Goddard was not your mistress. I assume Frobisher and Norris didn't demand you strangle them for sexual gratification."

"I'm no sodomite. Frobisher planned to tell the world about the discovery I handed him. It would get out in society that I imbibed in a drink conjured from a necromancer. I couldn't let the world think me so foolish."

"How was Norris involved?"

"My killing Norris was an act of mercy. I put an end to the horrors of the asylum he'd had to endure."

Ruddy raised up enough to see if he had a better shot at Everhard. He had a better one but not a clear one. "And Faith? She wasn't your mistress. Why kill her?"

"I loved her." His shoulders sagged with the confession and as though overcome with weariness, he lowered the gun. "She knew we were supposed to be together." He raised the gun again in Ruddy's general direction. "She's the one who threw what we had away."

"You held her under and drowned her."

"I saved her from a miserable life she was bound to have with some dreadful nobody in America. She didn't believe I knew what was best for her, for us."

Archie and Northam had crept up to where Ruddy lay.

"You killed her to save her?"

"You don't understand. A man of your low station never can. Perhaps I did over react, but I'm a good man. I championed better health care for the poor in Parliament. I'm generous to the villagers and kind to my staff. I am a good man," he said with greater insistence. "If you read my journal, you know I became a slave to an ancient elixir."

To Ruddy, there were only two kinds of murderer: one who delights in the kill and brags of it, and one who claims no responsibility and lays blame somewhere else.

"The only chance you have of explaining to the world that you suffered from this wicked formula is to stand trial."

Everhard's arm slowly started to drop. He wasn't keeping the gun up like he should. He was tiring. Finally. Something useful for Ruddy to plan his next step around.

"You say to stand trial and tell what happened. You and I both know there's no acquittal in the cards for me. I'll not die twisting in the wind at the end of a rope."

Archie and Northam took advantage of the distraction of the conversation to crawl up to Ruddy's position.

"I'm not playing this game with him forever, coaxing him to come along," he told Archie. "He's going to make a stand here."

Northam frowned. "Do you think he's going to turn the gun on himself rather than go with us?"

"Very possibly."

Northam looked appalled. "That's a mortal sin."

In spite of the tense situation, Northam's naïve comment brought the flash of a smile to Ruddy. He couldn't remember ever being that innocent.

"I'm not a religious man. I can't speak for God, but my guess is six murders trump the sin of suicide."

Northam nodded but he wore the same appalled expression. The notion still boggled him.

"If it puts your mind at rest, Northam, I suspect he'll put us in a position where we've no choice but to kill him."

Shock replaced his frown. "Good Lord."

"He's still got a bullet left. I'm certain he'd love to take one of us with him. Don't let your guard down, lad," Archie warned.

"I won't."

"I want to force his hand. How good are you with the shotgun?" Ruddy asked Archie.

"Damned decent. I hunted with my dad from the time I could hold the gun."

"Good. I'm going to walk out into the open, into his line of sight. While he focuses in on me, you sight in on him. I expect him to take a shot at me—"

"Are you mad?"

"No, and keep your voice down. He can't get an accurate shot off, not at this distance."

"Doesn't mean he can't get off a lucky one."

"It's a chance I'll take. I'm not going unarmed. I'll shoot if I need to, but I'd like to bring him in alive. That means having him expend that last bullet. Get ready." He waited until Archie nodded.

Ruddy removed the spent cartridge and reloaded another round. He stood and walked toward Everhard, keeping the rifle along his hip but pointed at Everhard. "You cannot win. You only have a single round left and there are three of us."

Ruddy fired a round into the ground in front of Everhard to frighten him into surrendering or wasting the shot.

A startled Everhard took a step back and brought his gun up to shoulder height. He aimed at Ruddy then suddenly flailed for only a moment before disappearing from sight. He was there and then he was gone.

Ruddy lowered the barrel of the rifle, briefly confused by what just happened before realizing the ground under Everhard gave way. That portion of cliff beneath Everhard crumbled with his shift in weight when he took aim at Ruddy. Ruddy thought Everhard cried out but the screech of gulls disturbed from their nests drowned the sound out.

"Holy Mother of God," Archie said, coming to stand by Ruddy. "Bloody hell, I've never seen anything like that."

"Neither have I."

Northam came running over. "Did I see right? Did he fall off the cliff?"

"It appears so," Ruddy said. "Come along, we have to see what's become of him. Keep your weapons ready in case he's landed on a shelf and still in shooting shape."

When they reached the spot where the cliff now ended, they spread out and cautiously edged just close enough to see Everhard's body lying on the rocks below. Around him, rough waves broke, spraying high along the cliff and threatening to take the body out to sea with them.

"Northam, you stay here and watch that nothing happens to the body until we get back with Pender and the wagon. Once we get to the village, we'll organize a recovery."

"I don't trust the bastard not to get up and limp away. His type are bloody resilient as sewer rats," Archie said.

Northam made the sign of the cross. "Sir, do you think he was right, that the elixir changed him, made him turn wicked?" he asked, turning to Ruddy.

"No. No potion, or mesmerizer's spell, or magical means can make a man do what isn't already in his heart."

## Chapter Twenty-Seven

London

Ruddy, Archie, and Northam went straight to the police station from the train. They'd wired Jameson from Tintagel advising him of what happened. Police procedure dictated Everhard's body be transported with them for official autopsy by their London doctor. Everhard's sister lived nearby to Foxleigh. The butler sent a messenger to her. When the London coroner was done, the family would be able to have the body shipped back to Cornwall for services.

Burton miraculously survived. Before they left, he told them he had a small savings, enough to live a quiet, comfortable life if he was careful. He sent a message to his elderly aunt and uncle. Once he healed and could travel, he'd move to Uxbridge to look after them.

Ruddy looked forward to finishing the paperwork as fast as possible and heading home to change, rough house with Winky, and then go to the Boot and Bayonet for a pint, or two, or three. It had been a long twenty-four hours. He'd be happy if he never saw Cornwall again. As Pender predicted, the villagers hated them for causing the death of their treasured viscount. The fact they were in the process of removing a murderer from their midst meant nothing. Local fishermen retrieved the body and brought it to the edge of the village, but that was all. There was a casket maker in the next town. Ruddy had to order Pender to bring the cheapest coffin back, load Everhard, and drop his body at the train station the next day.

Back home, the moment they stepped inside the police station the young constables crowded around Northam. He was the star among the patrol officers. He'd traveled all the way to Cornwall to participate in a major arrest, and he'd been shot at in the process. Later he'd be at the Muddy Duck, a favorite pub of the men, drinking free beer and retelling the adventure to all who asked.

Ruddy and Archie didn't make it to their desks before a gleeful Jameson ordered them into his office. "Tell me everything that happened. Start at the beginning and don't leave anything out," he said, closing the door.

"Before we do that, there is something, a troublesome issue regarding the first two murders," Ruddy warned.

"Let me have this day, Bloodstone. Tell me the troublesome problem tomorrow," Jameson said, wanting nothing to upset his apple cart.

After what felt like an eternity answering questions, they finally got out of the office and started on the reports. Fortunately, they'd done drafts while on the train home, which would cut the writing time appreciatively.

Meg and Archie's daughters were waiting by his desk when they left Jameson's. "We came by to invite you to dinner," Meg told Ruddy. "I want to hear all about the event."

*The event.* What a benign way to reference the experience. But the description suited Archie's tender-natured wife.

"I thank you for the invite Meg, but Archie can tell you anything you want to know." Ruddy didn't want to go to dinner at anyone's house tonight and make polite conversation. He wanted to put his feet up at the Boot and Bayonet, eat something he could share with Winky, and just relax.

"Oh no you don't, Rudyard. You haven't come the last two times I invited you to dinner. I refuse to let you decline now. I have a lovely pork roast with baked cinnamon apples and Yorkshire pudding."

"My Meg makes the best Yorkshire pudding in London. You don't want to miss that," Archie said.

His daughters began jumping up and down and

clapping, curls bouncing. "Please Mr. Bloodstone, please come."

He used a threat to their rabbits to strengthen his inability to attend. "I have Winky to take care of. I can't leave him behind after just coming home. I can't bring him with me either. He'll torment Gemma and Marigold or worse." Brow cocked, he offered his stern face to emphasize the danger to the bunnies.

"We'll keep them safely tucked away in their hutch."

He hadn't counted on their easy solution. He grasped at the only excuse he had left...their cat. "Then, he'll go after Muffin." Muffin, what a misleading name that was. The animal had nasty sharp nails a badger would envy, weighed more than an iron kettle and had the temperament of a medieval rack operator.

"Not to worry. We'll put him in mummy and daddy's room. Now you have no reason not to come."

Sadly, they were right.

"If it's no imposition, I'd love to join you." He forced a cheerful smile.

"Archibald tells me you have a special lady." Meg gave him that sideways look and grin all women employ. The look that made a man think the ladies knew things they shouldn't and men wish they didn't. "Please bring her as well. I'd love to meet her."

"I'll ask but she might have plans."

"Do try." Meg kissed Archie on the cheek and then took the hand of the oldest girl, who held onto the hand of the youngest. "See you this evening, Rudyard." She left with the girls in tow.

#

Allegra hadn't said much during dinner as Ruddy and Archie retold most of the story, leaving some details out that might frighten the children.

Ruddy and Allegra didn't stay late. He'd waited a decent length of time after the meal ended to suggest they go. He hadn't intended to call on Allegra until the next day. But since she'd joined him for dinner and they came back to her home, he decided he'd spend the night.

He removed his jacket and turned Allegra, who'd kept her back to him, around to give her a hug.

She didn't return the hug but he wasn't troubled by it. "I was thinking on the ride home," he said, releasing her. "Why don't we go to Brighton this weekend? You said you wanted to and at the time I couldn't get away. Now I can. I know of a charming hotel there. I'll have them make up a nice hamper and we'll have a picnic on the beach, take that walk in the moonlight you wanted, and go dancing in the evening, if you like."

He'd started fingering the ribbons on the collar of her dress, undoing them then bent to kiss her. Turning her head, she grasped his hands in hers and stilled them. She kept her head turned, sighed, and gave another heavy sigh before making eye contact with him. "We need to talk, Rudyard."

"All right." He couldn't imagine what was so serious she had to muster the courage to discuss it. "Is it my suggestion about Brighton? We don't have to go, not if you don't want to."

She let go of his hands and he shoved them into his trouser pockets and took a step back.

"When you told us what happened in Cornwall, trying to capture this murderer, I thought I'd faint on the spot. I've already lost someone I loved," she said and shook her head. "When I heard the danger you were in, fear for you overwhelmed me." She cupped his cheek with her hand. "I can't lose another."

"You didn't. As you can see, I'm fine."

"But for how long? I can't come to care for you more than I already do and then lose you. Simply put, I can't bear the thought of you being a detective. It's too dangerous."

Her worry didn't make sense, not to this degree. "What would you have me do? This is my livelihood. I must make a living."

"But it doesn't have to be as a police detective. Your ironwork is excellent. People hire you to do special pieces now. You can easily expand the amount of customers you need to build your business."

"Working with iron relaxes me. Whatever is pressing on my mind is forgotten for a few hours. Yes, I do sell most of my pieces. I like to dress well and I enjoy other small luxuries difficult to obtain on a detective's salary. The ironwork lets me afford them. I wouldn't want to do it as a profession."

"You say it relaxes you. Wouldn't you rather do something that makes you feel good rather than dealing with violence and tragedy?"

He couldn't fault her for her lack of understanding into that side of his nature and the nature of his work. He assumed she'd had an inkling about it and never thought he needed to delve deeper. "I care about you very much, Allegra. But I also like what I do. I'm good at it. I enjoy the challenges the cases present. I do what I'm able, however limited at times, to solve them. I take a sense of pride in that."

Ruddy handed her his handkerchief to wipe the tears that ran down her cheeks.

"You knew I was a detective when you sought me out. *You approached me*. Now this is suddenly a problem?"

"Yes, I knew you were a detective. At the time, I didn't give that fact a second thought. Afterward you never talked about your cases with me. I had no reason to dwell on what your job entailed. I do now."

"A detective is what I am. Iron work is something I do."

Head down, her tears turned to sobbing. He hadn't wanted to hurt her or make her cry. He felt a bounder for having done it, but he had to be honest.

She raised her face to his again, her red-rimmed eyes

already puffy. "I'm sorry Rudyard. The situation is unbearable for me. If you won't even try a different profession that eases my mind, then I see no future for us."

He tried not to let the ultimatum grate too much. She spoke from the heart. He'd give her the answer she demanded, just not the one she wanted to hear. "This is goodbye, then." He nudged Winky who'd fallen asleep on the divan awake. "Come on, boy."

"Rudyard..."

He kept his hand on the knob and eyes on the door. "Yes."

"I am sorry."

"So am I, Allegra.

"Do you think we could be just friends?"

The novel idea struck him as funny and he stifled an inappropriate chuckle. He turned to her and shrugged. "I don't know. I've never had a female *friend*."

"Will you try?"

"Yes," he said, because that was what she wanted to hear. Would he? Probably not.

#

Morris was locking the front door to the Boot and Bayonet when Rudy and Winky walked up. "Bollocks, I was hoping to get here before you closed," Ruddy said.

Morris unlocked the door and waved Ruddy in. "I'm not closed to you and Stinky."

"It's Winky."

"Not when he's been feeding on bangers."

"What do you expect feeding him sausages? Frankly, I don't know how you can single him out in that regard considering the habits of your clientele."

"No arguing with that logic." Morris relocked the front door and went behind the bar to the tap. "The usual?"

Ruddy nodded.

"What brings you here this late?" Morris asked.

"You're clearly not dressed to wile away time in a pub."

"The Holbrook's had Allegra and I over for dinner."

"How is your courtship?

*Courtship.* Ruddy never considered their relationship a courtship, at least not in the traditional sense. He thought of it as far less complex, uncomplicated as two people enjoying the pleasures of each other's company.

"It's definitely not going forward."

"I'm sorry to hear that." Morris quickly added, "Unless, of course, you wanted it to end. In that case," He raised his tankard of ale. "Cheers."

Morris set Ruddy's ale down on the table and pulled a chair out for himself. "You want to talk?"

"There's nothing much to say. I wasn't the one who ended it, not technically anyway. I was fond of her."

"What happened?"

Ruddy took a long swallow of ale. Her ultimatum rankled him more now than when she'd proposed it. The guilt provoking tears for choosing the life he liked only added to his irritation.

"She wanted me to quit the force and take up fashioning ironwork all day. She gave me a choice, her or my job. As you can see, I'm here."

"I'm guessing she took your decision badly."

"She cried."

Morris was quiet for a moment.

He tried to appear like he was mulling over the situation. Ruddy knew better. Morris didn't ponder or mull anything over. Most everything in his world could be handled with a yes or no, now or later, here or there. Ruddy waited. Whatever unusual insight Morris might come up with, it'd be simple and accurate.

His assessment of the relationship's demise was uncharacteristically philosophical. "Well, life can't always be fairy dust and sweet canoodling. I find when one person tells another they must do what the first person wants or else, someone winds up unhappy."

Morris's observation said it all, so Ruddy changed the subject. "Canoodling? Really Morris? I didn't know you knew that word."

"I didn't. I overheard my granddaughter use it. Since you mentioned the job, how's your murder investigation going?"

Ruddy told him about the journal, the arrest attempt, and Everhard's death.

"Good show. This deserves something stronger than ale." Morris got up and went behind the bar, then raised a bottle. "Gin or rum?"

"Rum," Ruddy said without hesitation. When he first joined the army, he had gotten sick on cheap gin that tasted like sugared goat piss. After one of the worst nights of his life, he swore off the vile drink.

Morris stuck the bottle of rum under his wounded arm and brought two glasses to the table. He poured a generous portion in each and then raised his glass. "Here's to Hell! May our stay there be as much fun as our way there."

Ruddy raised his. "That has nothing to do with my case."

"True, but it's the only toast I know besides cheers. Saw it on an outhouse wall."

Both men emptied their glasses and Morris poured more. "You don't seem as pleased with the investigation as I would've expected."

"It's the first two murders. I keep coming back to how different they were from the others. I don't think Everhard's the killer. If he'd done them, he'd have included them in his journal. I can't rid myself of the feeling another murderer is out there and he's not finished."

## Chapter Twenty-Eight

Ruddy and Archie slid in right behind Jameson as he entered his office. Jameson ignored them and hung his hat and coat on the rack. He turned and jammed his fists on his hips. "You couldn't have the decency to wait until I had my morning cup of tea."

"We'll wait. Have your tea," Ruddy said. He and Archie sat across from Jameson.

Jameson dropped into his chair. "Just get it over with, Bloodstone. What's the troublesome matter you feel compelled to tell me? Am I right in thinking you're about to spoil my day?" He took a deep breath. "Don't bother answering, your face says it all. What now?"

"Archie and I scoured the journal in case we might've missed an entry or two regarding his murders. Nothing in the book talks about the first two women killed in the museum gardens. The other six murders are there, details on the how and why of what he did justifying them, but no mention of Georgina Ellis or Tess Offerman. Why?"

"How am I supposed to know? Maybe it slipped his mind, or he hadn't gotten around to it, or at the time he didn't feel the need. I can't go into the head of a dead killer but the similarities are close enough, in my opinion, to blame him." Jameson turned his attention to some paperwork stacked in his inbox. Paperwork that had been there for weeks by Ruddy's reckoning.

Archie didn't move. Ruddy stretched his legs out and sat back in the uncomfortable wooden chair. His original desk chair had been identical to this. One of the purchases he made with his ironwork money was a desk chair with a padded seat that tilted and swiveled. The day it was delivered, Jameson eyed it hard. Ruddy stayed later than usual that day and came in early the next in case Jameson had confiscation in mind.

"Still here, I see," Jameson said when he finally looked up and slapped the papers in his hand down on the desk. "Bloody hell. Tell me why you think those murders are too different to be the viscount's, and when you're finished I want you both to leave me in peace."

Ruddy started with the method of strangulation not being the same. "Ellis and Offerman were manually strangled. Everhard's victims were strangled with the scarf we found in his bureau." He went on, "The sexual component is also different. There wasn't evidence of penetration with Ellis and Offerman. The killer spilled himself on their skirts."

Archie jumped into the conversation. "Everhard's victims had sex..." he paused, "the..." He rubbed his index finger back and forth through his semi-closed fist.

Jameson screwed up his face in disgust. "Oh for pity's sake, stop that."

Archie put his hands in his lap.

"Suffice it to say, the common way," Ruddy said.

"So? I'm not impressed with your logic thus far. I don't find the difference in the balmy bastard's gratification method a troubling factor. Again, why are we talking about this disturbing topic?"

Ruddy held his tongue but would've loved to tell Jameson to stop acting so offended. The idea he, himself, hadn't said worse was laughable. His club's toff membership was a litany of young actress—loving old codgers. Ruddy wasn't much of a gambler but he'd lay odds the doddering coots couldn't wait to regale each other with tales of their prowess in pleasing the ladies. The *actress* part conveniently forgotten when describing the ladies satisfaction.

"The point, Chief Inspector, is why would he suddenly

go from one form of debauchery to a completely different behavior?" Ruddy asked.

"I don't know. I don't care. Unless you have something more tangible than using two different means of wringing a woman's neck and varying his means of gratification, I am not interested. Is that all you have?"

"As we said earlier, he never documented those murders." Ruddy sat forward, leaned an arm on Jameson's desk to stress his point, "This is a man who wrote with delight about the way he killed. He's not going to leave mention of Ellis and Offerman out if he'd done them as well."

There was a knock at the door and the desk sergeant poked his head in. "Superintendent you should—,"

"Get out."

"But you—,"

"Out."

The sergeant shot a fast look at Ruddy, flicked his brows up and quickly shut the door.

Jameson leaned forward, inches from Ruddy's face. "I am meeting with the Home Secretary this morning. He's wants to know all the details of this case. He has the sticky job of informing the queen a member of the House of Lords was a maniac. I have already advised him we closed eight murder cases, including one for Southampton Police. Now you'd have me tell him what? Oops, we miscounted." He tapped his finger hard on the desk. "That is not going to happen, Bloodstone."

Ruddy's temper won out over good sense dealing with a superior. "I don't care about the poor Home Secretary's job of giving the queen bad news. He's paid a pretty penny to deliver sticky news."

"Ruddy..." Archie tugged on his arm to get him to give the superintendent space.

"You haven't given me even a modicum of solid information.

"But your entire theory is based on a hunch about whether or not the unhinged bastard would behave how you *think* he should've.

Archie tugged on Ruddy's arm again.

Ruddy pulled away from Archie's hold. "What about the families of the two women? Don't they deserve a thorough investigation? Don't—"

"Watch your tone with me, Bloodstone. They did get a thorough investigation. I sent three of you all the way to Cornwall to effect an arrest and see justice served." He sat back when Ruddy did. "Now, you will close those cases and I don't want to hear any more about them. Do you both understand?"

"Yes sir," Archie said.

When Ruddy didn't respond, Jameson asked, "Bloodstone? Do you have something else to say? Because at the moment you're ever so close to walking a foot beat as a constable again."

"I have a question."

"Go on and God help you if there's the slightest hint of insubordination in it."

"What do you plan to say, if and when, the first killer murders again after you've insisted he was gone?"

"Not your problem is it? Now get out of my office, the two of you. Finish the reports to include Ellis and Offerman. When you're done go over to the bloody newspaper office and give that reporter the exclusive story he wants. The last thing I need is to have him and his editor in my office moaning about not getting the story, *in its entirety,* in a timely manner. Go." He waved them away and turned back to the paperwork.

At their desks, Archie looked around to see who might be within earshot and asked in a low voice, "What were you thinking in there, challenging Jameson that way? He was purple in the face angry. I thought he was going to have apoplexy."

"I don't care. Justice isn't being served. You know Everhard didn't kill those first two women. Closing those cases is a travesty."

"You had better care. You're on the verge of having to put a uniform back on and tramp around in the elements on whatever shift Jameson decides. Is that what you want? To go home cold to the bone from shaking doorknobs in the rain and scuffling with drunks in the wee hours of the morning?"

A familiar threat. Some things never change. Whether it's the military or an organization that closely resembles the military, the first resort of officers was to threaten demotion or financial penalty. He unintentionally aimed his finger like a gun. "No, of course not. But keep in mind, adamant as he may be now, if more dead women turn up, he'll piss backwards on us in the blink of an eye. All the blame will be laid at our feet."

"That goes without saying. But fighting with him won't keep that from happening. It only antagonizes the man." Archie stood. "I'm going to have a cup of tea before we see Marsden. Want one?"

"Sure." Ruddy took a heavy crock cup with a chipped rim from a desk drawer and handed it to Archie.

Jameson opened the door to his office, stepped out and yelled for the desk sergeant without sparing a glance at Ruddy or Archie.

Before Archie returned with the tea, the sergeant came out, checked to see Jameson's door was closed and came over to Ruddy's desk. "What the deuce did you two say to him? He had all but steam pouring from his ears. He nearly bit my head off telling me to order him a carriage."

"We told him Everhard didn't kill the first two women in the gardens. We said he was making a serious mistake having us close those cases. He didn't want to hear it. All he's interested in is looking good to the Home Office, the Home Secretary, and by extension the palace."

The sergeant's expression said it all. *You're a pathetic*

*imbecile.* "You know better than to cast a shadow on him when he has the opportunity to show Effingham up."

*Effingham.* Ruddy had forgotten all about him and Napier. Once the Home Secretary's office heard the story, word would spread like wildfire about Everhard. Before the day was out, Effingham and Napier would come hotfooting over, demanding an explanation for not having been included. Something else to look forward to.

The sergeant left to hail a hansom for Jameson.

"What was that about?" Archie set the tea down.

"He brought up Effingham and that we're going to have to answer to him and Napier with our exigent circumstances excuse for leaving them out of the arrest."

"That should be a boatload of fun."

#

Both Marsden and his editor Orlando Humphrey sat back in their chairs. From their dazed expressions, you'd think they'd been slapped in the face with a fish.

"The Viscount Everhard, a murderer, and not just any murderer, but a prolific one," Marsden said. "Words escape me."

"Let me see if I'm understanding this right," Humphrey said. "Everhard got himself addicted to some bizarre French potion, that even the chemist couldn't say what effect it might have."

Archie and Ruddy nodded. "According to his journal," Archie said.

"There's nothing in here about the murder of Faith Goddard, the woman you say he loved." Marsden flipped through the pages with the last entries again. "Are you certain he killed her as well?"

"His valet witnessed the murder. Everhard didn't have the chance to write it down," Ruddy said. "Burton stole the journal and brought it to us after seeing him drown her."

"I'd like to interview Mr. Burton. Do you think he'd be amenable?" Marsden asked.

"No, Everhard shot him. He has a long recovery ahead."

"As soon as he's well enough then."

"I'm sure he wouldn't be amenable."

"It'd be a huge boost to our readership, if we could talk to him." Marsden jumped up and began to pace behind his desk. He reminded Ruddy of a German cuckoo clock. Not the kind where woodland creatures pop out from a wooden gable on the hour. But the ones with tiny chalet people who pass each other every hour. A measured pace, Marsden went four steps, turned, and in the exact same spot, turned again and went the same four steps. The speed increased as he continued. Excitement and wild ideas filling his head, Ruddy guessed.

"If we can speak to him, we can get the first hand accounting of the last murder." Marsden stopped eyes big as a child's in front of a candy store window. "Maybe we could even get a photograph of the viscount, or better, one of the girl and the fountain."

This was why people hate the press, Ruddy thought. All they cared about was the story and nothing for the people involved. If he hadn't already stirred things up with Jameson, he'd tell Marsden to bugger off. But Jameson had been clear. Co-operate.

"*Miss Goddard,* the *girl* as you call her, has parents who are brokenhearted over her death. What good is served by splashing a picture of her face and the crime scene across your front page? Is it your wish to crush them further in order to acquire a few more readers?" Ruddy asked in the civil tone he used testifying in court.

"When you put it that way, you make us sound like soulless brutes." Humphrey hadn't said much until now.

How typical. Humphrey was more offended by the perceived insult against him and his reporter than by the proposed act.

Archie always quick to see when a situation was going

to hell, interceded in the tense conversation. "Sorry, we don't mean to suggest you are without conscience. It's just having met her family we saw firsthand how difficult this is for them."

He gave a more carefully worded answer regarding Burton. "Honestly Mr. Marsden, speaking with Mr. Burton is not a good idea either for similar reasons. Everhard was like a son to him. When he turned the journal over and told us about Faith Goddard, he put a noose around Everhard's neck. It was a gut wrenching thing for him to do. I think he wants to lead what's left of his life in peace and quiet and not discussing the matter."

"Please, call me Geoff. I guess I understand. But if the opportunity arises, I'd appreciate it if you let me know."

"No worries. Of course, we will. And please call us, Rudyard and Archie," Archie said with his best fake sincere smile.

Marsden smiled back and turned to Ruddy who gave him a weak one in return.

"I have a question about the journal," Humphrey said. "Everhard gives a detailed account of three women he killed and the two men. Burton was witness to the Goddard murder. That's six. In your report, however, you clear eight homicides."

Ruddy anticipated where the conversation was headed and wished he could transport himself to someplace else, anywhere other than this office, even to what the Americans called their Wild West.

"There's no entry for the first two murdered women. Why do you think Everhard left them out?" Humphrey asked.

"Good point," Marsden said. "What's your thought?"

Archie managed to utter a halting, "um," nothing more. Then he turned to Ruddy, and when he did, the other two did. The three sat in awkward silence, eyes riveted on Ruddy who wished Jameson could've heard Humphrey's question. Ruddy would love nothing more than to point to the editor and tell Jameson in the frankest of terms that if a bloody newspaper editor can see something is amiss regarding the two murders, then why the devil was it so hard for him to see it.

"Rudyard," Humphrey asked, "why didn't he write about them do you think?"

Ruddy ran through a small sample of lies to put forth. None seemed credible if Humphrey or Marsden gave them any real thought. He offered the only answer that held a semblance of possibility. First chance he got, he'd make Archie pay for passing the question off to him.

"I believe, and this is just speculation since we never had a chance to interview Everhard, that it was a personal issue."

Marsden looked baffled. "What does that mean?"

"All the rest of the victims, he had a relationship with, which made the killings personal. The only exception was Norris, the arsonist. His murder is only briefly addressed and one Everhard claimed was an act of mercy."

"Maybe you'll think me strange but in a way, I believe it was a merciful act. If you've ever been to an asylum, you'd feel the same," Humphrey said.

"I'll take your word." Since neither Humphrey nor Marsden appeared as though they considered Everhard's possible reasoning unsound, Ruddy left well enough alone.

Marsden flipped through the original crime reports regarding the museum murders. He stopped at a page in the back where they attached the autopsy reports. "The doctor who performed both autopsies said the women were manually strangled. Yet all of the female victims of Everhard were ligature strangulations, except Goddard, of course."

Ruddy didn't offer an explanation, hoping he wouldn't ask why the switch.

"Don't you find that strange?"

"Yes."

"Any thought as to why?"

Ruddy shook his head. Marsden turned to Archie who shrugged the question off.

"I've covered a number of stories about murderers, men who kill more than once. They're not given to changing from one style of killing to another, not unless they are in the process of increasing the level of brutality," Marsden addressed the statement to Ruddy, seeking some confirmation from him.

"That's what we've normally found to be true. Why Everhard altered his, neither of us can say for sure."

A valid reason suddenly came to Ruddy although he didn't think it true. He was still of the opinion there were two killers. However, the reason had the ring of truth, enough credibility to convince Humphrey and Marsden. "I have one idea, but like some of the other answers, I can't say it's more than speculation."

Humphrey gestured open-handed. "Please go on."

"The first two women were sexually violated, but not in the truest sense. There was no penetration. For some unknown reason, Everhard couldn't perform in the standard fashion." He looked over at Archie. "Do your pantomime for them."

It took a moment for the penny to drop and Archie to understand what he wanted. He repeated his finger in fist demonstration. By all appearances, editor and reporter were as disgusted as Jameson by the sight.

"Stop now, they understand," he told Archie and continued offering his theory to Humphrey and Marsden. "The other three he had sexual congress with involving penetration. Perhaps, he needed the scarf and the act of strangling them to perform as a virile man."

Marsden leaned back in his chair and fixed his attention on Ruddy. The intense scrutiny didn't bother him. He'd experienced it a dozen times in court. Solicitors for the defendants wore it while they tried to think up a way to impeach his testimony.

"Something you want to ask, Geoff?"

Marsden didn't challenge any element of the case. To Ruddy's surprise he asked a cunning question. "I realize this is a stretch. But, have you considered there might be more than one killer?"

How to answer in a way that won't come back to haunt them if it does turn out there are two? Ruddy chose his words with care just in case. "That is a stretch. Any indication it's true, which I'm not saying it is, would put the women of the city in a panic."

"Isn't the risk of a panic worth it if women are more alert?"

"Panic solves nothing and leads to chaos. As for being alert, London is a major city with the problems any city has. Everyone should always be alert to the world around them."

## Chapter Twenty-Nine

Late October-1888

London

When the weather wasn't atrocious, Ruddy walked to work. Autumn had begun to make her presence known. Today the sky was cloudless but a brisk breeze blew off the Thames. The blustery weather kept Ruddy walking to the station.

On his way, he bought a paper from the boy who worked that corner of Great Ormond Street. He read as he walked and glanced up from the Ripper article in time to see Evangeline Bannister. The pretty blonde from Kensington Gardens waited in the streetcar queue. He called out as the horse-drawn trolley clattered to a stop. She must not have heard. Without turning his way, she grasped a handful of skirt offering him a pleasant sight of white-stocking clad ankle and climbed the stairs.

At the park, she said she lived nearby. Where he wondered, since he'd never seen her around the neighborhood. Didn't matter since they didn't have the chance to speak. He folded his paper, tucked it under his arm, and continued on to the station.

"Have you read the latest newspapers?" Archie asked, reading a story from that morning's paper.

Ruddy sat at his desk. "I read one." He laid a few on his desk. "I bought these on my way in but haven't had a chance to look at them yet. Nasty business those murders in Whitechapel. The reporters are making mincemeat of the detectives and how they're handling the investigation."

"I feel bad for the lads, everyone throwing fits because they haven't caught the Ripper. *Jack the Ripper*, what a name."

"It was a mistake for our people to release that *Dear Boss* letter he signed *Jack the Ripper.* They've handed him what he wanted: notoriety. Now the whole of London is aware of a previously nameless east end killer, including 10 Downing and the rest of government. Before, the blighters in Parliament didn't give a toss about the poverty and squalid conditions in the borough, let alone prostitutes. Suddenly everyone has an opinion and a deep concern." Ruddy waved a dismissive hand. "Balderdash."

Ruddy scanned the day's lurid headlines with both sympathy and great relief the cases weren't theirs. "I'd hate to be the investigators on these. Two agencies involved, pilloried by Parliament and the press, who'd blame the detectives if they walked off the job-just dropped their shield on the Commissioner's desk and went off to raise sheep."

"Would you walk?"

Ruddy answered without hesitation, "No." He'd understand if the others did, but also understood in spite of the horrible press, why they remained. "I couldn't even drop the investigation unless I was absolutely certain I'd done everything in my power to solve the crimes.

"The negative press isn't the worst part. Beyond the brutality involved, or the public being whipped up, or the nature of what little evidence is available, it's the knowledge that no matter what you do, it's never going to be enough. Even when, or if, he's apprehended, the question of why wasn't he caught sooner will take precedence over the arrest."

They turned their attention to a commotion in the lobby. A woman in a large yellow hat led a sobbing young woman to the desk. The younger lady's dress was torn exposing part of her petticoat. Her hair was in disarray and half the ribbons seemed to be missing. Ruddy couldn't tell from where he sat, but it looked like she had leaves stuck in her hair as well.

"Wonder what that's about," Archie asked, watching the women with the sergeant. "Quite a big hat, which reminds me—" He turned around in his seat and set his paper to the side. "I saw Allegra on the street yesterday. She was with a pinch-faced chap, pale as snow. If you'd talk to her, I bet she'd send him packing."

"I'd greet her politely if I passed her on the street, but I have no intention of doing more. She made it clear she doesn't want to be with a policeman. That's pretty much the death knell seeing as how I intend to stay a detective. And don't think I don't know what you're doing with this you should talk to her suggestion. I'm not looking to rekindle our relationship."

"It's been almost three months. You haven't once mentioned a lady you've taken a fancy to in all that time."

Ruddy saw no need to mention his failed attempt at speaking to Miss Bannister. "I didn't know I was under a time constraint. Let me stress again, I am not lonely, or pining, or weeping in my beer with longing."

The desk sergeant came hurrying their way while the ladies remained where they were, the hatted one watching the sergeant.

"Oh dear, what's this then?" Archie asked.

"Whatever it is, please don't let it be a Ripper caper, that's all I ask," Ruddy said, thinking since they had nothing to do with the east end crimes, they didn't have to worry.

"You better talk to these women. This is bad...very bad," the sergeant said.

"Oh? I'd like to know what we're getting into first," Ruddy said and glanced around the sturdy-built sergeant at the women. The hat lady wiped the eyes of the torn skirt one with a handkerchief, consoling her from appearances.

"It's a Ripper case."

Ruddy drew back. "What?"

Detectives at the nearby desks looked up, eyes on the three of them.

The sergeant bent low to not be heard. "It's a Ripper case."

"As in Jack the Ripper?" Ruddy knew the answer. Of course it was Jack the Ripper, but he dearly hoped he was wrong.

The sergeant nodded.

"How do you know?" Archie asked.

"The young one was attacked by a man with a knife who said he was Jack."

"Where?" If they were lucky, the case would turn out to be Whitechapel's jurisdiction and not a Holborn case. Ruddy didn't mind taking the preliminary report and then handing it over to the Ripper investigators to do what they wanted with it. But's that's as far as he cared to get involved.

"The museum gardens."

"Oh, bloody hell."

The sergeant waved the ladies over. Archie and Ruddy pulled spare chairs from other desks to theirs.

"Have a seat ladies," Archie said and like Ruddy, stayed standing until the women sat.

"I'll fetch you some tea," the sergeant said in a gentle voice. He looked past the women to Archie. "I've already asked Northam to come with his camera."

"Before we take your statement we need to know if either of you needs medical attention," Archie said.

The ladies shook their heads.

Ruddy said, "Very well. I understand from the sergeant that you were attacked in the museum gardens."

Hat lady said, "Yes."

She didn't appear disheveled in any way but to verify he asked, "Both of you?"

"Just me," the young one said.

"What's your name, your age, and your address or the best one to contact you?" Ruddy asked, taking out a pen and paper. The easy details he'd note, while Archie copied down the narrative telling of the story.

"Vivian Waldgrave, 19, and I live with my family at 324 Grays Inn Road."

Turning to the other woman, he asked, "We'll also require your name and information as well."

"I'll give it to you, but I saw very little of use to you. My name is Phyllida Ainsworth, 37, 122 Argyle Square."

"Tell us what happened," Ruddy said.

Waldgrave took a ragged breath. "There's not much I can tell you. Everything happened so fast." She trembled as she recalled the attack. "I took the path through the gardens to work. In spring and fall, I leave early to take that route. I love the seasonal plants in bloom there."

The tears had stopped but started again. She wiped at her wet cheeks with Ainsworth's handkerchief. "Take your time," Ruddy said.

"I'm fine," she said, her breathing no longer ragged. "I was on the path...,"

"What time was this?" Archie asked.

"Eight. I work in a dress shop and need to be there by eight-thirty to help with the displays. Just before I reached the topiary section, a man came up behind me, put a knife to my throat and said, 'I'm Jack the Ripper. You know of me. You know what I'll do if you scream.' Then, he started dragging me backwards towards an area thick with shrubs."

She began to tremble again. "Your tea is here. Have a drink of it and when you're ready we'll continue," Ruddy told her.

"Thank you." She spooned a large amount of sugar into the tea and drank it all. "I promise I'll not fall apart anymore."

"I take it you didn't scream."

She shook her head. "Not then. I did when he got me on the ground. I knew he was going to kill me. He moved his hand from my mouth for a moment and I screamed loud as I could."

"Good girl," Archie reassured her.

"Did you happen to see his face when he held you down?"

"No. You'll think me an awful coward but I was on my back and squeezed my eyes shut. I was terrified of seeing that knife coming at me again and again, like what they say the Ripper does to women. I couldn't bear it. I just couldn't."

Waldgrave was edging toward hysteria recalling the attack, eyes wide and trembling worse than before.

"I know this is difficult for you to relive. Take your time," Ruddy reassured her. "Would you like more tea?"

"No, thank you."

Ruddy looked over to Mrs. Ainsworth. "I take it you heard the scream."

"Yes, and I screamed my head off yelling for help. He jumped up as Miss Waldgrave scrambled from under him and he ran away."

Waldgrave composed herself and said, "I tore my skirt trying to get up and run myself."

Ruddy pulled his sketch pad and soft pencil from a drawer.

A handful of constables and the sergeant had gathered by the front desk. They watched as the women were interviewed and whispered among themselves. Obviously, the rumor of a Ripper case had spread.

Constable gossip was bad enough but when Ruddy looked over to the lobby from the detectives area, he spied Seamus. He made a circle with his finger and pointed to the door. A crestfallen Seamus picked up his shine box, did a turnabout, and left. Ruddy wondered how much he'd heard. The last thing he and Arch needed was to have the little tattler run over to Marsden's office with loose talk about a Ripper caper. Besides having the borough in a tizzy, the press would come to the station in droves, hovering about, pestering all and sundry with questions.

"Excuse me a moment, ladies. Please continue for Detective Holbrook." Ruddy got up and went to Freddie

Coopersmith, the detective who sat behind Arch. Quietly he told him, "Follow that shine boy, Seamus. If it looks like he's going into the newspaper office, grab him and bring him back here. And, you have my permission to boot him in the arse on the way."

Coopersmith nodded and moved to catch up with the boy.

As he did, Jameson stepped from his office, teacup in hand and stopped at the corner of the sergeant's desk. "What is going on here? Did someone declare a holiday I don't know about? I believe most of you have a patch to patrol? So, get on with it."

The sergeant came from behind the desk and joined Jameson, who he pulled aside. He leaned in and said something in the superintendent's ear and then pointed to Ruddy and Archie.

"We'll talk when you're done," Jameson said in a loud voice and stomped into his office, tea forgotten.

Ruddy returned his attention to Mrs. Ainsworth. "You said you saw the suspect."

"Only a glimpse, I'm afraid."

"Every little bit you can give us is helpful." He pulled his sketch pad and a soft drawing pencil from a drawer. "Describe him as best you can."

"He was medium height and weight with medium brown hair. From what I saw of his face, he didn't appear to have facial hair, but I can't be sure. It all happened so fast."

"What about clothing?" Ruddy asked.

"He had a dark blue jacket, a jacket," she emphasized, "it wasn't fashionable like a frock coat or morning coat, and he wore dark trousers."

Ruddy made a simple sketch of male figure. "Where did the jacket hit, since you say it definitely wasn't like a frock or morning coat? Was it short like one worn by common laborers?"

She thought for a moment and said, "It was hip length,

not unlike a soldier's jacket or the length of one of your constables coats."

Ruddy didn't want to consider that possibility and hated it might be true. No one would look twice at a uniformed officer walking in the vicinity of the crime. "Were there any insignias or rank designations on the sleeves?"

"I didn't notice any."

"What about epaulets?"

"Again, I didn't notice."

"Did you see the front?" Ruddy hoped she had and the question would jog her memory. If it was a army jacket, the front might have ribbons or medals pinned to it. If she remembered the colors, he might be able to distinguish the regiment.

"Sorry, I only saw the back."

Ruddy quickly penciled in a plain jacket with a military cut. He didn't have a blue pencil and just shaded in the jacket. "Did it look like this?" He handed Ainsworth the drawing.

"Not exactly but similar," she said and handed the pad back. She perked up and added, "I forgot, there were metal buttons on the sleeves. The sunlight bounced off one when he turned to run. I can't say how many, but there was more than one."

Ruddy drew three buttons, which was a best guess.

"If that's all detectives, I really must go." She turned to Waldgrave. "I do hope they can find this fiend. I'm sorry I couldn't do more." She kissed the cheek of the victim and left.

Northam had been waiting in the lobby and Archie waved him over. He set up his equipment fast. "What did you need, sir?" he asked, looking from Archie to Ruddy.

Ruddy had Waldgrave stand. He pointed out four small bruises on her cheek and a single larger bruise on the other cheek. "Will these show up in a photograph? They're finger bruises from where the suspect clamped a hand over her mouth."

Northam shook his head. "I doubt it, not as bruising anyway. I think they'll show, but they'll appear as smudges."

"Try as best you can to take a clear photograph. We also want photographs of her torn skirt, and her hair with the leaves in it." Ruddy walked around her making sure that was all they needed. "That will do."

"Why do you want photographs of my bruises? What use are they?"

"In my experience, an attacker uses his off-hand to control and his strong hand to menace, or do harm, or brandish a weapon. The small bruises are on your left cheek. The larger one is on your right. He must've used his right hand to clamp over your mouth and held the knife in his left."

Her eyes widened as he explained. "In my fear, I forgot to say how he held the knife. I only remembered he had one. Goodness me, you're right. He did have it in his left hand."

"Don't fret. It's not uncommon for a person who's been traumatized to temporarily forget details. The photographs won't take long. Once Northam is done Miss Waldgrave, we'll have a constable escort you home."

He started to walk away and turned back to her. "One more thing; please refrain from telling anyone that your attacker claimed to be Jack the Ripper? We'd rather not start a panic here, like in Whitechapel, until we know more."

She nodded and said, "I understand. I'll keep that part to myself."

"Thank you."

"Detective Bloodstone..."

"Yes?"

"Is there someplace I can wash my hands? They're filthy. As you can see I've skin under the nails from where I clawed at his hand."

Ruddy took her hands in his and examined them. The skin under the nails was flecked with black dots of blood and several of her nails were broken. "It appears like you clawed him badly. He'll have some wicked scratches."

"I hope so," she said with a faint smile. The first he'd seen from her.

"Northam, take photographs of her fingernails as well. When he's done, Miss Waldgrave, you may wash your hands. We have a basin in the back."

#

"What do you think?" Archie asked after the women left.

"It's not the Ripper," Ruddy said, reading through the details he noted. "Nothing about this is his modus operandi Waldgrave is attacked walking through the gardens in the morning on her way to work. The Ripper's victims were killed at night. She's not his typical victim since she's obviously not a prostitute. He's a ways from his preferred area to hunt. I believe this is someone trying to mimic the Ripper to throw us off."

"I don't want to think what Jameson will do but we can't ignore the fact he claimed to be the Ripper."

"We'll have to send a report to Scotland Yard so they're aware of the incident. But I am going to ask Jameson to let us follow up on the scant description Ainsworth gave us."

"Not much to go on."

It was the thinnest of descriptions. In truth, Ruddy had serious doubts they would discover much. At least the Ripper detectives wouldn't get underfoot. They were already working with minimum information on their cases. This one didn't help in any significant way so they'd likely thank Ruddy and Arch for the report and toss it into a pile on their desks. The museum suspect wasn't the only man claiming to be the Ripper. From what the papers said, there were a handful of *alleged* Rippers working all over the city. This was just one more. It was a clever ploy on the criminal's part. The female victims naturally panicked hearing the words, *I'm Jack the Ripper.* If they reacted like Waldgrave, they were so focused on being viciously cutup, they paid little to no attention to anything about the suspect.

"I guess we should go in and tell Jameson about our Ripper," Archie said, looking resigned. His expression shifted to one of suspicion. "You think by some chance this might be the secondary killer you thought responsible for Ellis and Offerman?"

"Funny you should bring that up. I was just thinking he might be."

#

"How certain are you this isn't the Ripper?" Jameson asked. "Give me a number, because if it is, and we don't handle it accordingly, it could be the ruination of all three us."

"Ninety-five percent." Ruddy didn't see how it would ruin any of them unless attacks increased and no suspects were arrested. At the moment, if they kept information to themselves and the Whitechapel boys, the public's focus would remain on the other investigations.

"We can't be certain but the crime has nothing in common with the pattern he's demonstrated with the others." On occasion, Jameson needed more than one telling to reassure him. Ruddy recounted the differences again.

"Well, go about the investigation. I want this taken care of before it mushrooms into an indictment of *my* detectives handling of the case." He slid his watch out and took a fast peek, eyed his bottle of whiskey and sighing, put the watch back in his vest pocket.

Right now, Ruddy wouldn't mind a shot himself in spite of the morning hour.

"We'll do everything we can," Arch said.

"Yes, yes. I'm sure you will. Close the door behind

you."

Back at their desks, Ruddy showed Arch the drawing. "Take a good look at how the suspect is dressed, especially the jacket and picture it dark blue."

"What am I supposed to be seeing?"

"This doesn't look like any everyday style worn by the common man on the street. Think who might wear this."

Archie studied it. "I don't see—" Recognition lit in his eyes. "Mother of God, no."

"You see it too."

Arch nodded.

"He might be one of ours."

"Looks like it from the back but we know the button isn't from a constable's uniform."

"We may have been wrong about the button being evidence from our case. We assumed it was related," Ruddy reluctantly had to admit. "The witness said the attacker's jacket had metal buttons and pointed to a constables as similar."

"It could be military too."

"Let us hope and pray he's theirs not ours."

"If he's ours, it would be worse than having the actual Ripper skulking about this district. What little trust the people have in us would be lost for years to come. Should we mention the possibility to Jameson?" Archie asked.

"And give him apoplexy for sure? No, let's not broach that subject until we have more evidence it might be a Peeler. For now, let's talk to the museum guards and advise them of the incident.

## Chapter Thirty

Xavier Weeks was out of the country, tramping around a dig at a ruin in Southern Egypt. Fine with Ruddy, he'd rather not deal with Weeks. He asked the curator's secretary to locate the two guards and have them meet him and Archie in the security office.

Their office was in the basement. An assistant to the secretary led the detectives through a multi-room maze of artwork, statuary, pots and vessels of all sorts, waiting to go on exhibit. The rooms were dank and dusty as the inside of a pyramid. Archie didn't seem to notice, but Ruddy thought they smelled strange, moldy, with unnaturally thick air. The new wood of the unopened crates offered some relief.

The office was unlocked and the secretary's assistant suggested they have a seat while they waited. Small and cramped by the desks and chairs, the windowless room smelled stuffier than the rest of the basement. It made the detective bureau cheerful by comparison. At least the bureau had a row of windows they opened in the nice weather and let in a lot of light year round.

The first guard, Theodore Stavros, arrived shortly later. They'd interviewed him after each of the murders in the gardens. He wasn't near the sites at the estimated times of death and could offer no additional information.

Stavros was of Greek heritage. Taller than average in height, but broadly built with not much visible neck, he looked like he'd pull a loaded oxcart with no trouble. His eyes were coal black at first look but up close were deep brown. A heavy, black beard obscured his mouth and most of his cheeks. No doubt he frightened the children on his block. One menacing look from him would scare any devilish child into angelic behavior.

His uniform jacket was dark blue, military length, and when Stavros extended his hand to shake the detective's, the metal buttons caught the office light. Ruddy showed no reaction to recognizing the button on his sleeve. A lion's head on brass, it matched the one they believed torn from the suspect's clothing in Ellis's struggle.

When the guard turned to take a seat, Ruddy whispered to Archie, "Look at his jacket."

Archie nodded in understanding. The big question in Ruddy's mind was the facial hair. Stavros's beard should've been noticed by Ainsworth even if her visual was only a glimpse. But in the excitement of the moment, she might've missed noting it. Witnesses focus on different things.

After Archie finished advising the guard of the latest attack and suspect description minus the clothing, Ruddy said, "I'd like you to stand and give me your jacket."

"Why?"

"Because I said so." If Stavros turned out to be their suspect, taking him into custody might prove interesting and tough. Ruddy wished he'd brought his truncheon in case Stavros resisted.

Stavros stood and removed his coat, handing it to Ruddy.

The guard's hands were unmarked.

"Roll up your shirt-sleeves," Archie told him in case Waldgrave had scratched his arms. Stavros did, pushing the sleeves back to the elbow. No fresh marks were visible on his forearms either.

"Is this your only uniform jacket? Or, is there a spare?" Ruddy asked.

"That's the only one I have," he said, rolling his sleeves down.

Ruddy checked to see all the buttons intact. Then, he turned the jacket inside out and checked the stitching for the buttons. Nothing indicated recent repair or alteration. He handed the jacket back.

"May I ask what you were looking for?" Stavros asked, slipping his coat on again.

"The buttons on your uniform match the one found by the first victim's body. We think it was torn off the suspect's coat during the struggle." As he explained, Josiah Poole, the second guard, came into the office. Poole spun around and tried to run but didn't get more than two steps before Archie clamped a hand on his shoulder.

"Where do you think you're going?" Archie shoved him into one of the desk chairs. He forcibly held the guard's hands out to inspect them. Both were covered in angry fresh scratch marks, swollen and red.

Archie pulled Poole to his feet and held him still while Ruddy checked the buttons on his jacket. One was missing on the right sleeve.

Ruddy stepped over to Stavros, who'd watched the action from the corner of the office and asked, "Has Poole ever talked about the murders in a personal way?"

Poole wrestled against Archie's hold as he shoved him down in the chair. "Don't answer them, Teddy. They're trying to make me a scapegoat for their failure to catch the real murderer."

"Mr. Stavros, we can conduct this interview at the station if need be. Although, I doubt you'll care to be seen leaving with us," Ruddy said. Both guards hauled off to the station, one manacled would bring scandal. Everyone in the room knew Stavros wouldn't risk a scene and his job.

Stavros looked at Poole and raised his shoulders in acquiescence. "No, we just made general conversation about how awful they were and we'd have to be more diligent if we saw any unsavory types."

"Do you know where he was when the attack

happened this morning? Or, where he was when the others occurred?"

"He was always here when I arrived. He likes to come in early and have a cup of tea before our shift. That's what he told me."

They'd asked the same questions at the time of the murders. The connection to his early arrival hadn't the sinister overtone it did now.

Stavros made the connection. "I see what you believe he was up to. How could this be, Josiah?"

"They're lying. Ask anybody and they'll tell you Peelers are a pack of liars." Josiah tried to force Archie's tight grip from his shoulder to no avail.

"I can't believe this of him," Stavros said.

"His hands are badly scratched from where the victim today clawed at him. His coat matches the witness's description of the suspect's, and he's been here when the crimes occurred," Archie told him.

Stavros turned from Poole to Archie, to Ruddy and back to the man he worked with, his inner debate about who told the truth evident. He crossed himself. "Such a sinful man, if this is true."

The looming possibility Poole was the Ripper needed to be addressed. Those killings happened at night when the guard was off. He had the opportunity.

Archie kept a strong hand on Poole so he couldn't rise. Ruddy stood over him. "Where do you live?"

"I've a room in Covent Garden."

Covent Garden wasn't exactly close to Whitechapel. He'd be taking a huge risk getting from one of the murder sites home covered in blood. But it could be done.

Part of Ruddy hoped Poole was the Ripper, for no other reason than to lord capturing the most infamous murderer in English history over that bootlicker Napier.

The most recent Ripper murders took place on the same night. The press called it, *the double event.* Elizabeth

Stride and Catherine Eddowes were found brutally murdered within a short time span of each other. "Where were you the night of Sunday, September 30?"

"Onboard ship. At Mr. Weeks's request, I guarded a sarcophagus he was transporting from Egypt to here."

Ruddy looked to Stavros who nodded he told the truth.

Ruddy wasn't too disappointed. Unless Poole provided a solid alibi, they had enough to hold him for two murders and attempted murder for a brief period. Without more or stronger evidence, they might not be able to formally charge him. But holding him in the uncomfortable surroundings of a police station helped during interrogations. Men got nervous. After a while they confused their lies and contradicted themselves.

#

At the station they placed him in the interview room. Archie sat with him while Ruddy reported the arrest to Jameson.

Jameson left his office with Ruddy to take a look at Poole. Arms folded, he stood in his usual observation spot and watched Archie and Poole through the metal-grilled glass half of the room's wall. "Is that all you have—the button, the scratches, and the early arrival times?" he asked.

"Afraid so." Ruddy worried the superintendent would argue against keeping Poole in custody even overnight with only superficial evidence. Evidence a clever defense attorney could cast doubt on as part of the crimes.

"It's thin."

"I know."

"You're certain you have the right suspect for Ellis and Offerman?"

"If we weren't, we wouldn't have brought him in."

"Let me play Devil's Advocate here. If I'm the defense, I'll argue the scratches could easily come from tending rose bushes or even walking in the museum's rose garden. I'd ask the jury when did missing a button mean you're a murderer? When did an early cup of tea become a cover up for murder? You get the drift. If I can see how to argue a defense, so can the prosecutor. They don't fancy taking on losing cases."

"I realize we have our work cut out or the prosecutor won't pursue charges."

Jameson sighed and unfolded his arms. "Think the ladies from this morning might be able to identify him?"

Ruddy didn't think so but it was worth a try. "Maybe."

"I'll have the desk sergeant send someone to collect the women and call in two of our lads to stand a lineup with Poole."

"They should be average height. According to the women, the suspect was average height and weight with medium brown hair."

#

Finding the men didn't take long. Two constables were in the area of the station sorting out a fistfight between a costermonger and a customer.

Ruddy explained they'd stand a lineup with the murder suspect. The two started to shrug out of their jackets. "Leave your uniform coats on." They gave Ruddy a strange look but did as he asked.

He removed Poole's manacles and along with Archie, escorted him to the storeroom that served as the lineup room as well. The constables were already there and had taken off their helmets and combed their hair. Poole stood next to them. Ruddy stayed in the room to monitor the action and offer instruction when needed. One at a time, Archie had the ladies stand in the doorway at the far end of the room where Poole couldn't hear them. Ruddy had the three men face forward, then take a quarter turn to the left, presenting the profile Ainsworth briefly saw.

Waldgrave couldn't identify the suspect. Ainsworth told Ruddy the third man, Poole, looked the closest to the attacker.

"But as I said this morning, I only had a glimpse, Inspector. It happened too fast. I'm sorry."

"You did fine. Thank you for coming. I'll have a carriage ordered to take you both home."

Archie manacled Poole and took him to the interview room again. Jameson had hovered in the back, observing. "That didn't go anywhere," he said to Ruddy when they were alone. "We need a confession. Think you can get one out of him?"

Ruddy smiled.

#

Jameson looked up from the paperwork he was reading when Ruddy and Archie came into his office. "Well?"

"We got it," Ruddy said.

"Is he in one piece?" Jameson couldn't keep a twitchy smile at bay.

"Yes."

Jameson eyes shifted to Archie. "Any bruises that show?"

Archie shook his head.

"You look surprised," Ruddy said, "For the record, he hasn't any bruises. I used my considerable talent for persuasion to obtain a full confession."

Jameson turned to Archie again. "Really?" His skepticism wasn't unexpected. Ruddy wasn't the most silver-tongued man at the station.

"That and a couple of convincing lies."

"Go on," Jameson said, leaning back in his chair.

"First we told him that Ainsworth identified him. When we didn't get a response, I went down a different path. Strangulation is a very personal way to murder someone. With that in mind, and the sexual component indicating he couldn't, for some reason, achieve actual penetration, I approached him with empathy. I let him know I understood that women loved to tempt men and then reject them. This cruel streak is an inherent part of their nature they exercise with glee."

"You think he had a hatred for women? One of those chaps who are driven to punish what he can't have. How did you know that approach would work?"

"I didn't, but it was worth a try. Archie led him to believe we were secretly of the same mind."

"Tell me about his confession?"

Archie rolled his eyes in disgust. Fortunately, when he rolled them during the exchange, Poole didn't see.

Ruddy sat back in his chair, relishing the retelling. "Apparently, he was comfortable sharing his feelings of anger and hate with us. It seems the size of his manly bits is seriously lacking...very seriously according to him."

"Ugh," Archie muttered.

Jameson wore the same look of disgust that Ruddy felt when Poole shared his story. "He offered to show us but we declined."

"I should hope so," Jameson said.

"He told us women find him laughable, even whores. They've mocked him and made cruel barbs about how pathetic he is. He can no longer bear the thought of another humiliating normal encounter. That coupled with his hatred of all women set him on a murderous path."

"Good job."

## Chapter Thirty-One

Archie yawned and stretched out and then up toward the ceiling.

His yawn triggered one in Ruddy.

"Long day," Archie said and stood. "I'll be glad to see my pillow."

It was one of the busiest days in Ruddy's memory. From the moment they had a possible Ripper attack on their hands, to Poole's confession, they'd worked nonstop. They dropped the last of the reports on Jameson's desk. With the paperwork complete and his permission, they were free to quit for the day.

"I'm not ready for bed yet. I'm ravenous and it's shepherd's pie night at my boarding house. Mrs. Goodge makes an extra-large portion for me. Then, I'm relaxing with that Jules Verne book, *20,000 Leagues under the Sea*. I was given a copy ages ago but never got around to reading it."

Just as Ruddy put his coat on, Effingham and Napier came into the station and quick-marched to Jameson's office.

"Oh, bloody hell," Ruddy said as Napier looked his way.

"What?" Archie had his back to the station door and hadn't seen them enter.

"Effingham and his lap dog Napier are here."

Deep down, Ruddy never believed for a moment that Effingham and Napier would accept the exigent circumstances explanation. They let it go unquestioned because Everhard died. That's what Ruddy thought at least. He had little doubt if the viscount had lived and been brought back to London to stand trial, a nasty dustup between the agencies would've followed.

"If we hurry, we can be out the door before Jameson has a chance to order us to his office."

"We aren't necessarily in trouble." Archie pushed his desk chair in and laid his coat over his arm rather than take the time to put it on. "But we should go just in case."

They got as far as the door to the street when behind them Jameson called out, "Bloodstone, Holbrook, my office, now."

Effingham and Napier sat in the only two spare chairs in Jameson's office. Ruddy and Archie stood to the side. Ruddy wouldn't have sat if a chair were available. He preferred to stand. He liked the feeling of superiority over Napier it gave him.

Napier scooted his chair closer to Effingham's and further from Ruddy.

"Sir, you wanted us?" Ruddy shoved clenched fists into his trouser pockets.

Effingham answered. "I wanted you here. I think Detective Napier and I are owed an explanation." He turned from Ruddy to Jameson and tossed the evening edition of the paper on the desk, pointing to a story on the front page. "You do know I'll have to discuss this entire case with the Home Secretary."

How had the press gotten their hands on the story? Coopersmith confirmed Seamus hadn't gone to Marsden's office. No one else in the station knew many of the details of the arrest yet.

Ruddy cocked his head to better read the upside down front page with the story. He saw enough of the first paragraph to read Theodore Stavros was listed as a witness to the arrest of Poole for two murders previously attributed to the Viscount Everhard.

"I plan on speaking with him. No need for you to get involved," Jameson said, far more calmly than Effingham's tone with him deserved. "This is our case and has nothing to do with your bureau."

"I'm making this my business. I never believed that tommy rot of yours about exigent circumstances when you went to arrest Viscount Everhard."

Napier jumped into the argument to confront Ruddy. "I knew it for a nonsense excuse not to inform me so I could oversee the arrest."

Ruddy had his fill of the arrogant ass. He stepped closer to Napier. "And what exactly did we need you for? So you could speak to Everhard in the manner befitting a viscount?" Ruddy feigned an upper class accent mocking Napier's fake one. "Oh, dreadfully sorry viscount. It's this messy murder business. I'm afraid you'll have to come with us. Do be a good fellow and come along without a fuss." He poked his finger in Napier's face. "For your information, he wasn't a good fellow and didn't come along without a fuss. And had you been there, you likely would've gotten yourself shot and one of us as well when we went to your aid."

Napier pushed back hard on his chair and stood almost nose-to-nose with Ruddy. "I don't have to take your insults."

"Sit down, Nathaniel," Effingham ordered and then turned to Jameson. "I won't tolerate this insolence toward my man. I demand you make him—" he pointed to Ruddy, "apologize."

"Apologize," Jameson told Ruddy.

"Why? Because I told the truth?"

"I don't need this problem, Bloodstone. Just apologize."

Ruddy took a minute to choose his words. "I'm sorry if Detective Napier felt insulted by my comments."

Effingham turned to Napier. "Nathaniel?"

Napier looked Ruddy up and down and up again. "Apology accepted."

Both Effingham and Napier stood. "We're done here. Your attempted arrest resulted in the viscount's death. Two murders wrongly laid at his doorstep. Just know that the Home Secretary questions if other mistakes were made regarding the case against Everhard."

Jameson came round his desk to show them out. "I'm aware."

After they left Jameson poured the three of them a whiskey. "Don't think I don't know what you did, Bloodstone."

"What I did?"

"That non-apology, apology. You said you were sorry Napier to took offense to your comments. You *never* apologized for what you actually said."

Archie threw back his scotch in one swallow. "Good observation, Superintendent. It slipped right by me."

Ruddy lifted his glass as if in toast. "I've no intention of apologizing to that toady." Jameson drank expensive whiskey from Scotland. Ruddy sipped his, enjoying the drink. It didn't burn going down and wasn't sweet on the tongue.

"You'd do well in Parliament, wily as you are." He held the decanter of scotch up and then poured each two fingers more. "Gentlemen, have a fine evening, you earned it." He touched his glass to theirs.

#

Ruddy stopped by the boarding house to ask Mrs. Goodge to set aside some shepherd's pie for him. As usual, Winky kept her company in the kitchen disposing of any morsels that fell. Ruddy coaxed him out long enough for a walk. When they returned, Winky took up his previous spot and Mrs. Goodge said she'd take care of him. Still brassed off over Effingham and Napier, Ruddy headed for the Boot and Bayonet to let off steam.

En route, he passed a popular ice cream parlor and candy store that stayed open late to catch the local music hall crowd. People said the shop made the best sundaes. He enjoyed sundaes as much as anyone but had never gone into the parlor to try theirs. The rich odor of chocolate wafted out and Ruddy glanced inside. Then, he stopped. He recognized the profile of the blonde enjoying a dish of strawberry ice cream and went inside.

"Miss Bannister, how are you?" She sat alone at a small, wrought-iron table dining on a jam covered scoop of ice cream.

"I'm well and I thought we agreed it's Evangeline and Rudyard."

"My mistake. Good evening...Evangeline."

"The sundaes here are heavenly. Won't you join me, Rudyard? That is unless your lady will get upset."

"She and I are no longer seeing each other." The pub visit abandoned with ease. He pulled out the chair opposite Evangeline. "I'd love to join you."

She slid her spoon into her sundae but he saw her little smile before she came up with a mouthful of ice cream with a dollop of whipped cream. She held the spoon out to him. "Have some, it's quite tasty."

He obeyed and ate the bite while she continued to hold the spoon. It was tasty, but the opportunity for an evening's company beat a tasty treat.

"Do you like music hall entertainment," he asked.

"I do, very much so. Are you inviting me?" She kept her eyes on the sundae as she dipped into it again.

"I am. There's a hall near here with a merry show."

"I'd love to go." She put her spoon down and dabbed at her mouth with a lace-trimmed handkerchief. "Ready whenever you are," she said, tucking the hanky into her pelisse.

Ruddy came around to pull her chair out. When she stood and looped her arm in his he didn't move to leave right away. "I'm a police detective. I thought you should know."

"I know. You're mentioned in the evening papers. You arrested the museum killer. How exciting your job must be."

"It has its moments."

"Tell me about it while we walk to the hall. Don't

leave anything out. Start with how you caught the killer."

"That had many twists and turns. I'll start from the beginning."

#

Archie joined Ruddy at the tea station. "You had quite a smile on your face when you came in. Dare I guess you had a nice evening."

"I did. Judging from your grin, I guess yours was as well."

"Wonderful. Meg sent the girls to bed early and we had dinner just the two of us with wine, mind you. Then, she drew me a hot bath," Archie lowered his voice conspiratorially, "and washed my back. She hasn't done that in a while, she—"

"Don't tell me anymore. Let's leave it at you had a great evening," Ruddy said. He was about to tell Archie about the delightful night he had at the music hall with Evangeline. Before he got into the details, Jameson walked over with a multi-page report in his hand.

"Good to see you both looking bushy-tailed this morning. This came in last night." He handed Ruddy the paperwork.

"Rather unusual case, I think you'll find it interesting."

The End

# *Author's Notes*

A number of years ago I had the opportunity to go on a private tour of 24th Regimental Museum in Brecon, Wales. The 1964 movie, Zulu, with Michael Caine and the late Stanley Baker, was a favorite of mine. While traveling the United Kingdom, I made a side trip to Brecon specifically to visit the museum. After my visit there, I was inspired to write a story that the battles of Isandhlwana and Rorke's Drift (January 22nd-23rd, 1879) had relevance to one of the main characters. This is how Rudyard Bloodstone's military background and his awarding of the Victoria Cross came into being.

I have tried to present an accurate telling of the battles. Any mistakes are mine alone. Four of the men mentioned did exist: Lord Chelmsford, Private (John) Williams, Private Henry Hook, and Colour Sergeant Frank Bourne. Williams and Hook did receive the Victoria Cross for their courage in the hospital evacuation at Rorke's Drift. Colour Sergeant Bourne received the Distinguished Conduct Medal. He was offered an officer's commission but turned it down. He felt he'd done was expected in battle.

Regarding the murder investigations where crime scene photographs were taken, this practice began (in

London) in the fall of 1888, during the Jack the Ripper murder spree. In my story, Detective Inspector Bloodstone requests crime scene photos taken of a murder he's investigating in the spring of 1888. My use of an alternate timeframe was a deliberate choice.

Research information for the writing of Silk can be found on my website: chriskarlsen.com

# LOOK FOR CHRIS KARLSEN'S OTHER BOOKS

## KNIGHTS IN TIME

Heroes Live Forever, Journey in Time, and Knight Blindness are three romances that take the reader into a world filled with heart-warming heroes and heroines. Theirs are stories where heartbreak and danger is faced with courage. They're stories of how love is stronger than any challenge. Each mixes history and the modern world where the settings are brought vividly to life.

## DANGEROUS WATERS

Golden Chariot and Byzantine Gold explore the beauty and mystery of the undersea world. The books follow the characters as they recover valuable and important artifacts from ancient shipwrecks. As with many things of value, evil is intent on obtaining them as well. Against the exotic backdrop of the Aegean and Mediterranean, readers are taken on a thrill ride with scientists and government agents who are at risk and confronted with terrorists, organized crime, and men bent on revenge.

## ABOUT THE AUTHOR
## CHRIS KARLSEN

Chris Karlsen is a retired police detective. She spent twenty-five years in law enforcement with two different agencies. The daughter of a history professor and a voracious reader, she grew up with a love of history and books. An internationally published author, Chris has traveled extensively throughout Europe, the Near East, and North Africa satisfying her need to visit the places she read about. Having spent a great deal of time in England and Turkey, she has used her love of both places as settings for her books. "Heroes Live Forever," which is her debut book, is set in England as is the sequel, "Journey in Time." Both are part of her "Knights in Time," series. Her third book, to be released in late 2011, "Golden Chariot," is set in Turkey and she is currently working on another set in Turkey, Paris and Cyprus. Published by Books to Go Now, her novels are available in digital, ebook,

Audiobook. "Heroes Live Forever," is available in paperback and "Journey in Time," will be made available in paperback in October, 2011 on her publisher's site. A Chicago native, Chris has lived in Paris and Los Angeles and now resides in the Pacific Northwest with her husband and four rescue dogs. A city girl all her life, living in a small village on a bay was a interesting adjustment. She'd never lived anywhere so quiet at night and traffic wasn't bumper to bumper 24/7.